Colin Sephton
Soulslayers

Published by: Cinnabar Moth Publishing LLC
Santa Fe, New Mexico

Cover Design by: Ira Geneve

ISBN-13: 978-1-962308-39-7

Library of Congress Control Number:

Soulslayers

COLIN SEPHTON

For Mum and Dad.

Who are somewhere in the cosmos.

Prologue

She felt the burning white light hit the centre of her back, and a purple aura enveloped her. She felt the cosmos scream as she felt every atom of her body separate and become at one with the fabric of space. From that moment forth, everywhere she turned, one wrong movement or thought and an energy bolt flew from her fingertips and destroyed anything it came into contact with. A silent scream in her own voice filled her consciousness, but she was incapable of any sound. Just the silent screaming in her head. She awoke with a jolt, sweating profusely, her chest and neck wet.

As she half opened her eyes, a searing pain split her skull. It was not just the pain from enduring death itself, or from using all her strength to fight hell spawn and gods, but as she looked around the room with bleary eyes, the main reason came into focus. Several empty bottles of absinthe and an opium pipe lay discarded on the worn Kilim rug. She pondered what had become of her life. She had always been in control of it, always strong and level-headed, never phased by any mission she had been assigned. Now her life lay in tatters. Every night she had the same dream, the nightmare of her death, the pain in her head and the agonising ecstasy of her atoms being absorbed by those of the cosmos. The structure of her body had altered forever. She began to think that when the atomic structure of her body had reconstructed, her soul had been forgotten. It lay in the cold and had been put in some vice-like grip and hidden away in a dark room somewhere in the depths of the earth. The inner strength against her constant struggle was the only thing that held complete blackness from filling her soul. Looking gaunt and pale with permanent pain and sorrow etched on her face, she wasn't even sure if she was human anymore. It was like her life from here on was just a scene she watched from afar. A small tear squeezed out of the corner of her eye and ran down her pale cheek. Ignatius had staged her death, complete with a funeral, but she wished it had been real. She had no wish to continue this existence. Life had become too complicated, and the pains from her previous adventures would not go away. Her only hope was that pain eases over time, and no time had passed since her ordeal.

As dawn paled the eastern sky, the only cloud appeared as an orange smear across the horizon. Even before she had opened her eyes fully, she could make out the sun streaming in through the gap in the curtains, blinding her. As she eventually opened them completely, her mind still in turmoil, she took in a deep breath, resigning herself to another day. Her battle-bruised body ached all over. She could feel her heart beating in what had felt like an empty, hollow chest since her ordeal. She felt light-headed as she rolled over onto her back and could feel the comforting warmth of his body lying next to her. He felt solid, permanent, unlike herself, he was her security and much more, he loved her. Events of the previous week ran through her mind and with mixed emotions she took delight, not in the fact she was alive, but because she was with him. She could hear the dawn chorus outside and eventually smiled. She had to be positive; this was a new day, a good day, she had fought gods once more and survived.

Turning over she placed her arm over his muscular frame. She could feel the scars of his battle-torn body. She studied them, tracing them with her fingertips. She studied his beautiful face, the shock of blond hair ruffled from restless sleep. His square jaw and high cheekbones. Warmth began to flow through her veins and her heart quickened its beat. They had worked together for years, and it had always been professional. Strictly business. Maybe things had changed because both felt like they only had each other. They had experienced the same cosmic enormity of what lies beyond earth, the same cosmos that ran through their veins, through their minds, their very thoughts and they, unlike the rest of humanity, knew the futility of life on earth, and of everyday struggles that were unimportant. The rest of the populace were blissfully unaware of the same cosmic connections, wasting their energies on the mundane. In truth, Indigo had started to question the requirement of the organisation they worked for, the Union Jacks, to protect the Empire. What was it all for? She sighed lightly and watched his chest rise and fall as he breathed.

Stirring, he opened his eyes, turning to her and smiling. She had changed significantly since her ordeal. She was still courageous, and independent, but her beautiful face showed signs of strife, and she no longer looked the same. It was difficult to put into words, but Indigo was different. He smiled, although deep within his heart yearned to go back, to change events somehow, to save her the agony she had experienced. He would never forgive himself and had made a promise to protect her no matter what, but couldn't discuss this with her, she was far too headstrong and independent for that. Just recently he had been having his own internal struggles.

The information they had about the cosmos was too explosive for humanity to comprehend. He rubbed the back of his hand, the eye-shaped birthmark on the back of his right hand was giving him some pain. He had noticed this more often nowadays, yet in the past, particularly in his younger years, he didn't give it a second thought. He was born with it and accepted it as a part of his own uniqueness, like the colour of one's eyes or hair. It was just skin. He was able to put the pain to the recesses of his mind and smiled as if nothing was wrong.

"Good morning, Indigo. How did you sleep?"

"Really well," she lied. "For the first time, in a long time," she added.

"It's probably exhaustion," he said.

"Perhaps."

"It still fills me with dread. You gave me a scare. I thought I'd lost you."

"Very nearly, Ignatius. But not yet."

They both smiled at each other and held each other tightly like they never wanted to be apart. She felt secure wrapped in the warmth of his love.

"You know this will complicate things, don't you?" She said.

"I know. But you forget one thing."

She frowned questioning what he meant.

"To the rest of the world, Indigo Gemstone is dead. I attended the funeral to prove it!"

They both laughed so hard, although with pretence. They were unaware of the knock at the door and Lambeth entering with a silver tray laden with a pot of Earl Grey, fine bone China and some toast and marmalade.

"Forgive me, sir. I did knock. Good morning, miss." Lambeth was careful not to make eye contact with her. This was the first time

Ignatius had entertained a young lady in his rooms, and Lambeth was most unaccustomed to it.

"I'll bring the newspapers up when they have been delivered, sir. Shall I pour?"

Sensing his discomfort, Ignatius spared him any more embarrassment. "No, that'll be all thank you, Lambeth. I, we, can take it from here!"

As his manservant left, both Ignatius and Indigo couldn't help but chuckle.

Chapter 1: The Debrief

It was a bright crisp morning. There was a bit of a chill in the air but the drive from the suburbs of London in a steam gurney had been pleasant enough. It was early, without much activity in the streets, just the cooing of the pigeons as they perched on top of the British Museum. The fabulous old girl looked gleaming as the Portland stone reflected the low-placed sun with its Ionic pillars and carved portico, imposing even, as the gurney turned into Great Russell Street. Even after all these years, he still marvelled at the Great Revival architecture every time he came here. Sir Robert Smirke had successfully attained a grand achievement with the building's design.

As the speeding vehicle screeched to a stop in front of the portico, a tall thin man dressed all in black and wearing a Bowler hat stepped out. His accent was cut-glass English, piercing the chilled morning as he thanked his driver. He was a very fit, lean-looking gentleman with a long thin nose and penetrating steel blue eyes, sunken cheeks and high cheekbones. It was difficult to determine his age. But the haggard lines that ran down either side of his mouth and the slight limp indicated he was not a stranger to action in the field. Still, it didn't prevent him from bounding up the steps to the main portico with an urgent purpose, cutting a dashing sprightly figure, dwarfed by the thick tall columns that tried to imitate Greek antiquity.

Edward Thomas Lawrence slipped in unnoticed before any of the museum employees arrived for work. One or two keen academics were already in but paid him no heed. Impatiently turning immediately left, he disappeared past the South stairs, past the early Greek and Roman exhibitions and was soon lost from sight. He had studied classics and ancient history at Jesus College, Oxford, so the story of the various statues, vases and paraphernalia of everyday ancient life that surrounded him were all too familiar.

The secret panel closed tightly behind him, and Lawrence found himself in the familiar dark passageway that he traversed every morning. His eyes were used to the darkness; as a boy he would often run around the New Forest in Hampshire, amongst the thick trees that obscured the light. He was most comfortable in the dark. Throwing back the iron gate, he stepped into the lift that was dimly lit by a single gas lamp. Closing the gate, he fiddled with the brass levers on the control panel. There was a puff of steam, and the lift descended rapidly into the bowels of the capital.

As the lift came to a shuddering halt, he got out to be confronted with a huge bronze door, heavily riveted and green with age, except where thousands of hands had worn it to a golden patina pushing it open over years of use. Cast in the centre of the door was an emblem. It consisted of a great gear in the centre of which was a shield, the left-hand side of which had in relief half the Union flag, the flag of the Empire. On the right-hand side were the three lions of England, and sitting on top of all this was the crested Centurions helmet of Britannia, the goddess of Britain and the personification of the country and its strength.

Some sleight-of-hand activated the locking mechanism, causing heavy bolts to clank open, a hiss of steam and the door, which was a foot thick, glided open as if it was light as a feather.

The other side of the doorway, Lawrence entered a vast labyrinth of corridors and chambers. This was the worldwide headquarters of the Union Jacks.

Sitting at his desk, the latest reports were already piled up in front of him, each in a brown Manilla folder, stamped with the same crest as that on the bronze door and labelled with the Chapter House it had come from.

The desk was large, and made from burr walnut, inlaid with green leather, decorated around the edge in gold. Its golden glow illuminated the office. The room was floored with black and white tiles and all four walls were lined with rich oak panelling, with the same crest carved into one of the panels. Behind the desk hung a large oil painting, a dark portrait of a brooding figure. The desk was otherwise uncluttered, just a brass inkstand and a green banker's lamp. The only ornamentation was a bronze of a lion like those seen in Trafalgar Square.

"Good morning, Mr Lawrence," said an aide as he entered the office with a silver tray of tea. Earl Grey, his preferred choice. Hot, no milk.

"The latest reports, sir," the aide gestured with his head at the stack of Manilla folders. "Some unusual goings on in Oxford," he said as he raised an eyebrow. The thin weaseley man had been with the Union some twenty years and throughout all that time had spent most of it behind a desk.

Lawrence didn't rise to his prompting and replied simply, "Very well, Jenkins, I will let you know."

Sifting through the reports, Lawrence took on a serious brow, mulling over the potential impact on the Empire of each report. The first report told of dangerous shamanic practices in China, disrupting the activities of the East India Company. He picked up the next report and after reading it, then reading it again, his face turned red, his brow furrowing. Significant disturbances in Oxford. His large fist slammed down in a rage onto the green leather, knocking his ink pot over. A book fell off the shelf behind him as he filled his lungs and bellowed,

"Jenkins, get me Isambard Ignatius. NOW!"

There was a flurry of activity in the next office. Tables shifted and a chair fell over. Papers flew into the air and a door closed loudly as Jenkins and others scrambled to carry out his order.

The communication system was swift within the Union Jacks organisation. It had to be to keep the various Chapter Houses well-informed. The movement of intelligence was paramount.

Later that day, a vellum-coloured envelope fell onto the ornate coloured tile floor in the hallway. It lay there for a few moments before Lambeth noticed it. Bending down, his back groaning, he picked it up and realised it had been hand-delivered. He opened the door swiftly, but it was too late, the streets of quiet, pleasant, suburban Summertown were mostly empty.

Ignatius was sat reading the papers, drinking Earl Grey. Indigo was cleaning her steam cannon. It lay in pieces on the coffee table, brass components gleaming in the sun that streamed in through the window. Lambeth cleared his throat to announce his arrival.

"A message has arrived for you, sir."

Ignatius took the envelope and, turning it over, realised it had been sealed with wax. The seal was familiar, a shield and the helmet of Britannia.

"Ah! It seems I have been summoned," he announced to Indigo. "I have to leave for London immediately."

"Is that just you, or me also?" Indigo looked inquisitively. "I fancy a change of scenery. To get away from Oxford for a while." She hesitated for a moment. "Too many recent memories," she lowered her eyes. "You know."

"Of course. Perhaps we could stay a while, give us a break for a few days."

About an hour later, Ignatius and Indigo were in a steam gurney heading for the train station in the centre of Oxford. The train came into the station right on time, its large green boiler spewing steam out of its chimney, obscuring the platform for a while. The porter loaded their luggage, two small leather cases, one of which had seen lots of travel, displaying labels from all sorts of exotic countries in the Middle East and Asia. Ignatius held out his hand and took Indigo's as she stepped onto the train. Before long, the train was gently swaying as it sped off along the tracks heading for the capital. Indigo closed her eyes and remained so for most of the trip, leaving Ignatius to wonder why he had been summoned. He knew his last two reports had been unusual, and he did want a meeting with the First Lord, the Grand Master, but had a feeling the meeting was not going to go well.

Two hours later, Ignatius sat in a large leather chair, waiting for the pungent cigar smoke to clear. He could just see the tip glowing red through the veil of smoke. Removing it from his lips, Lawrence leaned forwards and glared at Ignatius with suspicion. He was a sharp dresser, with his crisp white shirt, undoubtably from Jermyn Street, and a green tie with golden brocade. A black waistcoat from Saville Row, and trousers to match. He wore a brown leather belt with a discreet pistol attached on his right side and a Derringer on his left. Ignatius was convinced he probably concealed other weapons, too. Lawrence was a master swordsman in his younger years, something that Ignatius pondered, considering how he would fair against Indigo in a duel.

"You're not what I expected, Ignatius."

He didn't reply. Not sure how to.

"You don't look deranged, but your last two reports…"

He slammed his fist on the leather inlay.

"This has got to stop, man! Do you hear me? It's so fantastical, it can't be true."

Ignatius cleared his throat. "You doubt my integrity, sir?"

"Then tell me more. Make me believe…"

Ignatius rubbed his chin in deep thought.

"I shouldn't have to make you believe. We are Union Jacks, an organisation with a long proud history, descended from Brutus. My reports are genuine. This world we live on is a mere speck. An insignificant speck in a vast cosmic ocean of energy, with other dimensions, other planes… and yes, other beings! We are talking…" He hesitated. "Gods!… Unless we start to understand this in detail, the Empire, humanity will stagnate. It will lose out on the greatest body of knowledge ever known to mankind.

We have seen it, sir! We have been face-to-face with the creator, with the many faces of the Omnisoul, the creator of the entire cosmos.

This knowledge, this burden left me and Indigo with significantly changed views on the nature of life."

Lawrence was silent. Clouds of cigar smoke drifted around his head. Ignatius studied his face, trying to work out what he was thinking. Lawrence was cool. He gave very little away with his facial expressions. It was said that he was cold and calculating. He had a reputation for being ruthless with no hint of emotion. His claim to fame was he slaughtered twenty crazed shaman in the Far East, entering a forbidden temple in order to steal a golden idol which the locals venerated with such fanaticism it prevented them from working, carrying out their duties to aid the Empire. The shaman were women and gifted children, killed with his bare hands. The villagers, too frightened, were soon carrying out orders. Ignatius hoped the Union Jacks had moved a long way forward since such acts of barbarism.

Lawrence looked at him through squinted eyes. "Go on."

"In true Union Jacks' style, we had been investigating the whereabouts of an ancient text, purported to have been written by the creator. It turned out there were two books, books of great power. Power which would be very dangerous in the wrong hands. We were carrying out our duties, to protect the Empire."

"So where are these ancient texts now?" Cold, unblinking, steel blue eyes locked onto Ignatius.

"Gone! They no longer exist on earth, which in reality is a relief. However, we encountered seven terrible beings, the Charon, who are supernatural, immortal. Gods, if you will."

At this point, Lawrence nearly choked on his tobacco. He removed his cigar and leaned forward, his squinting eyes burning holes in Ignatius's soul.

"And if all of this is true, and, if I may, you don't strike me as mad! What now?"

"There is another relic from the creation. It's known as the Flaming Celestial Pearl. But we have no idea where it might be. Or what powers it possesses."

"A pearl, you say? Of significance?" Lawrence went silent and began to frown. There was a lengthy pause.

"I know of someone who may be able to help you. There

are many mainstream legends coming out of the East regarding Celestial Pearls. It's a common theme, usually adapted to suit the country that owns that legend. Most of these have been handed down though the great oral tradition over thousands of years and the only part of the world I can think of that has so many legends about pearls is the Far East. But more of this later. Now what of this weapon? A sonic blaster, you called it."

Ignatius reached into the leather holster strapped to his right thigh. "A demonstration, perhaps?"

Ignatius wasn't sure if his tone was slightly mocking.

"By all means. You have my full attention."

Ignatius lifted the weapon and took aim at the bronze lion statue on Lawrence's desk. Then, adjusting some brass dials on the back of the weapon, he pulled the trigger. The statue began to vibrate until it looked like it was about to topple over, then it raised off the desk and just hovered a few inches from the burr walnut surface.

"Remarkable!" Lawrence's eyes were wide open in astonishment.

"All matter is a vibration. The whole cosmos vibrates. Get the vibration correct, and you can affect matter, move objects, or even destroy them."

Without warning, Lawrence bellowed, "Jenkins, come and see this. It's incredible."

The door promptly opened, and Jenkins arrived.

"Take this weapon and show it to the tech boys, will you? They need to start replicating it immediately. Send one to each Chapter House."

Ignatius reluctantly handed the weapon over.

"Oh, don't worry, you'll get it back before you leave. They're damned quick in that workshop. Now tell me, what of Indigo? You said in your report, she died. And that somehow, she has special powers. Explain."

"Yes sir. That's true. She died during the mission. Somehow, I was able to summon power beyond my natural ability. How, I don't know."

Lawrence cut him off, "what do you mean, man? You summoned power?"

"Yes, sir. I don't how, but at that moment in time, I summoned a power from nowhere and brought her back to life."

"And have you been able to do this since?"

"No, I have had no cause to, sir. I don't know how to summon it again at will."

"Jenkins!" shouted Lawrence. The door opened without delay again, just as Lawrence opened the drawer of his desk and took out a small steam pistol and without warning fired it. There was a loud crack and hiss of steam as a shot hit Jenkins on his left shoulder. Wide-eyed, he fell backwards to the floor, disbelief painted on his face, a red stain widening on his shirt, blood dripping from beneath his cuff forming a puddle on the floor.

Ignatius looked on, horrified and in total disbelief. Lawrence was cold and unmoved. "So let's give it a go, shall we? Over to you, Ignatius, save him."

Ignatius felt the whole world go into slow motion. He'd heard that Lawrence was cold and calculated, but this was something else. Rumour had it that he once killed three of his own men to clear a path and reach an assassin that had tried to kill the Queen. Lawrence was Empire through and through, nothing else mattered. Ignatius had often wondered if he had risen to the top position via nefarious means.

As Ignatius moved from his chair, his legs felt like lead. Instinctively, he placed his right hand with the birthmark over his right eye. He looked out across the thirty-one planes. Disorientated at first, his eyes became accustomed to the sights before him. A host of colours swirled before him as whole worlds rushed by. He saw strangers going about their everyday life, he saw sea creatures grow leg-like appendages and walk onto the beach. His mind pulled him back into the room and these images faded from sight as his eyes now focused on Jenkins before him. He was gasping for air and Ignatius could now see a colourful aura around him. It flickered and was constantly changing shape, it shone like the yellow sun and at its edges a deep black began to creep over it, absorbing the yellow. Jenkins was dying.

Ignatius concentrated on his wound; geometric shapes radiated out of it like a never-ending fractal. Ignatius placed his left hand on Jenkins's wound. His hand appeared to disappear, absorbed by the fractal, and he withdrew it quickly. He tried again, more successfully, and Ignatius felt it grow warm. His whole arm began to ache. It felt heavy, numb and his hand felt like it was on fire. He felt sweat form on his brow and run down the back of his neck. His head throbbed and he felt his heart race. He moved his hand around Jenkins's shoulder, hovering just about the bullet wound. By now, Jenkins had stopped breathing, his aura had turned almost completely black. Ignatius focused and the fractal began to undulate in a wave-like motion until it began to dissolve. He caught a glimpse of the cosmos, a densely starred gas field of all colours shifted before him. It then vanished to be replaced by colourful sine waves that radiated from his fingertips and encircled Jenkins arm and shoulder.

Lawrence looked on but could see none of what Ignatius could see and feel. He took a step closer to see what he was doing, and as he did so the wound on Jenkins's shoulder began to fade, leaving behind just a blood-stained hole in his shirt. Ignatius saw his aura begin to re-glow yellow and orange, it sparked, and flecks of fire danced around his entire body.

Jenkins let out a great gasp of air and his body jolted. Opening his eyes, he shot upright, looking dazed, not knowing where he was or what had happened. Two other clerics came and dragged his weakened body out of the office and closed the door behind them.

Anger filled Ignatius. "What's wrong with you?" he shouted at Lawrence. "How could you just kill in cold blood like that, and one of our own!"

Through half-closed eyes, Lawrence calmly offered an answer. "Sometimes it's a necessary evil. In the field, only one thing matters, that's the mission and the protection of the Empire."

He resumed smoking his cigar as Ignatius returned to his seat.

"Still, it proves one thing Ignatius, you are telling the truth, and you do still have the power. It's fascinating. How do you do it?"

"I have no idea. It would appear, I just can." Ignatius was raging inside but successfully hid it.

"So, what happed to Indigo, after you revived her?"

"After her revival, she was significantly changed. She has been left with powers greater than mine, the like of which we are not quite sure yet. She is now our most valuable asset, which is why we faked her death with a funeral. The world believes her to be dead and only a few know the truth. I thought it was convenient, but to what end, I don't know, but the situation may be useful. But I don't have to explain. She is here, she can show you."

Leaning forward with a frown, and sucking on his cigar, Lawrence shared knowledge that Ignatius was unaware of, "trouble is, news has leaked out, but we don't know how, that she had special powers, some are saying she was a psychic, far-sighted, or a witch. We have managed to keep it out of the Penny Dreadfuls for now, but it's a good job she is believed to be dead, we don't want journalists, if you can call them that, poking around. Who knows what they may discover. Where is she now?"

Ignatius had a deeply furrowed brow and was concerned both for Indigo and the Union. "In the waiting room, sir."

"Then bring her in, I want to meet the enigmatic Indigo Gemstone."

Indigo was beckoned into the office and Lawrence introduced himself.

"What happened to Jenkins?" she enquired, looking at Ignatius with one raised eyebrow. There was no time to answer before Lawrence interjected. "Now, Ignatius here tells me you have acquired some remarkable powers during your last mission. I'd like you to demonstrate them."

Indigo turned to Lawrence for the first time since entering the room. Through squinted eyes she released an almost inaudible gasp, then composed herself, looking at Ignatius with displeasure. "What? You mean my death? Well, not sure I can replicate that, sir!" She was defiant. She was not happy at being put on the spot.

"No, no, no! I mean your actual powers. What is it you can do?"

She looked again at Ignatius, who gave a gentle sly nod of his head.

"Very well! She closed her eyes and could see the lion statue on Lawrence's desk in the darkness of her mind. She thought for a moment, then, concentrated her thoughts, her vibrations. She felt her body grow warm, a fire burned within, a cosmic fire that ignited the birth of stars and illuminated the colours of every nebula in the cosmos. She became breathless and had outstretched her right arm. She felt her hand glow warm as an orange aura swirled around it. Lawrence felt uneasy and moved his chair away from the desk. The aura travelled out from her being and the statue began to tremble once more. It raised off the desk and then without warning, burst into a million tiny fragments of bronze that showered the office.

Lawrence looked on, horrified by what he had witnessed. Indigo opened her eyes and lowered her arm. "Just a fraction of my power, I'd say. Wouldn't you?" And she looked at Ignatius, who felt uncomfortable at the demonstration. Indigo then turned and left the office, still furious at Ignatius for putting her forward as some sort of exhibit. The door slammed behind her.

"Extraordinary! I'm speechless, old boy," said Lawrence. "I think this calls for a whiskey," and he opened the bottom drawer of his desk, removing a bottle of single malt Scotch and two glasses. He poured two drinks and offered one to Ignatius.

"Pity, I quite liked that statue. It was given to me by the Queen for my service." He seemed to drift off as if reliving a distant memory. "So, you've actually encountered supernatural beings?"

"Yes, sir. Demons, ghouls, and… if I may, sir? Gods. They actually exist, sir."

"Really? I know the Chapter House of Pretani have had dealings with local shamans conjuring up spirits, ghosts if you will. But gods, Ignatius?"

He didn't answer.

"Right! I think we need a plan of action. I have no doubt about any of your reports. Now this pearl. What I'm about to tell you is in the strictest confidence. As you know, we have twelve Chapter Houses."

He leaned forward and lowered his voice to almost a whisper. "Well, there is another. A highly secretive Chapter, the House of Esoterica, for want of a better name. Very few know about it. Just me and the members of that Chapter. They are based in Tibet, high up in the Himalayas, so not easy to get to, at the temple in the sacred city of Lhasa. They have rooms hidden beneath the Tavern of Good Fortune that connect with the temple." He took a sip of his Scotch. "You will have to tread carefully, the city is so sacred, they don't take kindly to strangers. The Master there is a woman called Helena and her number one is Nicholas. She will be able to fill you in about the pearl, the local legends and the like. It's the only place where you are likely to obtain information about a celestial pearl."

"How will I find her?"

"You won't! She will find you. But just in case this is her." He opened his drawer and withdrew a daguerreotype. She was a stout, stern looking woman with several chins. Matronly, with large piercing, hypnotic eyes. She looked solid and the kind you wouldn't want to mess with. But she looked more like a wrestler than an agent for the Union.

"For a long time now, she has spoken of the esoteric and things not of this world. At first, I was sceptical, but there have been more and more happenings recently of an occult nature. I just needed you to confirm your story today. I have already briefed Her Majesty."

His cold hard eyes squinted as Ignatius felt them piercing his very soul, as he stared at him across the desk.

"When do you suggest we depart, sir?"

"As soon as possible, of course. See Jenkins, or I mean, whoever, on the way out and he'll sort out some transport, you know, tickets, money, and anything else you should require. Very good. Good day to you, Ignatius."

Ignatius got up to leave, and as he reached the door to open it, Lawrence added, "I'm not sure where all this is headed, Ignatius, but take care. But if, as you say, we are dealing with cosmic events, then we need to be on top of this. The Empire needs to contemplate its place, not just in this world, but also in space. As you can imagine, Her Majesty is keen to seize any power that will increase the strength of the Empire beyond all measure. Indeed, if it's possible, she is keen on developing a Celestial Empire herself. I shall require an audience with the Queen to discuss this latest intelligence and our response to space exploration. But not a word of this to anyone."

"Gracious, sir! I had no idea."

"No! Nobody does. In fact, it's just Her Majesty, you, me and the Prime Minister. So don't let me down, Ignatius. We don't want the French or the Dutch hearing about this."

On the other side of the door, Ignatius spoke to another agent. Jenkins was nowhere to be seen, as expected. The man had just returned with his sonic blaster.

"The tech boys are really excited about this, Ignatius. They had a good look and took some measurements. They think they'll be able to replicate it and test them in about a month."

"Very well. Lawrence has requested I go to Tibet, and you will sort out all the arrangements."

"Very good," the man replied as he got to work on numerous pieces of paper to organise travel plans. Ignatius looked around for Indigo, but there was no obvious sign of her. Eventually, he found her in a small side office. As he entered, he could feel her pain.

"I'm sorry, Indigo. That was thoughtless of me. But I thought it was best Lawrence experienced it for himself. It's all very well explaining these strange tales, but to witness something with his own eyes, that means even more than I can explain to him."

"I know. I'm sorry. But I want to forget the whole ordeal. But I do understand. I really do." But deep down, Indigo was not happy. She had a strange sinking feeling in the pit of her stomach.

Ignatius reached out his arms and embraced her, not knowing how to break the next news. She shrugged him off and stepped aside, out of his reach.

"We need to return to Oxford as soon as we can, we are… we are travelling to Tibet."

Chapter 2: Spirit of the Empire

They could see the great airship from a distance as they travelled through the countryside to the airfield. Sunlight glinted off the brass structure. The *HM Spirit of the Empire* was a magnificent ship, the biggest in the fleet and said to be the fastest despite its size. It was rumoured to have crossed the Atlantic in record time. Too big to be tethered to the usual masts in Oxford, this great leviathan hovered just off the ground and was tied to several squat concrete structures weighting it to the earth.

The hull of the ship cast a shadow, plunging parts of industrial Cowley into darkness. It swayed gently in the breeze, tethered to the iron mesh tower that stood atop of the Military College. As Ignatius and Indigo approached, they could see hundreds of people milling around the airfield. They were smartly dressed in fine silks and top hats, a sea of pastel colours. These were the rich and elite of society, entrepreneurs, financiers, high-end businessmen and women, the only people who could afford such a long-distance journey in comfort and splendour. They could see activity within the docking station. Porters were carrying luggage up the steel staircase to stow safely in the hold. The crew were making last minute checks around the hull of the ship, checking the fabric and rudders.

The rigid outer shell of the airship was made from wood and brass, all intricately carved or cast to adorn the vessel with some unnecessary splendour. *HM Spirit of the Empire* was the jewel in the crown of the Star Line fleet. The enormous, elongated hull gleamed in the morning light, a vast array of heavily varnished teak and polished brass, with each rivet sparkling like precious stones, the gas bags were of the finest Chinese silk. The air was filled with the drone of the two large bronze propellers at the rear that would push the ship along on its journey. Occasionally a hiss of steam departed from a vent along the fins that were shaped like those of a giant fish.

Beneath the great gas bags hung three large gondolas. The first was the passenger quarters and amenities, the second the dining room and saloon, kitchens and dining areas and the third, at the rear, was the crew's quarters, some sixty strong, along with the luggage hold. This was the biggest airship ever built and boasted the ability to travel the entire globe without ever landing. This was due to the large water tanks that were secured beneath the wings and the gigantic copper boilers that took up most of the space in the engine room.

A network of thick pipework ran the length of the ship, carrying steam from the boiler room to the engines. In front of the three gondolas, the captain, wearing his leather aviator's cap, and his first mate, could be seen on the bridge of the ship, with a full three-hundred-and-sixty-degree panoramic view of the skies. Gas lanterns were dotted along the sides illuminating the entire vessel. Beneath the middle of the airship hung a small dirigible, an escape vessel if needed, although it was only large enough to hold about ten people.

At the extremities, front and back, slung beneath the entirety of the ship were two glass domes that housed long-range steam cannons for protection against pirates. Behind the tail fin there was another gun emplacement and an oversized Union flag, flapping in the breeze and proudly displaying the red, white, and blue of the Empire. This was a floating fortress.

Suddenly, there was increased activity as the porters finished loading the luggage, most of which was large leather trunks held together with brass corners, rivets and clasps. The guards started to usher the remaining passengers aboard and the platform began to clear. There was a cry of orders from various officials and a flurry of activity, with uniformed men rushing this way and that. Most of the female passengers were dressed in fine silk dresses adorned with jewellery and fur stoles around their shoulders and were very much dressed for the occasion. Indigo looked on bemused. She was dressed for the occasion, too. An occasion that would probably involve extremes of weather, a good deal of hiking in icy terrain, uncomfortable nights with few home comforts and insect bites. She did, however, come prepared for evening with finery to rival that of her fellow passengers. But she knew her dress sense was more practical. She wore a leather fedora that had concealed under its brim a veil to stop any enthusiastic mosquitos, a thick tweed sporting jacket with vents at the rear to allow for reaching arms up comfortably when shooting, and sturdy riding breeches with knee-high riding boots. To create layers for warmth, she wore a thick cotton blouse and velvet waistcoat with another shorter tweed inner jacket beneath her outer coat. This gave her plenty of storage for her usual armoury of twin derringers, a steam cannon, and a short sword for close combat. She guessed not many other guests were as well equipped. Ignatius was dressed in his usual attire of striped breeches, heavy boots, white cotton shirt open at the neck with a cravat strung loosely around his neck, his engineer's waistcoat, short jacket and a greatcoat for warmth. Indigo glanced down at his luggage, he travelled with an old heavily used and battered Gladstone bag. He obviously travelled lighter than Indigo, but she wasn't sure where the provision was for a dinner jacket for evenings.

A ticket master stood at the stairway checking tickets before letting the passengers board. He looked very smart in his deep leaf-green uniform with gold epaulets and a peaked cap. His hair was white, and he sported a large handlebar moustache, which he twitched as Ignatius approached. He checked their tickets.

"Good morning, sir! Ma'am. Isambard Ignatius and Eliza Patience, all in order. I do hope your journey is comfortable?"

He touched his cap and took Indigo's hand to assist her entry to the stairway, not that she needed it. They were led to their cabins by stewards who were dressed almost as finely as the ticket master.

"Eliza Patience?"

"Well, I thought it best, I mean Indigo Gemstone is dead, remember?" He gave her a huge warm smile. Ignatius had booked a cabin each to spare Indigo any embarrassment, it wouldn't do to be cohabitating in public, although they did have adjoining doors.

The cabins were sparse with regard to fittings, to save weight, but opulent in the use of materials, silk and finest cotton, the bed covered in furs in preparation for the journey to the icy realm of Tibet. Their luggage had been brought to their cabin; her colourful carpet bag sat next to her nightstand. After entering her room, she stepped out into the corridor to get her bearings so she knew whereabouts in the ship she was staying, At the far end, she could see a wizened old man with wispy white hair. Lambeth! Of course, Ignatius had brought his manservant along, who seemed to be struggling with the rest of the luggage.

Good evening miss, er, Patience. I do believe I'm quartered here next to Ignatius," he explained.

"Hello, Lambeth, let me help you with that," she said, taking hold of a handle on the trunk. It was much smaller than the rest of the trunks she had seen being loaded, but all the same. It was a trunk.

"Why didn't you let the porters load it, Lambeth?"

"Ah! Well, I wanted to see it wasn't damaged. Ignatius has some important items in here, miss."

Ignatius heard the conversation and stepped out. "Very good, Lambeth. Let me give you a hand."

Soon the trunk was stowed in Lambeth's cabin, As Ignatius retreated back to his own cabin, Indigo questioned him. "What's in the trunk, Ignatius? What is so precious that you haven't permitted the porters to bring it aboard?"

Ignatius gave a wry smile. "It's nothing. Just some equipment we may need when we get to Tibet. Nothing to be concerned about."

Indigo smiled at him. "Hmmm. I know you." But she didn't pursue the conversation.

Each returned to their respective cabins and rendezvoused later for dinner. Ignatius had changed into a dinner suit. Indigo had never witnessed him look so smart. "You scrub up well, Ignatius," she laughed. Indigo was dressed in the fashion of the day, wearing a pale olive-green dress.

"Fully armed?" enquired Ignatius.

"Of course. A lady should never be without," she replied lifting her dress to reveal a derringer tucked into the top of her stockings. "But one wrong move and this short sword is likely to pierce my ribs."

Ignatius raised an eyebrow.

"I'm going to eat in my cabin," said Lambeth.

"Very well, we will see you later," replied Ignatius, looping his arm for Indigo to put hers through his.

As they entered the dining room, it was a grand place. No expense had been spared. Crystal chandeliers hung above the tables and the vaulted ceiling was painted to depict white fluffy clouds floating across a pale blue sky. Cherubs peeked from behind some of the clouds and birds were depicted in majestic flight.

They were escorted to a table next to the windows, where the maître d' adjusted their chairs and handed Ignatius the wine list in a most extravagant way before turning his attention to other guests.

"So why do all these people wish to travel to Tibet?" asked Indigo.

"Oh, I don't know. I guess some are merchants looking to import goods, silks, tea, Buddhist icons and paraphernalia. Some will be bankers looking to broker such trade deals, others will be explorers and botanists seeking new flora to bring back to Blighty. Some of the shadier passengers may be arms dealers. Who knows? And some…" he paused and seemed to be looking beyond the time and place they were currently in, "some might just be on a spiritual journey, seeking solace, they may never return, looking for a simpler existence."

"I'd settle for that right now." Indigo smiled, her face glowing and at ease after the previous period in their lives. But this might just be a fleeting moment, she wouldn't know if the nightmares had stopped until she closed her eyes that night.

Chapter 3: A Short Delay

The journey took them out over Norway, passing over the country's breathtaking mountain ranges, which were broken only by the intricate tapestry of fjords with their glaciers reflecting the sun as evening approached. Dotted around the valleys and fjords, the towns turned into an image of sparkling lights, twinkling in the low light as dusk enveloped all.

The dining room was busy as passengers took to their evening meal. Only the finest bone China and silver cutlery was in use. The airship boasted a well-stocked wine cellar and corks popped and bubbles began to flow. This was not going to be an arduous journey by any means. This was fine dining in the air, the height of luxury.

The dining room was buzzing with low-level chatter, refined and intelligent conversation, each table trying not to cause disturbance to their surrounding diners. As Indigo looked around, she saw ladies in their finest dresses, wearing hats of delicate intricacy, decorated with flowers or ribbons of the finest Indian silk. The gentlemen were all dressed in black evening suits, sporting top hats or bowlers. Some were more avantgarde with steam elements of gears and fine gold chains or mechanisms to illustrate they were forward-thinking, modern men of society with an interest in the latest technology of the Empire.

What neither Union Jack noticed was a gentleman dining alone in the furthest corner of the dining room, his bowler hat pulled down low over his eyes, his face in shadow. He wore no adornment, dressed in black with a white collar and buckled shoes. The butt of a steam cannon created a large bulge in his jacket pocket. Eating silently, he spoke to no one and was careful not to draw attention to himself.

Shortly, dinner was served, a rich meal of pheasant and vegetables, fit for a king. The Star Line Company really had excelled in their hospitality. Ignatius sat nursing an after-dinner whiskey and Indigo sipped at her gin gazing out of the window next to their table. In the distance against the fluffy white clouds that drifted slowly and peacefully by, she saw a large dark-coloured bird. Its flight was elegant as it swooped upwards on the air currents, occasionally flapping its wings once to power it onto a different current. It circled and spiralled lower, almost out of view, then, changing direction, it flew directly at the airship, coming to perch on one of the side wings.

"Look at this, Ignatius, it's a beautiful bird. An eagle."

It stretched its wings displaying an impressive wingspan as Ignatius looked out.

"Well I never!" he exclaimed. "Nature really is beautiful."

Th eagle soared majestically above the gas bags of the airship and vanished from sight.

"He's gone. I can't see him," said Indigo, and the two agents sat staring out of the window watching the magnificent sight of the mountains and glaciers below. The air was silent. Even the whir of the dual propellers was faint in the thin air high above the snow-capped mountains.

Looking out again, Ignatius observed that the craggy mountains appeared to be getting closer. "Are we descending?"

Indigo looked out and could see the deep forested slopes that led down to the valleys begin to grow, getting nearer. "We are."

Ignatius searched the frozen blue landscape beneath for a dwelling where they were likely to land. He saw nothing. Soon the whole dining cart became aware that the airship had lost altitude and before long it was drifting gently over a large glacier, with the steep sides of the fjord on either side. The ship was running through the narrow channel, but with no obvious reason why. Chatter spread out and grew in volume throughout the dining cart.

Ignatius was first out of his seat and made his way to the door, followed by Indigo and several other passengers. They encountered a steward, a tall thin man dressed in a white jacket. "What's happening man? Why have we descended?" demanded Ignatius.

"I don't know, sir. I'm sure there is nothing to be alarmed at. The captain knows what he is doing," he added reassuringly. "Perhaps we should all make our way back to the dining room?"

Ignatius and Indigo ignored him and pressed on, making their way towards the bridge. Making their way along the steel grid platform they soon encountered two armed guards, dressed entirely in black. "I'm sorry, sir, ma'am. You cannot approach the bridge. We are the air marshals and we have been given strict orders for all passengers to go about their usual business. So, if you wouldn't mind," he extended a hand out to gesture for the two Union Jacks to return the way they had come.

Ignatius looked offended and stood his ground, "Please! Old boy, if you wouldn't mind. Tell the captain he has Isambard Ignatius onboard, and I am on the Queen's business, so any delay to my work will obviously be looked on unfavourably. Or, if there is any alarm, I need to know as the Queen's orders may be severely affected."

Ignatius seldom declared his work for the Queen, and even now, this was not strictly true. Yes, they were working on behalf of her Majesty's government, via the Union, but Ignatius needed to know if there was any danger.

"Very well. Wait here," said one of the burley marshals, who retreated to the bridge whilst the other kept a keen eye on Ignatius and Indigo. After a few minutes he returned, "Very well, this way please, sir," and he led the two of them on to the bridge.

The captain was a grey-haired thin man with large white handlebar moustache and thick bushy eyebrows. He looked like an ex-brigadier from the armed forces. "Good evening, Mr Ignatius. I am told you are on business for Her Majesty." He raised a questioning eyebrow and his moustache twitched.

"We are, captain. Exactly what, I am not at liberty to say. But I am concerned. Is there a problem? We seem to be flying awfully low, if you don't mind me saying so."

The captain looked at the two of them suspiciously. Then after a few moments where he seemed to be muttering to himself, he replied, "I am not sure what is going on at the moment. My man in the crow's nest thinks he saw two dirigibles tailing us, so we have come low to try and lure them out of the thick cloud cover above. But there's been no sight of them yet. Which I don't understand. They should be a lot faster than this old girl and have no problem catching us up. But we also think somebody has been tampering with one of the engines. A most serious matter. If this is all correct, our journey to Tibet is going to be a very long and arduous flight with all of my men on constant high alert!"

"I see. Do you know who or why?" asked Ignatius.

"Not at all. However, may I enquire if you have anything of value aboard? Do you carry anything for Her Majesty that is of value?"

"Not at all. It is only the two of us. Passengers only with nothing of value, not monetary, or even a letter. I can assure you that we are of no interest to any other parties, or to be the target of any attack."

Indigo looked at Ignatius, a little incredulous. But said nothing. It was true, they had nothing of value. But as for enemies, or a reason to stop them reaching Tibet, there were many.

"Very well," replied the captain, "I am sorry for any inconvenience, or delay in your royal duty, but events are out of my hands. We must proceed with caution. Now, if you will forgive me, sir, I must decide on our journey forwards and make a plan. This journey is for ten days; at this rate, it's going to take a lot longer!"

The captain turned his back and walked away to a large layout table where he resumed studying charts using a set of dividers and a compass.

Ignatius and Indigo turned to leave and as they approached the door to the bridge, the captain let out a cry, "What... what is wrong with this?"

They turned to see a confused captain and navigator both staring at the compass. The captain was tapping the top of the glass with his finger as if trying to influence the needle. Returning, Ignatius could see the needle was spinning wildly in full rotations. Magnetic north seemed to mean nothing to it.

"Please! Mr Ignatius, you are going to have to leave, so my men and I can decide on our course!"

The air marshal ushered them off the bridge and back into the corridor. As they made their way back towards their cabins, they were trying to work out what was going on.

"Something is afoot, Ignatius. There is definitely something strange taking place," said Indigo. "But I can't decide if it is to delay our journey, to prevent us from getting to Tibet, or merely a rival company seeking to compromise Star Line or worse, a foreign power trying to falter the Empire."

Ignatius seemed to be vacant, replying with a simple, "quite".

Indigo could see he was gazing out of the nearest window, looking to the distance. "What is it?"

"That eagle is definitely following us."

Indigo looked out and could see the eagle swooping down on to the deck of the airship before returning to the air, only to swoop again, and again, before deciding on a suitable part of one of the gondolas to land and perch.

"Come on, let's go and see where he is," said Indigo. The two Union Jacks made their way towards one of the other gondolas, where the great bird of prey had landed. As they approached, they could see a large dark shadow that repeatedly shifted its weight from foot to foot.

The large black silhouette perched on the deck, his huge dangerous-looking talons gripping the brass rail with such a powerful force, it looked like he could easily crush a man's arm. His intelligent eyes blinked and his head turned now and then, inquisitive to his surroundings. Occasionally, he spread his wings to stretch them.

"I wonder what the bird wants? Or do you think he is just curious because he's never seen an airship before?" said Indigo.

The three of them stood staring at each other for a while. It was like the bird was scrutinising the two Union Jacks. He shifted his weight from foot to foot and peered again with suspicion.

"Well, we can't stay here all day. We must press on. I wonder if the two dirigibles have some means of disrupting our compass," said Ignatius, thinking out loud. Making their way to an outer walkway, Ignatius held his right hand to his eye, the eye-shaped birthmark on display, like an eye tattooed on his hand. He looked around before covering his eye, searching for the dirigibles amongst the clouds, but could see nothing. Looking below all he saw was the pastel colours of a frozen fjord veiled in mist. He lifted his right hand, rubbed the birthmark with his left. He held his hand over his right eye again to see if events were a little clearer. He gasped and momentarily removed his hand. He could never quite get used to using the power this blemish gave him. He tried again. Attempting to look at the fjord surrounding them, he struggled, his sight kept peering onto other planes. He saw strange beasts and skies of unnatural colours. Eventually, focusing hard, he looked upon the fjord and into the sky above, but saw nothing. After a few moments, he became aware he was now staring through time. Viking longboats were moored along the shore and campfires filled the air with soot. It was no use. He removed his hand.

"I can't see anything of any value." At which point, the airship lurched a little and began to rise, rapidly lifting itself out of the greyed-out landscape and into the clouds before going full-steam ahead. Returning to their table, there was some chatter in the dining room again about the unusual stop, but before long passengers had forgotten about this minor inconvenience and resumed their business, the airship continuing unhindered on its long voyage.

Chapter 4: Ransacked

The airship continued its journey, heading over St. Petersburg in Russia, their flight path taking the shortest route, heading north east before dropping down and heading south east. With nothing much else to do, Indigo was gazing out over the many islands that comprised this beautiful city in the delta of the Neva River. The Winter Palace, home to the Tsar, drifted by. Indigo could see soldiers below, taken by surprise, trying to ready their weapons to take aim at a vehicle from a rival Empire, but they were too slow. The captain sent message for more steam and within no time the airship was heading for the Ural mountains.

It was getting late, and the two Union Jacks decided to retire for the night. As they approached their cabins, Ignatius could see that his door was slightly ajar. Silently, he held his hand up to signal Indigo to be cautious. He removed a small pistol from the inside pocket of his jacket and crept towards the door, poised to shoot if necessary. Indigo stood the other side of it with her derringer in her hand, ready to follow Ignatius in. He threw the door open and hurled himself into the cabin, rapidly followed by Indigo, and although it was quite obvious it had been searched, they were alone.

Ignatius quickly shut the door behind them.

"What were they after?" asked Indigo. "And what's more, who knows we are on board? I don't fancy spending the entirety of the trip looking over my shoulder. And it's a very long trip!"

Ignatius rubbed his chin. "I don't know who they are Indigo, but I might know what they are after."

"What? Tell me"

"Well, I have obviously brought Enoch Slipnot's book with me, just in case it gives up any information of value. But I've also got maps and…" He paused, checking outside the cabin before closing the door again and locking it. "Remember we took some books from the library at the Administorium before it was all destroyed? I can only assume they may be after those, but I don't know if any of them are significant."

"Where are they? Have they been stolen?"

"No. I think they are quite safe. They are in my trunk with Lambeth."

The two Union Jacks looked at each other and then both exclaimed in unison, "Lambeth!"

Hurrying outside into the corridor, they knocked on Lambeth's door, but there was no reply. Ignatius knocked again, this time in a peculiar sequence. The knocks were obviously a code or signal of some sort that only he and Lambeth knew.

Indigo could hear movement from inside and then the sound of the lock. Lambeth opened the door to peer out with just one eye to check if it was safe. As the door opened fully, a dazed and bloodied Lambeth staggered backwards and perched on his bed.

"I'm sorry, sir. He overpowered me and I took a blow to the head. I think I was out cold for a while."

Ignatius rushed to the man's aid, checking his head. A scarlet wound crossed his head, his white hair matted and stained. "Not at all, Lambeth. There's nothing you could have done. Are you alright?"

"I… I think I just need to rest." His eyes were full of sorrow, and he gripped Ignatius's arm tightly, his knuckles turning white, "he didn't get anything, sir. Nothing. He searched your room and, hearing the noise, I went to investigate. Obviously, he didn't expect me, or that I am travelling with you. So, he didn't look in here." He grinned as best he could, displaying blood between his teeth.

"I'm going to see if I can find a medic," said Indigo. "He's going to need more help than we can give him."

Ignatius began to tidy his cabin so it didn't look too obvious to anyone who came to help. Before long, Indigo returned with a doctor, who quickly attended to Lambeth and although he didn't ask too many questions, he eyed Ignatius with suspicion and said that he would have to report this to the captain for security reasons, then left.

After the doctor left, Ignatius tried to analyse what had occurred. "I wonder who did this? We need to be vigilant for the whole journey, they may attempt something again. But I intend to find out who is spying on us."

"It's not going to be a great journey if we are constantly watching our backs," replied Indigo.

Chapter 5: Spy

A dark figure returned stealthily to his cabin. In his haste, he fumbled as he unlocked the door and once the other side of it began to breathe heavily. He was out of breath from his exertions. Removing his bowler hat revealed a thin-faced man with black rings around his eyes, like he hadn't slept properly in days. He swept his unruly hair to one side and began pacing up and down his cabin, wringing his hands in agitation. This is not what he had expected, now Ignatius would be alerted to his presence. He didn't expect Lambeth to be in his room at the time.

Sweat formed on his pale brow. His long thin face was twisted with concern, and he felt uneasy. He was not used to such activity. The old man had taken a strong blow to the head. He usually didn't get his hands dirty with such work, a minion or a drone would do his bidding for him and whilst his internal rage was kept burning for Ignatius, he didn't really wish any harm to anyone else. He had a score to settle with Isambard Ignatius and he wouldn't rest until it was done. More importantly, he had made a mess of things, and if he was to obtain what he believed Ignatius had with him on this journey, he was going to have to return.

As he paced restlessly, he tried to think of a new plan, but his attention was drawn to a dark shadow that flew past his cabin window. The incident was repeated several times. He looked out of the window and saw an eagle hovering on the currents, peering in at him. Opening his window, the bird entered his cabin, perching on a chair at a small desk in the corner.

The menacing bird paced a little, his razor-sharp talons gripping the chair back tightly. "Well? Have you located it? Said the bird.

"No, not yet." His voice was hesitant and trembled a little. "It didn't go according to plan. I will have to try again. I wasn't expecting his manservant to be with him. He also has a woman with him."

"I have seen her. Is she a threat?"

"I'm not sure. Probably not. His partner died; she was a definite threat, but this woman seems a bit frail, not much of a fighter, I'd say." He gave the bird a nervous thin-lipped smile.

"Since Ignatius destroyed the library built by Viveka, there have been many bounty hunters looking for him from across the planes. The destruction of all that knowledge has had far-reaching consequences in all the great libraries, some have come crashing down because of their ethereal link to that of Vivekas."

The great bird of prey spread his wings full span to make a statement. "We have another complication. This airship is being followed. I don't know who they are, but they pose a definite threat. If they are after the same prize as ourselves and you do not get it first, I am going to pluck your eyes out as you sleep, and you can live the rest of your pitiful life in darkness, much the same as you had lived it before in the Administorium.

Brother Aelfric was the last remaining cleric alive from the Administorium. He was certain that no other cleric or priestess had survived the incident at their headquarters, and the Librarian had abandoned them all, flying off into the cosmos, leaving his eagle, Manjushri, behind.

"You had the title of Grand Wizard once, so make use of your powers, or are your powers like you, a pale imitation of the position you once held? If you truly are a wizard, use your powers, gain entry, killing Ignatius if you must. But as you know, I am not just a bird, but also a god, and I can guarantee your remaining days on this planet shall be unbearable!"

Aelfric's pride wouldn't allow anybody to mock him like this. He was raging internally, and his pale face flushed. Nobody had ever spoken to him like this, he was a nobleman, the highest cleric of the Administorium, feared throughout the Empire. However, he had never dealt with a god before, bird-like or not. Rising to the challenge, like a fool, he opened a small wooden box, breathed in and inflated his chest with pride, pulling out some chalk, a black candle, some herbs in a small bag and a phial of blue liquid. He paced his room, examining the floor, looking for where to start.

He drew a large circle on the floor with the chalk, filling it with geometric shapes, symbols and runes. On one of the symbols, he placed the candle and lit it. His face in the peculiar light looked dark and foreboding but his eyes were alight in his desperate act of vengeance. Then, sitting at the centre of his sorcery, he sprinkled the blue liquid around the circle. His movements were slow but dramatic, with over-exaggerated arm and hand movements, and then he closed his eyes.

Manjushri looked on, fascinated and slightly impressed that this pathetic cleric who had lived most of his life hiding behind the walls of the Administorium's edifice, had risen suitably to the challenge. He stretched his wings and was slightly perturbed by what was happening. He knew the planes inhabited by the exceptionally gifted were magical places on which no normal human could survive unaided for long and the spaces between the worlds, perhaps between the planes, were where the inexperienced could be lost forever. One wrong gesture or chant and it was possible never to escape the Voids between, and that they probably led to the Ghost Worlds where monsters and terrors were normally exiled. He didn't know if Aelfric was that good, that experienced, truly a Grand Wizard, and if he would ever return, without being severely affected, or even if he might leave his body an empty husk on this planet, this plane and timeline, never able to get back to it.

Aelfric sat chanting, a low vocal incantation, his mind, the very air around his body, vibrating to produce extra sensory alertness within. In his mind's eye he was able to float through the airship, unhindered, unchallenged by anybody he passed to arrive at Ignatius's cabin. In truth, he had only achieved something like this once before and found the whole experience taxing on his body, physically and most of all, mentally.

He drifted through the cabin door as if it didn't exist, where he had seen the trunk. Lambeth felt a chill in the air, an unnatural chill like that when in the presence of a ghost. The hairs stood up on the back of his neck, but looking around he couldn't see anything unusual. Lambeth was on his bunk, nursing his head and paid him no attention. Aelfric's astral body went over to the trunk, but it was locked. He placed his open hand against the lock and white fire began to grow around his fingers, then his whole hand and up his forearm. It burned, the pain was unbearable, but he could feel the tumblers in the lock barrel begin to turn. This would surely attract Lambeth's attention.

Aelfric's body back in his own cabin suddenly jolted, his

chanting stopped. He wheezed and gasped for air and his body slumped backwards. Someone or something was blocking his powers. He had been prevented from working any further in the planes between planes. His hand and arm still burned. He opened and closed his hand in pain, trying to stretch his fingers and regain some normal feeling in his digits.

He became aware once more of Manjushri. The great eagle stretched his wings and squawked, then laughed. "Ha! Are your powers not strong enough, then, Aelfric? As I suspected, and have always suspected, you are full of wind. All air and no substance. You look down on everyone, you have an air of superiority, but when it comes down to it, you're not a great wizard of any kind!"

Aelfric's pale face turned red and with gritted teeth, he lashed out at the bird, who was too slow to move, and he caught him by the legs, throwing him at the wall opposite. Feathers flew into the air and the eagle took flight, wounded, bruised, but able to move out of Aelfric's way. The eagle dove and pecked at the cleric, wings flapping, talons tearing at the thin clothing and skin on his shoulders.

Eventually, Manjushri stopped and headed for the cabin window, back out into the thin air and away from the airship. Aelfric was lying on his back, motionless, breathing heavily, wondering what he should do next and what power was stopping him from fulfilling his mission.

Picking himself up, he stood pondering for a while and nursing his wounded shoulder. Some force was in operation in and around Ignatius, but what? He returned to be seated in the chalk circle and closed his eyes. After the same routine, he found himself back with Ignatius and Lambeth. As he scanned the scene, an interconnecting door opened and in walked the woman he had seen. All around her was a dark aura, midnight blue and purple.

He gasped and his whole body felt the resistance his astral self was experiencing. He began to grow weak, fearing he might get lost on the planes between planes, exiled forever. He could sense Ignatius had brought with him some ancient knowledge, but fear overcame him and he retreated, firstly to distance his astral body from the woman and then, when she felt too strong, he retreated altogether, to the safety of his own cabin.

Chapter 6: Pirates

Ignatius could just make out two small black dots on the horizon. He wasn't sure which direction they were going, away from them or towards the ship. He continued to look out throughout the evening, and although they drifted into view occasionally, they didn't seem any threat due to the great distance between them and the airship.

A few hours later and the ship was silent, all the passengers and some of the crew were in their bunks. The night was dark, but fortunately the moon gave enough light to illuminate the upper decks. Ignatius and Indigo stood on the highest deck listening, scanning the air surrounding the ship. High up in the crow's nest, an aeronaut looked out using a mechanical scope. He had the contraption strapped to his head, so it was a permanent feature over his right eye. The lookout's monocular hissed a little steam as it projected in and out to focus on the two shapes on the horizon. But it wasn't an ordinary monocular, it was a mechanical eye that, although looked like it was strapped to his head, was actually attached to his skull. A fine example of the technological advances of the scientists and engineers of the Empire. The two dark shapes started to grow as they approached moving rapidly. It was obvious they had been stalling for time and had waited until nightfall. Two dirigibles came clearly into view, armed with weapons down the length of each side and a solid looking ram at the front. At the rear each flew a black flag with a curious silver circular emblem on it. It was an empty silver circle with silver flames coming from one side. They were small, fast and agile, able to out manoeuvre all other craft.

Using the voice pipe, the lookout called down to the bridge, "we got company. Air pirates, cap'n. Movin' fast"

He then fired a flare into the air, usual protocol, partially to light the area so they could see the approaching danger, and partly as a distress signal for any other passing airships who might be able to lend assistance. The crew opened fire from the gun turret beneath the airship. Rapid fire exploded in the air close to the two dirigibles which were too swift and nimble, avoiding all gunfire.

Ignatius was looking out of the promenade windows and saw the craft. Turning to Indigo he said, "get ready for boarding, we're being attacked by pirates", and the two of them prepared their weapons.

It was clear the ship would not be able to outrun the two dirigibles. The captain took evasive action, taking a sharp pull starboard hoping to run into the smaller craft, but they dived and flew beneath the airship, eventually coming back up on either side.

At the forefront of one of the dirigibles was a figure with outstretched arms, with open hands poised as if to grab something. Only the mouth and chin of this individual could be seen. Lips were moving constantly in chant, an incantation. The air seemed to writhe from fingertips, with spirals of magical, electrified air finding their way through the *Spirit of the Empire* to find and disturb the compass.

There were several clanking sounds as grappling hooks were

secured to the rails of the ship. The captain tried to descend, but it was no use, the dirigibles were secured to the ship.

The pirates swiftly boarded. They were all dressed totally in black clothing, tattered and torn as if they had travelled a great distance, or maybe it was just a long time since they had been home, or on land. They were of slender build with their faces hidden, covered in black hooded cloaks and black bandanas covering their mouths and noses. Only piercing sapphire blue eyes could be seen. They wore black leather gloves that were strapped up their arms to their elbows and they were adorned with thick silver chains. Each wore an inverted double cross on a chain around their necks. They all possessed a short sword or scimitar, useful for close combat, and slender ornate pistols with ivory-inlaid handles; others were also armed with a quarterstaff. Around their middle they all wore a black cummerbund with several short, handle-less throwing knives tucked into it. Some were steel, some were black obsidian that often shimmered with iridescent blue and purple, like Peacock ore. The air pirates were obviously experienced and moved swiftly once aboard.

For the most part, the pirates ignored the passengers, pushing them aside. They were of no consequence or danger. The crew had armed themselves and were trying to hold the pirates back, but the first two fell, their innards spilling onto the deck and horror etched on their faces as they fell.

Blades flashed this way and that. They didn't stop and seemed to be on a quest for something, or someone in particular. They were driven and ferocious. Two pirates made their way to the gun turret to take out the operative. The rest headed for the passengers' cabins.

Ignatius and Indigo readied themselves. They barred the passageway to their own deck with annoyed and confused passengers behind them.

"Get back! How many more times," shouted Ignatius and the last of them disappeared into their cabins. Bolts were noisily fastened, and chairs propped against the door handles to prevent the opening of any doors. Indigo could hear several passengers crying or hyper-ventilating.

The first pirate burst through the outer door and fired a shot. At the same time, a short obsidian knife whistled passed Indigo's face. The black figure moved like lightning and was soon upon the Union Jacks, followed by two more assailants.

Indigo fired both of her derringers, hitting one in the forehead, and just missing the other. Ignatius fired his steam cannon and a large hole appeared in the torso of the lead pirate. The smell of burning flesh filled the air and spattered the walls of the passageway. Ignatius fired again, killing the third assailant.

Without wasting any time, Ignatius knelt beside one of the bodies to try and find out who they were. Two sparkling sapphire blue eyes, bright and mesmerising even in death, stared back at him. He pulled the bandana from the corpse's face and to his surprise, fine beautiful features appeared. A woman with black tattoos on her cheeks and forehead, black runes for protection, presumably. Indigo reached for the other two bodies, and letting out a gasp of surprise, revealed that they were all female and all had the same or similar runes tattooed on their face.

"Women! They are all women! Who are they?" she asked. "What do they want? They seemed to be heading specifically for someone or something."

Ignatius didn't get time to answer, not that he knew, before several more pirates came running down the passageway at them. Ignatius felt knuckles smash against his face, and a scimitar blade sliced through his dinner jacket and arm. That was it, to ruin a gentleman's dinner jacket was more than he could stand, and he went into a fury. Female or not, he lashed out and felt ribs cave in as he punched with his full weight behind it. Snatching a scimitar, he made short work as he sliced and parried until two more pirates lay in a crumpled heap at his feet, turning the deck slippery with their blood. The others were being played with by Indigo, who was an expert with a sword. It was like a cat playing with its prey, until one by one they were sliced and run through.

Without delay, he was out onto the outer promenade deck with Indigo, ready and waiting for more assailants. Several black figures came swinging over in formation onto the ship. Looking around, it became obvious the remaining pirates all had the same slight build and were clearly skilled at doing this. One by one, they landed, armed and dangerous, onto the deck.

One of the assailants stood before them, striking a pose, waiting to pounce. The slender shadowy figure stood defiant, aggressive, feet apart, legs locked, holding two quarterstaffs with long blue crystals at the end. Blue fire cracked and fizzed, arcing around the figures arms and encircling the iron shaft of the weapons.

Ignatius lifted his steam cannon to take aim but was roughly knocked off balance as one of the crew hurled himself at him, wrapping his arms around him to prevent him from taking aim.

"No! You can't! If one shot hits those gas bags above, we will all be done for. This thing will just be one big fireball!"

Ignatius looked somewhat annoyed but before he could object or compose himself, the assailant unfurled a grappling hook and caught the rail on the deck above, swiftly swinging into action and climbing higher towards the gasbags. Ignatius snarled at the crew member and raised an eyebrow. The man, realising his error, looked a bit sheepish and retreated. Without any delay, Ignatius began to climb the rope attached to the grappling hook, following the dark figure onto the upper deck.

Azure light illuminated his face as a quarterstaff sliced dangerously close to his face. It caught him on the shoulder, which burned. But no blood appeared as the heat of the crystal instantly cauterised his flesh. The startling sting caused him to let go of the rope and he hung in mid-air holding on desperately with one hand. Finding his grip once more he pulled himself up, every move causing his shoulder to burn.

Once on the deck, he had to duck and weave as the two quarterstaffs whistled through the thin air, threatening death if he wasn't quick enough. Eventually seeing a gap, he threw himself at his attacker and landed on top, pinning one arm down as the other quarterstaff flailed around behind him. Grabbing it and using his sheer strength, he eventually freed the weapon and threw it out and away from the ship, watching the thin wispy clouds illuminate blue as it fell to the mountains below.

It fell past Indigo, who was in close combat with another, her short sword flashing in the moonlight. She was holding her opponent close, not allowing room for any movement. Then suddenly the silence of the night was shattered with a single gunshot and smoke arose from one of her derringers. She figured at such close quarters it was safe to use. Blood erupted from the forehead of the figure before her as she helped the pirate overboard with lifeless limbs flailing about in the cool breeze. Soon, another was upon her, and she made short work using her sword. The figure fell to the deck, a pool of blood appearing around the body.

Ignatius was struggling high above in the netting holding the gas bags in place, engaged in unarmed combat. A quarterstaff whistled passed him over and over, just managing to duck and dive at every attempt, Ignatius didn't know how long he could keep this up. He could see he was heavier and more muscular than his opponent, so he threw himself at the pirate knocking the figure off balance and they both fell. Managing to grab the pirate Ignatius was able to manoeuvre his body around so the assailant broke his fall as they both hit the deck. A pool of dark blood soon surrounded the pirate's head.

He groaned, winded and croaked in a low voice to Indigo, "Are there any more?" He was hoping they had all been dealt with, they were all much younger and more agile than he was, and the threat to take over the airship was all too real. Their mission to Tibet would be scuppered, and he couldn't risk that.

Looking around, it became obvious the remaining pirates were all women. They were caught up fighting the crew, who were desperately defending the ship. Picking his way through the bodies on the deck, both crew and pirates, he leaned over the side and pulled out his sonic blaster. Adjusting the dials, he pulled the trigger, and strange music filled the air. The impulses that emanated from it hit the side of one of the dirigibles, causing the boards to warp and twist like they were made of rubber. Eventually they shattered. Ignatius fired again and this time blew a hole through the hull and some of the grappling hooks became detached. The dirigible slowly turned and took a nosedive, heading for the jagged rocks below.

Most of the pirates lay dead upon the decks or had fallen to a gruesome demise. Those that remained headed for the remaining dirigible to retreat. Indigo was hanging off the side of the airship, her knuckles were white holding on to some ropes that had been used previously to tether the airship to the ground. Her short sword sliced through the air, narrowly missing one of the pirates. As they cut the ropes and drifted rearwards to turn, Ignatius showed no mercy. He adjusted the dials of his sonic blaster once more and took aim and they all watched the horror clearly visible in the pirates' eyes as the boards around them and beneath them splintered and disintegrated, falling as fine sawdust, and blowing away on the breeze, leaving the shadowy figures onboard to fall to their death, clutching aimlessly at the air.

The captain ordered the bodies of the fallen to be searched for any clues to who they were and what they wanted. Tucked into their bandanas were pieces of parchment or scroll, with writing that looked similar to the runes on their faces.

"Prayers," said Ignatius, "for protection. Fanatics with a mission, Warrior nuns."

The captain scowled at Ignatius with suspicion. "I get the distinct impression this is all your fault. Who are you, and what business do you have on my airship?"

Ignatius and Indigo were silent.

"I'll ask again, do you carry anything for Her Majesty that I need to know about? Anything that will put the lives of all the passengers and crew at risk?"

Ignatius shrugged. "Not at all. We are merely travelling as is everyone else, to Tibet."

The captain looked to Indigo, as if to appeal, but was met once more with a shrug of her shoulders. But as the captain turned to walk away, ordering his men to throw the dead overboard once stripped of any weapons or valuables, she looked at Ignatius, and she knew he was lying.

"Wait!" said Ignatius. "Before you do, collect up all the parchment pieces and copy down all the runes on their faces. If we can decode them, it may tell us who they are and what they wanted."

Chapter 7: The Black Tattoos

Ignatius and Indigo returned to their cabins. Indigo helped to clean and bandage his wound. Lambeth kept busy fetching water and swabs.

Eventually, Indigo got around to asking him outright, "well! Are you going to tell me? We are clearly carrying something on board that you haven't told me about. Do you know who these warriors were?"

"No. But I have an idea they are related to some intelligence I have about the Flaming Celestial Pearl."

"Then why didn't you tell me?"

"In truth, I didn't know! Only now am I able to piece things together. But I wasn't keeping it from you, honestly." He turned to Lambeth. "Lambeth, open the trunk, I need to retrieve something."

Lambeth was up on his feet, "the books, sir?"

"Yes, Lambeth, the books." He looked at Indigo. "I knew they might be precious, hence us keeping the trunk close by, for security. But I had no idea until now. I promise."

Indigo said nothing but was beginning to think that Ignatius was not telling her everything recently. She had doubt in her mind, didn't he trust her? Or was he just trying to protect her? She suppressed her thoughts and acted normally.

Lambeth reached into the trunk and brought out two ancient-looking books, one of which looked extremely archaic and in need of repair.

"This book mentions Tibet, which is why I didn't question Lawrence too much about sending us thousands of miles. I think he has probably pointed us in the right direction. It also has a symbol embossed on it that I think represents the Pearl."

Indigo recognised it as one of the books that Ignatius liberated from the library beneath the Administorium. The book looked like the oldest tome she had ever seen. The leather surface was flaking, it was in very poor condition. The black leather was turning yellow, and it looked like mould was starting to grow on its surface. Embossed on the cover, and just visible, was a logo of some kind. It was the same logo that had been on the pirates' ensign. As Ignatius carefully opened the cover, it became detached from the spine and a line of dust fell to the table.

"Look," said Ignatius, "that same logo appears throughout the book, and the runes, too. They are the same as the tattoos on the pirates. I'm beginning to think this book picked me, rather than me picking it from that library!"

"But what do they mean?" said Indigo.

"I don't know, I haven't been able to decipher them yet. But this is no coincidence. I am beginning to think the emblem represents the Flaming Celestial Pearl. In which case, are these pirates, these warrior nuns sworn to protect it? But how did they know we were on our way to find it?"

There was a loud knock at the door. Lambeth opened it to reveal the captain, giving Ignatius time to hid the book. "Mr. Ignatius, one of the pirates is still alive! But she is badly injured, I'm not sure how long she will survive. You'd best hurry if you want to speak to her."

Without any delay, he turned and was along the passageway as Ignatius and Indigo left the cabin to follow. Outside, the air was damp and cloud had started to mask the moon, so the light was low. A crewman was holding the pirate's head up off the deck a little, and another was tending to her wounds. She coughed and blood trickled from the corner of her mouth, and she wheezed, finding it difficult to breathe.

Kneeling beside her, Ignatius spoke softly and slowly. He knew time was precious and he couldn't risk needing to repeat himself. "I am Isambard Ignatius, I'd like to know who you are, and why you attacked us?"

She coughed again, then spat her hoarse words in almost a whisper. "I know who you are. I am Katia from the Great Sisterhood of the Celestial Pearl, the Knights of Himavala, sworn protectors of Prajnana, or as you would know it, the Flaming Celestial Pearl."

"What do you want with me?" Ignatius knew the answer as soon as he asked the question.

"To kill you. You must not obtain the Pearl. You know nothing of its power or its purpose. It would disturb the balance of the cosmos. You are ignorant and foolish."

Ignatius ignored the threat and the insult. "How did you know we were aboard this airship?"

The pirate coughed, spraying blood across the deck. "We see everything. My death will only make us stronger. These runes upon my face will secure my place in the cosmic ocean, to strengthen the Great Sisterhood, to give our astral selves even more power."

She let out a large gasp and struggled for air. More blood foamed on her lips. Ignatius looked up at the crewman administering some medical aid. He said nothing and slowly shook his head. One more gasp and the pirate seized Ignatius by the arm; she tried to talk, her wild eyes piercing his very soul, and then she was gone. She slumped back onto the deck, her body limp and lifeless.

Rather coldly, the captain said, "she'll have to go overboard; we can't keep corpses on the ship. Sorry! Before we do, though, what does she mean pearl? And what is the significance of the tattoos? Do you know, Mr. Ignatius?"

"I don't, at least not yet."

"Are we talking treasure? Were they looking for pearls?"

Ignatius couldn't get a word in.

"Do you have pearls or some high value jewellery, treasure I need to be aware of? Is that what this is all about?"

"No!" said Ignatius. "I certainly do not. There are no pearls, I have no idea what she means. They are probably from some cult, fanatics. Pirates out for what they can get. Trying to strike it lucky. As for the tattoos, they are probably for protection, or some mystical connection. But if your men give me all the parchments I can try and work it out."

"I don't like it, Mr. Ignatius. I don't like it one bit. I know they call it the mystic East, but I don't believe in magic, mystical connections and the like. I want answers, Mr. Ignatius. Answers!" He turned and walked away. "Men get the rest of these bodies overboard, quickly! Full power ahead, we need to make up for lost time. And keep fresh and observant in the crow's nest, change the crewman every two hours and scrub those decks. I don't want to run into any more pirates. I'll go and check the gun turret; we can't afford for it to be out of action." The captain marched off with purpose in his stride, leaving Ignatius and Indigo behind, feeling somewhat unpopular amongst the whole crew.

Indigo looked at Ignatius. "You have studied the occult, do you know anything. Have any idea?"

He leaned in towards her to speak quietly, "I have an idea, but I'm not sure yet. Let's get back to the cabin."

Back in his cabin, Ignatius unlocked his trunk and removed the ancient tome. The pages inside were yellow and crumbling and the ink had faded badly. Whole sections were absent, and some pages had large holes in them. He wasn't sure he was going to get any useful information from its pages, but he knew this was what the warrior nuns were probably seeking, along with his own demise. He lay the pieces of parchment out on the top of his trunk. They looked as if they were all from the same scroll. Next to them, he lay the drawings the crew had done of the runes. Carefully he picked up the ancient book and lay it next to them. He turned some pages, and tiny fragments broke away and were lost to the atmosphere as the dust drifted away. He noticed his birthmark had started to irritate him again. The same dull burning sensation he had experienced before.

"This may take all night. Lambeth, could you fetch me some whiskey please, then perhaps you should get some rest. How's the head?"

"Much better now, sir. Thank you."

Lambeth left to head to the bar. Upon returning, he got the impression he was being watched. He locked the cabin door, handed Ignatius his drink and made his way to his bunk, where he tucked a derringer underneath his pillow.

Turning to Indigo, he said, "I'm taking no chances miss."

"What are we looking for?" she asked.

"Well.… I think… all of these pieces form a whole. I think they are directions, and the runes are the key to understanding them."

Indigo looked on, she could see some regularity in the text, and the odd rune was repeated, but it was all very confusing. Nothing was that discernible.

"You can see more than me, then," she said.

Ignatius tentatively opened a few more pages of the book, cautious for fear the whole lot would disintegrate. Liberating the book from its subterranean home and bringing it up to the surface had harmed the book. The air and the light were takings its toll. It had laid undisturbed in the dark for thousands of years. Ignatius began to shuffle the parchments around as if he was playing a game of patience. He mumbled a few times and moved them again. Placing the book down he placed some of the pieces onto a page in the book, moving them around to try and gain a match. Removing them, he turned some more pages and tried again.

"Any luck?" asked Indigo. "Only I really think we should get some rest, it's late."

"You go ahead, I don't mind staying all night if I must. But I want to work this out. The sooner the better in case there are more attacks along the way."

Ignatius worked alone, deep into the night.

When morning came, Indigo gave a gentle knock on the interconnecting door and let herself in. Ignatius was slumped over the trunk, asleep. Several pages of the antique book lay around him with several fragments of some pages that had deteriorated some more. He had been scribbling on pieces of paper trying to decode the runes. She laid her hand upon his back and he stirred.

"Ummph, what time is it?" he said in a quiet hoarse voice. He was still very sleepy.

"It's eight in the morning."

"Ah! Then I'd best awaken."

"It's probably not critical you decipher the runes anyway. I can't imagine the pirates are going to return or have that much influence anyway...."

Ignatius cut her off before she could continue. "That's where you are wrong!"

Indigo frowned and looked into his half-closed eyes. "On which account, their return, or their influen..."

"Both!" Ignatius gave a huge grin. "I have solved it. I think we haven't seen the last of them, and they do have a lot of influence. I have deciphered the runes. They are pictograms. Putting them together forms a map!"

"Isambard Ignatius, you are a genius. So come on, tell me. A map to what and how does it work?"

Rubbing his eyes, Ignatius, became a bit livelier and started to move the parchment pieces around on top of the trunk. He pieced them together, then placed the drawings of the runes on top. "The writing is a description of how to get to a mystical city, the runes form images aiding the descriptions and act like pointers, markers to help show the way."

"So, which city and where is it located?"

"Well, that's the problem. It's a mystical city, it may not be real, just some legend, but I believe it points the way to where the pirates originate. And to answer your previous questions, I think we haven't seen the last of them, and they are extremely dangerous. They are fanatical protectors of the Flaming Celestial Pearl. But now we have this knowledge, we can't leave it lying around here, not even locked in the trunk. Our intruder earlier yesterday may pay us another visit, and whoever he is, we need to find out."

Chapter 8: Captured

Refreshed, Ignatius and Indigo sat at their breakfast table in the dining room. Looking around, some of the other passengers who had seen him in action the previous night were staring with equal parts disapproval and gratitude. They were all talking in hushed tones.

"I have a feeling this journey is going to be longer and more uncomfortable than we anticipated," laughed Indigo.

Ignatius smiled, then, leaning forward so he couldn't be heard, he said, "what do you make of the gentlemen sat by the doors? He's sat in his bowler hat, pulled low over his eyes, and his collar is up. He looks like he is trying to hide."

Without being obvious, Indigo glanced over. "he couldn't be more conspicuous, could he?"

They both smiled. "I think we may have our intruder," said Ignatius. "And I think he is definitely an amateur."

"Maybe, but he couldn't possibly know of those ancient books, could he? I mean, who is he and who is he working for?"

"Well, later today, I think we should find out. But for now, I'm starving. Let's eat!"

After breakfast, Ignatius waited for the suspicious gentleman to leave, then he and Indigo followed him. He was trying to be elusive, darting into other passages when other passengers or crew passed him. He kept his head firmly down, making sure not to make eye contact at any point. Stopping at the door to the cabins, he looked behind him and spotted Ignatius. Picking up his pace, he hurried to his cabin and as he quickly turned the key, Ignatius pounced. The full weight of his body hit the man and pushed him through the doorway, the two of them collapsing on the floor. Ignatius saw his hand move swiftly to his belt as he attempted to pull out a steam pistol. Indigo placed her boot on the man's wrist, pinning his arm to the floor. In the fray, his bowler hat had been knocked off and as he stopped struggling, realising it was no use, he had been captured, Ignatius recognised him.

"Aelfric! Whatever, man! What are you doing here? I thought you'd perished with the rest of the Administorium."

Aelfric looked embarrassed and gave a large sigh. "No, I still live!" he whispered, the wind having been taken out of his sails.

Ignatius got off him and helped him to his feet. He was no real threat. Ignatius had got the measure of him some time ago, during his visit to the Administorium.

"Are you spying on us, old boy?"

Aelfric stammered. "I… I… I want to know what you are up to. You destroyed the Administorium, all of it. Gone! The clerics and priestesses all dead. As far as I know, I am the only survivor."

"Well, that wasn't my intention. And in truth, it was brought on by your own High Priestess. But that's not the point. What are you doing here? I'm guessing it was you who ransacked my cabin. Why are you following us?"

"Really? Why do you think! I want revenge. My life has been turned upside down, I have no purpose, and I want to know why you are travelling to Tibet."

Ignatius gave a sardonic grin. "You only had to ask, old boy. You only had to ask!"

Aelfric looked confused but before he could speak, Indigo was upon him, the blade of her short sword dug into his fleshy neck. "One move and I'll slit it!" She had taken him completely by surprise. He had underestimated her. She looked so gaunt and pale. "Who are you? Do I know you?" He gazed deep into her partially vacant eyes.

"Eliza. Eliza Patience, and I don't like thieves and pirates!"

She felt Aelfric's legs tremble against hers. His eyes watered and his face turned red.

"Who were the pirates, and how did you communicate with them, so they knew where we'd be?"

"What? No… no… no. The pirates had nothing to do with me. I have no idea who they are."

He watched as Indigo's face looked confused. She studied his face for minute changes to see if he was telling the truth. Satisfied with his answer, she removed her blade and, releasing him.

"So why were you in my cabin, what were you looking for?"

Aelfric shrugged. "I don't know. Clues, I guess. I want to know why you are travelling to Tibet. You are in Oxford one minute then on an airship travelling to the other side of the globe. You must be up to something. An academic like you doesn't just travel thousands of miles on a whim."

Ignatius paced around, looking at the floor, then at Aelfric. "No. No, you are right. Quite right. We are off to find a sacred artefact, probably save the world, kill some gods along the way, and potentially find ourselves floating in the aether in some other part of the cosmos."

Aelfric looked at him with a frown, still trying to process what he had heard. Then he had a moment of clarity, at least he thought so. He laughed, nervously. "Why are you going to Tibet? How do you get from destroying the library of the Administorium to travelling to the far East in a few days?"

Ignatius ignored him. Looking at Indigo, he shrugged. "I did tell him. He has chosen not to believe. That was always the problem with the Administorium. They always knew best. Tie him up."

After some struggling, Aelfric sat in the corner of his cabin, his hands and feet bound, with a gag in his mouth. His wild eyes pierced Ignatius as he patted him on the head and said, "Don't worry old boy, we'll come by and feed you from time to time!"

The door shut behind the two Union Jacks and Aelfric was left in the dark.

As they walked away, Indigo asked, "what we going to do with him?"

"I don't know yet. In truth, due to his ineptness, he is mostly harmless. But I fear he's going to get in the way. Although, I don't want to risk feeling a cold icy blade between my shoulders when I'm not expecting it. When we get to Tibet, we will have to offload him somewhere."

Returning to their cabins, they checked on Lambeth, who was feeling rested and not so shaken.

"I've made a copy of the map you had pieced together, so it's all on a single sheet now."

"Thank you, Lambeth." Ignatius studied the two maps for accuracy. "Good man. You can destroy the originals now. We will soon be over North India; another day and we should be flying over Tibetan airspace. We need to have a plan in case we have a reception committee waiting for us when we arrive. I don't fancy dying the minute we set foot on Tibetan soil."

Chapter 9: Tibet

Ignatius and Indigo looked out from the foredeck to see Lhasa in the distance, growing ever larger as the airship got nearer. There wasn't any pomp and ceremony here like the airfield back in England.

"I guess it's quite appropriate we have come here. Lhasa means *Place of the Gods'*, so I am expecting this is the place we will get some answers," said Ignatius with an air of authority.

As they approached the city, they could hear the chanting of monks and the ringing of bells in the many temples. Closer still and they could smell the aroma of spices and food in the thin mountain air, mixed up with the smell of the many working yaks that trod the earthen streets. The many white buildings with their red roofs covered the mountain valley. Bright paintings of eyes or idols adorned the white walls of the houses that were packed in so closely the streets were barely more than an alleyway in places. The two Union Jacks could see the landing site, a thin strip of yellow grass with some lanterns burning.

Indigo grabbed Ignatius by the arm. "Look, we have a reception committee, hiding in those streets there." She pointed for Ignatius to follow.

There were several figures all dressed in black, the same attire as the pirates. It was the same Sisterhood.

"Come on, I have an idea." Ignatius headed towards their cabin. "We need to get Lambeth and whatever equipment we can carry. We'll have to abandon the trunk."

"Where are we going?"

"The escape ship, the dirigible. Our hosts won't be expecting that. We can get a head start."

The two Union Jacks climbed into the dirigible. Ignatius stretched out a hand for Lambeth.

"Do you mind if I stay here, sir?" asked Lambeth. "Only I feel I'm only going to slow you down. I'm not getting any younger." His face looked a little despondent. "Besides, I can remain with your belongings and can be a contact if you run into trouble and need assistance."

Ignatius rubbed his chin in thought. "Very well, Lambeth. That's probably a good idea. Stay safe."

Lambeth gave a large grin and pulled a steam cannon from his coat. "I will sir! I will, no fear."

Ignatius pulled some levers, and the dirigible responded, ready for flight. Indigo pulled at the restraining rods and the tiny craft began a descent with a glide until the steam engine kicked in and the two propellers pushed them forward. The air was thin and cold. The two agents gasped for air. It was going to take some time to get used to the high altitude of these mountains. It soon became clear why the Tibetan plateau was called the *roof of the world.*

They circled round to get away from the airship and headed to Lhasa from a different direction, hoping the welcome committee hadn't seen them escape. Flying over row upon row of closely packed white houses, they looked for a clearing to land.

Below them, clearly visible, was the British army garrison. Soldiers were spread across the courtyard in their red uniforms and white pith helmets. Ignatius took the dirigible lower and passed by the Union flag that flew proudly from a white pole that marked the centre of the parade square. Some of the soldiers, aware of the low-flying craft began to panic and put training into action. Dropping to one knee, they took their rifles off their backs and began lining their sights up to take aim. Ignatius was quick to turn his craft, so they got a good look at the Union flag that flew at the rear, its red, white and blue blowing in the breeze. The soldiers lowered their weapons and Ignatius circled, looking for a place to land.

Climbing out of the craft, they were greeted by a sergeant who, although a little perplexed, was very civil and polite in true English style.

"Greetings, how do you do? We thought the natives were getting restless again, but what brings you to Lhasa, and where have you come from? That dirigible is for short flights only, isn't it?"

"Thank you, sergeant. Yes, you are quite right, we haven't come far. There's an airship about to dock, only we were a little impatient," laughed Ignatius.

"Mmmm, only you can't just land in the base of the armed forces. It's a court martial offence."

"I'm on a mission for the Queen, and I'm afraid we had an unwanted welcoming party at the airfield, so we made a hasty escape."

"Any proof of this?"

"Ignatius dug deep into the inside pocket of his jacket and pulled out a letter marked with the royal seal.

"The Empress!" The sergeant read the letter. It was an introduction for Ignatius to Tibet, for anyone who might stand in his way, but the contents were very non-specific.

"Very well, sir." He handed the letter back. "I'll send some troops to the airfield, we don't want any uprising. That would never do. We are here to keep the peace. Would you like some refreshments first, or will you be on your way?"

"Refreshments would be good, thank you," said Indigo. As they walked with the sergeant, Indigo took the opportunity to try and find out some information.

"So, sergeant err… sorry, I didn't catch your name."

"Sergeant Collins, ma'am"

"Sergeant Collins, tell me, this must be a fascinating place to spend your days. The culture here is so rich and mystical."

"Oh, yes ma'am, it is. The locals are, in the main, peace-loving and kind, and they respect the Empire and all we are doing and building in the area. We have good relationships with their elders and the lamas, er, you know, the priests and such, in the temples."

"I see, that's good to know. And are there any locals with stories about mythical cities? I know they have a great tapestry of myths and legends, much of it can be seen in their works of art."

"Oh yes, their works of art are so colourful and allegorical. And the statuettes, the prayer wheels, all so colourful. As for myths, the whole country thrives on them. I know there are two Russian historians or archaeologists here who are studying the myths, translating them into English, and Russian, presumably. They are always poking around, on the lookout for new stories and artefacts to purchase. Trouble is, we don't know if they are spies, so keep an eye out for them. You may not want them around, depending on what you are up to for the Empress."

Over tea, the three of them chatted amicably and passed the time of day. The sun shone, but the air didn't get any warmer.

"I must say, it would be remiss of me if I didn't, but you are not dressed for the type of weather we usually have this time of year. And at night, we are talking minus temperatures, sometime double figures. It's an area known for its brutally cold days and nights."

"Yes, quite, a most hostile climate," replied Ignatius. "Only I'm afraid in our haste, we had to leave our trunk behind, and the rest of our clothing."

"I'm sure we can help sir. We have plenty of tweeds in stock and thick woollen coats."

After tea, the sergeant escorted the two agents to the mess and provided them with suitable clothing. Ignatius wore a great woollen coat over the top of his engineer's waistcoat, a tweed cap, woollen scarf and leather gloves. Indigo removed her skirts and donned riding breeches and a tweed waistcoat; with a hooded yak's wool cape she could wrap around herself to stop the harsh wind from biting. The two of them concealed some of their weapons in the poachers' pockets and helped themselves to some food rations that were on the table. They were more prepared than when they had arrived, but Ignatius was concerned this might restrict their ability to fight should the need arise.

Chapter 10: The Tavern

Ignatius and Indigo made their way to *Tashi*, the *Tavern of Good Fortune*. The streets were empty, and the close nature of the buildings added to the darkness. The roads were no more than alleyways. The occasional window gave the only light as small yellow squares illuminated the way and the streets were silent, it was eerie, not even stray dogs could be seen or heard. A thick mist had descended upon the city, which was not wholly unusual; but rather than rolling in from the mountains, it seemed to emanate from the enormous temple built into the mountain, sitting high above the city. As Ignatius peered forward into the darkness, his eyes gradually getting used to the lack of light, Indigo was following up, constantly glancing behind them.

"I don't like this," Indigo whispered. "Maybe we should have left it until the morning."

Ignatius didn't turn around. "Trouble is, we can't afford to lose any time. Once that welcoming party figure out where we are, we will be sitting ducks. And I don't know about you, but I don't want to die in these squalid streets."

They both heard a footfall behind them. Glancing quickly round, they were relieved to see a native pass by perpendicular to their path, paying them no heed. As they turned into a clearing, a ceremonial square, they could see the tavern on the far side. It was illuminated outside by burning tapers, and prayer flags fluttered in the breeze connecting the roof to some of the surrounding buildings.

Another local, a merchant, saw them and immediately engaged in loud conversation. "Greetings, greeting visitors, you like?" He thrust some wooden prayer beads into Ignatius's hands, his weather-beaten, creased and leathery face beamed with a huge smile, speaking pidgin English, he boomed at full volume, "finest Tibetan prayer beads, you will not getter better around here. Finest quality, only ten tangka. You like?"

"No, thank you!" Ignatius was nervous, he wanted to remain incognito. Not many visitors came to these parts. He was looking all around; the disturbance was starting to attract attention. "No thank you, I don't need any beads, thank you." He tried to give them back, but the trader wouldn't take them. "Okay, I give you this carving of a yak, beads and one yak, just ten tangka."

"No, but thank you!"

"You drive a hard bargain. I give you two yaks, the beads and this bell, just eight tangka."

Panic started to set in. "Please I don't want any beads or carvings…" He didn't get any further, Indigo smiled and handed the man fifteen tangka. "Thank you for your trade, please, now go."

The trader gave a wide grin to her, displaying crooked yellow teeth, with gaps between each and then wandered off.

"For a moment then, Ignatius, I thought you were going to panic," she smiled at him. "Would you like your watch back? He lifted it straight away, so I retrieved it for you!" She handed him his silver watch and chain back.

"Oh! Oh, thank you, er, much obliged" Embarrassed, he returned his watch to his pocket, and they continued. They kept to the side of the square, hugging the walls like rats so they were not out in the open. The tavern gave off a foul odour, several aromas all mixed together. The smell of drinks and spices, overpowered by the smell of horses and urine. Several yaks were in the yard out the back, and they bellowed and grunted, stamping their cloven hooves on the cobbles, dragging their bulk against the fence that retained them, occasionally clashing horns, their thick matted fur adding to the odour and their foul breath adding to the mist.

Indigo looked on in distaste. Passing them by, the two Union Jacks peered in through the tavern door, sizing up the clientele before entering. Once inside, they headed for a table in a dark corner, furthest from the bar. Straw and sawdust covered the mud floor along with puddles of liquid, most of which were unidentifiable but were quite pungent. Ignatius pulled out a kerchief and covered his nose and mouth. Indigo pulled her woollen scarf over her nose. Despite its name, it served very little alcohol, and then mostly only to European visitors. For most of the population, alcohol was forbidden in this country. But it served hot food, butter tea and, very freely, amongst other narcotics, opium.

Clouds of smoke filled the air, and several clients were slowly succumbing to the effects. Some had already passed out, sleeping on rich brocade cushions and woollen blankets in the booths around the edge of the tavern.

The barkeeper made his way over to them. He was greasy looking, short, and stout with bandy legs, wearing a dirty apron. He gave Indigo a wide grin, displaying his yellowed and crooked teeth. But he was a friendly chap and continued to smile even when talking. He placed down two tankards of ale and to their surprise spoke some English.

"Food?"

"No, that's quite all right, thank you," replied Ignatius through his kerchief.

As the barkeeper returned to his post, Ignatius went to drink from his tankard, Indigo slammed her hand down on his forearm and the tankard hit the table hard, splashing ale over his hand.

"Don't you dare! This place is filthy, you'll catch something!"

They both laughed, at which point Ignatius just caught a glimpse of somebody on the far side, clothed heavily in shadow, but clearly watching them.

He was a bulky man, and not Tibetan. He had a cloak wrapped around him, but Ignatius could see from the outline it covered weapons and other bulky items on his side.

"We're being watched," and his head nodded surreptitiously in the direction of the stranger.

"Yes, I saw. Who do you think he is? He can't be with the Sisterhood. Unless they have hired him."

"He's coming over."

As he came into the light, they could see his muscular frame. His face was scarred, with the texture of sun-scorched leather, and his hair fell in a thick plait to his shoulder. Behind him, hidden in the shadows, was a short, stocky man. He struggled with the weight of some object wrapped in prayer flags and a linen cloth covered in scriptures and runes.

"Greeting, strangers. I am Magus. I hope the city's hospitality is to your liking." He grinned and didn't wait for an answer. "What brings you to our humble city of peace and prayer?"

Again, Ignatius didn't get a chance to answer. "Did you come in on that big, bloated bird yesterday?" This time he waited, his face a grimace, menacing looking.

"We did. Thank you for your hospitality, it is much appreciated. But if you don't mind, my friend and I would like to be left to quietly…"

He leaned in. "So why are you here? What do two soft English, like you, want in a hole like this?" He threw back his cloak. Fearing an attack, both Ignatius and Indigo had a hand on their steam cannons. But instead of a weapon, the man grabbed an ancient-looking holy relic that hung on a heavy gold chain around his neck, encased in an ornate reliquary. Strapped upon his back was a holy book covered in Sanskrit and runes, bound with bronze clasps.

"We don't take kindly to outsiders disturbing the peace here. Any sign of trouble, magic and the occult, we administer justice, as laid down in the great book."

He turned to the other man behind him, who was busy unwrapping the object he carried. Magus grabbed in and placed it down on the table with a thud. It was another holy book, covered in runes, jewels and ancient-looking text and bound in a thick silver chain and padlocked shut. At his side, Ignatius spotted a hollow, pointed crystal knife, clearly for collecting blood.

"Now why would you think we are in any way concerned with the occult?" asked Indigo, ready to pull the trigger on her steam cannon at any moment. "We are just travellers, passing through. You offend me, sir!"

As Magus started to reply, a hand came round and was placed on his arm. A figure dressed all in black stood behind him.

"Come along, Magus, not tonight. There will be no blood for Kali this time. These are just tourists and are here to visit me."

Magus looked around and, seeing the shrouded figure, smiled and said, "Very well. But we can never be too careful. This city is full of strangers looking for spiritual enlightenment, but they usually end up high and causing trouble, believing their bad trip was a vision of some god or another, who, having spoken to them has set them on the right course for their fate. They never return home; they just add to the overpopulation and contribute nothing!"

Without saying anything more, Magus picked up the book passed it back to his minion and they both left the tavern, looking somewhat disgruntled.

The stranger sat down opposite the two Union Jacks. "Please, join us," said Ignatius sarcastically.

Removing her hood, the stranger revealed her beautiful pale face. She smiled, squinting, her eyes revealing laughter lines at the edges. Indigo noticed it was a sincere, heart-felt smile.

"I am Helena, your contact." She spoke with a slight accent.

"How do you do? I am Ignatius, and this is my associate, Eliza."

"Very pleased to meet you, Indigo!" Helena couldn't help but laugh. "Eliza? Ha, no need for secrecy with me. Welcome, Indigo."

She bore no resemblance to the daguerreotype Lawrence had shown Ignatius. She wasn't the stout, sturdy and formidable-looking woman he had been led to believe. She was beautiful, her most striking feature was her over-large eyes. Blue green in colour, and beneath her black woollen cloak she was dressed in an elegant, colourful style, part European, part Oriental.

"Forgive me," said Ignatius, "I didn't recognise you. You look nothing like the image I had seen."

She smiled. "Ah yes! Necessary, I'm afraid, in order to remain anonymous. The East is not like Great Britain. I cannot for the life of me understand how Lawrence has managed to keep the Union such a secret for all these years when you do nothing to hide yourselves."

Ignatius smiled. "Maybe, that's just it. We are hiding in plain sight. So obvious, we cannot be seen. To my knowledge, we have only been infiltrated twice. One, an unfortunate affair, I made the mistake of recruiting a woman with her own agenda. Although, I guess, she is the reason we are here."

"Hmm. Yes, I heard. Reckless. You expose myself and Nicholas, and I will not hesitate to kill you!"

Ignatius remained silent. There was nothing he could say. "So, what of these demons she summoned. They kill everything in their path, do they not? London did let us know something of your blunderings. Plus, all the demons you managed to bring forth yourself from the last book you opened! Please, do not take an interest in any reading material here!"

Indigo remained silent, quietly irritated by Helena's air of superiority.

"I hope you will not conjure any demons here; the locals are very superstitious. They will not take kindly to any supernatural activity. Their biggest fear is the paranormal, demons manifested by thought, they call them the Tulpas."

Ignatius said nothing. The shadows he had fought in Oxford were just that, demons manifested by dark thoughts, nightmares, and fears. Indigo shot him a glance, and he gave her the merest shrug of his shoulders.

"If they think you are a Tulpamancer, a lucid dreamer, they will drive you from Tibet. That's if you are lucky, otherwise they will publicly execute you in the city square." Helena's face was a grimace. "And their method of execution isn't nice. It's unthinkable. You have already seen Magus. Your blunderings are exactly what he is talking about. Tibet is a very superstitious place, which is why the city pay Magus and his brigands to keep it safe and secure. They don't take kindly to too many Westerners. They think you are ignorant heathens with a lack of spirituality."

A cold shiver ran down Ignatius's back, and he remained silent, not sure of his status here. He didn't know what rank Helena held within the Union Jacks. The mere fact she had been kept secret from all the other agents in the Union spoke volumes.

"And what of them?" asked Indigo, pointing to a few locals sat in a corner booth, barely visible due to the opium vapours surrounding them. "Are they not considered lucid dreamers? My experience is that the narcotics, the psychedelics they are using probably mean they hallucinate and dream. They may even be able to astral walk, depending on the stuff of their addictions."

Helena said nothing, thinking the girl was simply impertinent.

Just then, they were joined by a tall thin man who introduced himself as Nicholas. He was older, sporting a long grey beard and, like Helena, was also an Orientalist, his clothing a mixture of European and Tibetan, silk and colourful. When he removed his traditional Persian Karakul hat, he was bald and looked like a Chinese wizard.

"How do you do?" said Ignatius. Without any delay, he asked, "so, tell me, why is this Chapter of the Union so secret? Nobody even knows it exists. A secret within a secret, so to speak."

Nicholas shifted, a little uneasy. Helena smiled and answered in a soft low voice.

"The Empire is at its height. If it is to remain this powerful, then further steps need to be taken. The Queen knows the Administorium are pompous fools who restrict innovation, but as Empress of the East she also knows there are other means to reinforce her power."

Nicholas was curious. "I am to believe you have destroyed the Administorium?"

"We have indeed. There is nothing left, just a pile of rocks, a crater and maybe a few clerics on the run, too frightened to return."

Nicholas nodded his approval to Helena. She gave a wide grin and continued.

"Tibet is full of mysteries. It is perhaps the most mysterious place on earth. Our Chapter has been created to seek out the repositories of all the mysteries and wisdom this land has to offer and, if possible, make use of it for the Empire. We have seen vast libraries with thousands of scrolls, most of which are ancient and have not been read for a very long time. Even the lamas here do not know what they contain. Some of the highest monks in the land think they are from before the Great Flood. Others insist there are texts that go right back to an ancient cataclysm thousands of years before the flood. But magic and power flows through this desolate country like water through the mountains."

"Impressive. Interesting work," said Ignatius.

Helena changed her mood and in a serious tone asked, "so, tell me, why are you and Indigo here? What do you want from us? Lawrence gave us some details but not much, cautious for security reasons. Are you expecting some kind of attack on the Empire, here in Tibet?"

Ignatius rubbed his chin. "Not quite…" But didn't get a chance to finish.

"Lawrence said something about some relics with cosmic powers. Sounds like local superstition to me."

"According to ancient cosmology, the cosmos was created by the Omnisoul using four artefacts or, as you say, relics. One of which was the Flaming Celestial Pearl, said to encapsulate the wisdom of the creator.

Nicholas gripped Helena by the arm. "Then perhaps it is true. The Pearl is not just a legend, a fairy story in these parts. We have heard of the Flaming Celestial Pearl, it is prevalent in Oriental mythology. It may be an allegory for lost knowledge rather than an actual pearl, but who knows? It is said to reside in a mystical land far out of reach to all humans upon the earth."

"Does that mean it lies outside of the earthly realm?" asked Indigo.

"It's complicated, Indigo. The realm you seek is said to be otherworldly with a bridge from the earth. Legend has it that it is not always present on the earth in some way. We always thought this was just legend and superstition, but if you are telling me that the gods are real then maybe this mystical land is, too," said Helena. "But it is said to be well protected, even when accessible from the earth."

Nicholas added more detail. "It is our belief there is a secretive sisterhood who are knowledgeable about this ancient wisdom, and who practice magic to conjure obstacles in our way to prevent us from progressing any further in any such quest. Not sure of the truth, we have tried to locate the realm in the past, and every time we think we have gotten further we encounter strange things blocking our way."

"Such as?" enquired Indigo.

"We had come into possession of some texts that give lessons on using our own aura as a powerful tool, whether to heal, or to fight, or just simply be at peace with the universe. They were stolen from us and the library where we found them was ransacked. Much of the other material was removed and destroyed. They also destroyed part of the temple containing the library. Whoever they are, they were trying to protect a powerful knowledge. Other times…" He hesitated before continuing, "we have encountered strange beings, ghouls, or the walking dead with a taste for human flesh. The hills around here are full of local legends purporting to give witness to these creatures over the centuries."

Helena leaned in closer and almost whispered, "this magical

land is where more of this knowledge resides. It is protected by this secret society and if needed they will fight to the death to protect it."

"What is the name of this land?" asked Ignatius.

"It is sometimes called Rahasya, the Place of Silence."

"Why is it called that?" asked Indigo.

"It is a mystical place and is said to lie at the crossings of the planes, connected to the earth's core and the universe in some way. It is a gateway to the stars, at a point where nothing moves, all is silent, all is at peace. It is a paradise."

Indigo smiled back. "Well, it sounds like an idyllic place. It also sounds like Sagharta. It, too, lies at a crossing of the planes, making its position unstable. It drifts in and out of multiple planes and never stays in one place for long. It sits at a weakness in space and time."

Helena looked impressed and curious. "This does sound familiar. I can see we have much to discuss. But this mythical land has never been located in Tibet. Hundreds of legends speak of its existence, yet none have ever found it, so maybe you are right. The reason it has never been found is, as you say, it drifts."

All this time, Ignatius was scanning the tavern. He wasn't comfortable talking in public. Helena put a reassuring hand on his arm. "Relax. We deliberately meet here because most of the time the clientele are not present, they are floating somewhere on the opium they have smoked. But we can take this elsewhere. Our headquarters are below the tavern. Come!"

Helena and Nicholas got to their feet and made their way to the bar. Ignatius and Indigo followed. Nicholas looked behind and whispered "Don't be fooled by the bartender. He's not as dumb as he looks. It's all an act."

Indigo giggled at Ignatius. "He's very good at it!"

Nicholas continued. "Although I'm not sure about the poor hygiene, I think that may be real! He is in our employment. He is our lookout. As Helena said, we meet here as we can go about our business unhindered, unseen. But our real business takes place below the tavern."

As they reached the bar, the bartender was already moving. He opened a trap door in the floor and the four Union Jacks traversed a flight of stone steps to emerge in a gloomy antechamber. On the far wall was a large bronze door, much the same as that in the London headquarters, but this one was decorated with some Tibetan art, a fierce three-eyed monster with flaming hair and his tongue protruding from his mouth. He was holding a book and a sword, dancing on the traditional lotus. Helena waved her hands across several peripheral carvings and there was a small hiss of steam followed by the bolts clanking open. She pushed effortlessly and the heavy door opened to reveal the inner sanctum of the Chapter House.

Chapter 11: The Map

The room was cosier than the tavern and was warmed by a large wood burner in the corner. Around the walls hung ornate tapestries of Tibetan art, woollen blankets and animal furs, snowshoes and tweed hats. At the far end was a large cabinet filled with weapons, short swords, obsidian blades, steam pistols, derringers and steam cannons, along with a few grenades. The Chapter had an impressive array of weaponry. To the right a tunnel led off into the dark, its walls roughly carved out of the stone. Helena saw Ignatius looking. "It joins this room to the Temple."

Tongues of orange light licked at the walls in the subterranean hideout, casting flickering shadows on the faces of the Union Jacks. Indigo felt uneasy as it was too reminiscent of her experience fighting the shadow demons.

"So what exactly are you going to do in Tibet? Lawrence mentioned the pearl."

"It was Lawrence who suggested we come here. I guess he is thinking that as this is the esoteric branch of the Union, you may be able to shed new light on the matter."

Helena thought for a while and mumbled to herself, pacing

around the chamber. "Tell me more, what do you know, give me everything you have got."

Ignatius sat down. "Ok, but there's a lot, and it'll sound crazy, but this is all true, and a very brief explanation. At the beginning of time, all matter, all life was made manifest by the genderless Omnisoul using four artefacts. The cosmos was and still is created from vibrating matter, to do this the Omnisoul created harmony out of chaos using a book containing everything that has been, that is and that will be. It's all written in Turiya, the Book of Consciousness. Any dark thoughts or deeds became manifest in Rahu, the Book of Shadows. Although this book seems to have been written by the Elder God, Calabi-Ya. The other artefact used was Keisu, the Singing Bowl, used to play music to create or restore order to the cosmos and the fourth artefact was the Flaming Celestial Pearl, but presently we do not know its purpose or how it was used. The previous artefacts have all held significant power, which is why the Union got involved, fearing some kind of threat to the Empire."

Helena looked at Nicholas, and to Ignatius's surprise she said, "It's all making sense so far!"

She gazed upon Ignatius and recounted what they knew. "The legends in these parts are ancient, some say they predate humans, and were created by a race that came before humans. In these legends, the Pearl usually represents the sun that gives birth to the planets and, therefore, life. The primordial dragon tries to swallow the pearl to absorb its power, and therefore take control of the cosmos, control of the creative act. Ultimate cosmic power. In this country, the dragon symbolises the Chinese Emperor and represents evolution from the ancient ancestors and primordial energy. The emperor is seen as immortal and all powerful, so it makes sense in the legends that he takes control of the cosmos."

"I thought you would think we were crazy, but clearly this all makes sense in these parts of the world. The West have a lot to learn and understand. So, Lawrence was right to send us here, but we don't know where the Pearl is, or even if it is on the earth, or even the same cosmic plane."

Nicholas thought for a few seconds before adding, "maybe not, but that welcoming party seem to think you are some kind of threat."

"They followed us over Norway and attacked the airship somewhere over Sweden, they said they were from the Great Sisterhood."

Nicholas didn't let him say any more. "That's it! That explains it. The Great Sisterhood, the Knights of Himavala. They are sworn to protect ancient wisdom. The belief was always thought to be Imperial Wisdom, the wisdom of the Emperor. But we've discovered these knights might be older than the legends tell, as old as the Union Jacks, or older still, with a great tradition of fearless fighting and certain victory, even when outnumbered. They are expert warmongers. If that welcome party are really the Knights of Himavala, you are in great danger. You have got into a skirmish you will not win."

For the first time, Helena's face looked concerned, and whilst still retaining her composure, she added, "Ignatius, regardless of what missions you have previously fought, terrestrial or celestial, you are heading for almost certain death. There is no way to dress this up."

Ignatius felt uneasy. Indigo looked even more concerned.

"We've faced gods, haven't we?" he said to her, taking her arm. She moved closer to him.

"Ignatius," she said, "we don't have to do this. Forget Lawrence, forget the celestial adventures. We could return to Oxford and live our lives like we used to. You know I am a fighter; I am unmatched with a sword, and I can fight any brute who tries, but this is too risky. We don't know where we are going, the climate is unforgiving and now we have to face fanatical knights, and who knows what kind of power the Flaming Pearl can hold, what we may unleash and have to deal with. I have been tortured and killed before, I have been given a second chance and I want to make sure the rest of my life is long and lived well."

Ignatius paced the room. "But we are sworn to the service of the Queen, the Empress. It is our duty to protect the Empire, even if that costs us our lives. That's what we signed up for!"

He reached into his inside pocket and produced the map. "We have this," and he offered it to Helena. Opening it carefully she said, "how did you come by this?"

Nicholas was busy moving objects and tankards to clear a space on the rough surface of the table. Helena carefully laid the map down and Nicholas gasped.

"This is invaluable. This is it! This is it!" Her excitement was intriguing. Nicholas's face lit up and he gave a wide grin.

"This is what?" asked Ignatius. "What is the significance of it? I think I have decoded it, but the runes make it confusing at best. I obtained it from a very ancient book and the runes were copied from the tattoos adorning the Sisterhood. But they matched runes found on the book. What do you think it shows?"

Helena confirmed what Ignatius already thought. "The runes, dear boy are not all runes. Some are pictograms, and the map shows the way to Rahasya. There have been many stories told of where it lies, some even say it is positioned somewhere within the earth, a hollow earth if you will. But this all makes sense."

"I'm pleased it does to someone," said Indigo.

"Look, here." Helena pointed to an area of the map. "This is

Lhasa, and this is Katmandu. The pictograms indicate it, I know I have seen them before on ancient Sanskrit scrolls. So now we have some idea of scale."

Nicholas handed her some iron dividers, which she placed on the two cities. "That's about 375 miles of treacherous unforgiving terrain. These runes give a description and direction for the fabled city. This rune represents Kalapa, the palace of Rahasya, or, as some call it, Shambhala." She pointed with her long slender finger.

"Over the centuries, some have argued that inner Shambhala is that world which lies within us all and outer Shambhala is the land you seek. This has always been considered a spiritual quest. In these parts, the legends still call it Rahasya, and legends say it is surrounded by snowy mountains, making the land unreachable. The realm is also called the Land of the Worthy Ones, because only the worthy will be granted passage to find it."

"So what direction is it?" asked Ignatius.

"North. You will need to travel north of Bodh Gaya, but this is a religious site, a place of pilgrimage with a large and significant temple complex. Upset the locals there and you will not get out alive. That's if you make it that far."

"What do you mean?"

"In the foothills there are many caves. Some are occupied by the Sadhus, the holy men of India. Some haven't spoken to another human in decades, and they will not take kindly to your presence, having renounced worldly life."

"We will be careful and respectful," said Indigo. "I'm sure it'll be alright."

"My girl, it will not be alright. Some are shaman or wizards, practiced in the dark arts. Some are cannibals. Get used to the unthinkable, this isn't England. However, there is worse, some of the caves are occupied by bandits who'll slit your throat as you sleep for some money or even a morsel of food. On the other hand, you may be unlucky, and they'll sell you into slavery. There are many nomads and caravans that pass through and some deal in human trafficking. Your soft white flesh, my dear, would fetch a nice price, and if they sell you to the cannibals, you could feed an entire caravan for about six weeks, believe me, dear! For the most part, you will still be alive, they like their flesh fresh!"

Indigo felt a shiver down her spine before remembering who she was, what she was, an extraordinary Union Jack with powers that Helena couldn't even dream of.

Helena continued, "the foothills are a massive jumble of rocks that look like they have been split by the severe frosts. Barren vistas also fill your view in all directions, it's easy to get lost. Most of the landscape is a pale grey-green except for the odd hard outcrop of granite or slate."

Returning her attention to the map, she added, "these other runes, they indicate places of importance, markers to indicate the way. Ultimately, you must follow the Red Path. I think that's a reference to the red granite that protrudes from the southern wall of the mountains, but to get there you must cross the Forbidden Territory and the Sea of Palms. It is said to be an indescribable realm of both wonders and dangers. As far as I know, nobody has ever survived the Sea of Palms."

"What's the Sea of Palms?"

"I'm not exactly sure, nobody has returned to explain. But it's probably a vast ice desert."

"But surely this is all immaterial, we can use the dirigible."

"It would only get you so far. As the hills start to climb towards the mountains and the air gets thinner, it'll struggle staying airborne and you will struggle to breathe. You are better off at ground level."

"And what about the Forbidden Territory?"

"It is protected by poisonous gas that leaks from the cracks in the vertical walls of the mountain. The path you seek will likely run straight through it. If you find a way of surviving your passage through the Territory, and I'm not sure how you do, then you'll need assistance from there on. You won't be able to find the way alone, you will need a guide. You must seek a mystic, one of the Descended Masters. His name is Issa. It is said he lives in the Altai Mountains in a cave marked by a red path with a crowned lion and a heavenly bird that has conquered the dragon. The passageway in the mountains is so narrow, it is almost impossible to go through. It is believed to be part of a labyrinth in which travellers can get lost.

Find him, and you will be on the right path to Rahasya. He has the key to the kingdom you seek, but you must pass a test before he will let you pass.

"A Descended Master?" said Ignatius.

"Yes. They came to the earth from the stars about twelve thousand years ago, a different earth to the one we know, for legends state there are many versions. They taught many skills to a tribe called the Duranki and were worshipped as gods."

"I have heard of the Duranki. Where did they come from and what did they want?

"Nobody knows for sure. They stayed a long time. Their life expectancy was a lot longer than our own. Some say they left one day just before a horrific cataclysm that destroyed nearly all life on earth. Others say they remained and now lie in tombs in cities that are now lost and they have never been discovered. Yet they are not dead, they are just sleeping, awaiting a time when it is right for them to rise once more and rule the earth."

"How will I know this mystic?"

"You won't have to. He will know you. The mystic has a knack for knowing everything. A mystic, born to the cause, spiritual, able to travel the heavens and wise beyond belief."

"Surely we will need some means of knowing who he is or where he will be."

"The Descended Master will find you, as I said, he is a mystic, he will meet you along the path, he will be a traveller of simple means and will walk with you for a while. During that time, he will judge you and decide if you are to find Rahasya. This shall be your test. If the decision goes against you, there is nothing anyone can do. The Descended Masters are the wisest men on earth, they travel between earths and know all. They will already know of your presence and your quest, but whilst they see, they do not yet judge."

"Have you ever had council with these Masters?"

Helena smiled. "Not at all, they do not operate like that. They have been on earth thousands of years, some of them you will have heard of. They are the wise, the enlightened, guiding humanity through the centuries, they are disrupters by peaceful means."

"And what of Rahasya itself, have you ever been?"

Again, Helena smiled sweetly. "No, not at all. Our duties here require us to be involved in the esoteric, the ancient, the sorcerous, extreme dark arts, the occult. That, and the odd negotiations elsewhere, the Kyber Pass, the opium fields, the temples. Remember this is the furthest reaches of our Empire and not easy to travel to, or through. Rahasya is inhabited by the great keepers of mysteries. It is said that many rare plants and medicinal herbs grow there, illness has been eliminated, it is a paradise. But it's possible that once in Rahasya, you will not return. Maybe that's why its location has always been such a successfully guarded secret. There are no witnesses. That's not to say it'll be your demise, but if your survive all the other labours, it's possible once there the inhabitants may not let you leave."

Nicholas intervened. "The hour is late, you will need to get rest so you can set off early tomorrow morning. We can travel the first part to set you on the right foot, but our presence will attract unwanted attention; we are too well known in these parts but nobody knows our purpose, obviously. Have you arranged lodgings yet?"

Indigo answered. "Not at all, escaping the welcome party at the airfield we ended up at the garrison, so haven't yet organised anything."

Nicholas laughed. "That's ok, you can stay here, the bar keeper has lodgings, they are a bit meagre, but you'll be safe and warm here. I'll go and speak with him. You need to get a good rest. You will need to leave early in the morning."

A little later, Ignatius and Indigo found themselves lying on a straw mattress on the creaking boards of an upper floor. The lodgings weren't very salubrious, but the thick woollen blankets afforded warmth from the chill wind blowing in off the mountains.

Chapter 12: The Expedition

Indigo found the night to be restless. The straw mattress was uncomfortable, and she wasn't sure if she was sharing it with other wildlife. Her skin crawled. Occasionally, she must have drifted off to sleep because she awoke with a jolt. The jolt back to consciousness was the light source that had torn her body apart atom by atom and used her as the means to find the Book of Shadows. Her body still ached. She didn't let on to Ignatius exactly how bad, but here she didn't have access to absinthe and although opium was going to be readily available, she had travelled that path and didn't care much to repeat it. She shuffled over to be nearer Ignatius, to feel his warmth and caring arms around her. Eventually, she slept for a time, but for the most part she had a restless night. It was cold and as she lay shivering but not due to the weather, it was when she left her body and floated amongst the alternate planes of existence. She was floating in the cosmos, drifting peacefully amongst the stars, the familiar searing pain in her back from her ordeal with death. She looked below and could see Rahasya rising up from the snowy landscape that surrounded it, with lava flows spreading out like the four rivers of the Classical underworld.

Ignatius lay awake most of the night, not letting on to Indigo he was still awake. He saw the brilliant flash of purple light that illuminated the room for a split second, emanating from the woman he loved. It burst from the gem-shaped mark on her chest and then was gone. This was a regular occurrence, and he didn't know if Indigo knew. His mind raced, trying to guess what was wrong and where this adventure would take them, what dangers might lie ahead and more importantly, what the Flaming Celestial Pearl might be and how it linked with the mythical paradise of Rahasya.

During the little sleep he did manage, his dreams were filled with images of the Queen of Shadows, and the Charon. He felt like he was falling, constantly falling into the abyss. But this abyss wasn't a black Void, it was scarlet. Visions of Limbo filled his head. Agonising screams filled his ears from the eternal damnation the poor lost souls relentlessly endured. He saw one-eyed Adonai grinning a hellish grin at him, suddenly morphing into his other self of a hawk-headed man, his beak dripping blood, his scythe encrusted with congealed blood and flesh. Heavy chains made from enchanted iron links as thick as a man's thigh secured him. Other bodies writhed nearby and one by one formed the rest of the Charon. Tara appeared directly before him, her beak almost touching his nose. He felt her hot breath and could smell its rancid odour. Then she appeared as her beautiful self, platinum blonde hair flowing onto her shoulders but dripping at the ends with gore. He fought hard to remove these images, remove all thought of contact with these supernatural beings. Eventually, he successfully blocked them out, he thought about the woman he loved, and about their mission and how he might return to headquarters in London with news of success for Lawrence.

As dawn came, he could hear movement below and smell mint

tea and freshly cooked bread drifting up between the boards, mixed with the smell of yak dung drifting in through the badly fitted and unsealed window. This part of the city was an assault on the senses.

Negotiating the ancient looking wooden staircase, Ignatius descended into the tavern. Helena and Nicholas were already waiting.

"We have arranged for everything you will need. A good breakfast here first, then we have kit for your expedition, a local guide who we trust, a good man," said Helena.

"We have used him a lot. Trust him with my life," added Nicholas. "His name is Sumata." He pointed towards an alcove on the far side. A little short man with leathery skin gave a gap-toothed grin back, and he bowed. Ignatius wasn't sure, the man didn't look much of an adventurer or look like a fighter. The only thing that Ignatius convinced himself of was that the little man's face looked so weather-beaten he must be a guide with lots of experience in the mountains.

"Very well," said Ignatius.

After breakfast, Ignatius and Indigo checked the equipment that had been supplied. They listened to Helena once more about the terrain they would be crossing and the path they must take, checking the map once more. Sumata studied the map and rubbed the few hairs he had on his chin. He knew where to go, and knew most of the dangers, but certain parts of the journey made him feel uncomfortable. There were many dangers, and he wasn't convinced Rahasya existed. It was the stuff of legend.

Ignatius and Indigo said their goodbyes, not knowing if they would ever see their fellow Union Jacks ever again. They followed the squat figure of Sumata out into the cold. He grunted and cleared his throat, spitting on the ground. Indigo look repulsed and nudged Ignatius in the ribs who gave a slight shrug. The wind was increasing and fine snow that lay on the ground was blown up into the air, swirling and stinging their cheeks. Sumata trekked in complete silence and led them out of the city, mostly unseen by its inhabitants. When they reached the foothills, it had started to snow. Sumata seemed completely unaffected by the change in weather and temperature and continued, snorting and spitting at regular intervals, much to the disgust of the two Union Jacks.

After several hours with no rest, they came to a wide chasm spanned by a frail-looking bridge of woven reeds. Sumata turned and grunted, "one at a time."

He beckoned Ingnatius to go first. He set foot on to the flimsy looking walkway and his heavy footedness caused the bridge to swing wildly.

"Carefully! You must be like the mountain ghosts, soft of foot, and light of touch on the ropes…" Sumata mumbled.

As Ignatius took several more cautious steps, Sumata finished his sentence, "or you die!"

Ignatius wasn't impressed. As he got further towards the centre of the bridge his weight was causing it to sag considerably, making the next few steps difficult, as he was walking uphill. When he reached the other side, he turned to see Sumata indicating to Indigo to go next. She stepped out, quickly perfecting the technique. She was truly light of foot, probably due to her swordsmanship, used to dancing around lightly to thrust and parry. She was lighter than Ignatius, so as she reached the middle, she found she didn't have the climb that Ignatius had experienced. Reaching the other side, she turned, and they both watched Sumata stomp across the reeds as if he was crossing the stone cobbles on Broad Street in Oxford, without any caution or care for his heavy-footedness.

Continuing, they could hear the thunderous roar of water. "The

Lost Waterfall," said their guide. "No man comes this way. Many have heard of its existence, but few have seen it."

The noise increased but at no point did the Union Jacks see the waterfall, hidden somewhere from view. Occasionally Ignatius would consult the map to reassure himself their guide was not tricking them and leading them into danger. Every time he did this, Sumata eyed him with suspicion and disdain.

Sumata was like a programmed automaton, he didn't stop. Head down, he just continued to plough on. Fortunately, it had stopped snowing, but Indigo had begun to grow weary. She was not her usual strong self, still suffering from her previous ordeal. Ignatius, although cold, was still willing to press on but realised this was unfair.

"Sumata, I think we need to take a rest. The thin air and cold is taxing on our bodies."

The usual look of disdain came back. "Very well, but not yet. We need to get to the Valley of the Deities, then you can rest."

It was growing late, and the temperature was starting to drop. "Not far now, we will be there before nightfall."

Soon they were in a wide valley and could see a dilapidated temple in the distance. Sumata pointed. "A little further and we can sleep for the night."

Chapter 13: Attacked

The sky was pale and hazed, a low mist hung in the valleys. A few stars still glimmered high in the sky. The air was cold and crisp as they travelled on.

After some time, the wind changed and a storm began to blow in, frozen snowflakes stung at their cheeks, but they pressed on regardless. Visibility was dropping. Ignatius was navigating using the stars and looking at the map occasionally in the dim light. They had recently passed Bodh Gaya, keeping well clear, and were now following what looked like a spine of red rock that protruded from the snow. Eventually this ran into the edge of a mountain face, so the two Union Jacks were walking on a cliff edge. Indigo lost her footing, and her boot slipped over the edge. Small rocks clattered down the slope and echoed in the frosty night. Unable to see clearly, they slowed down their pace, choosing safety over speed. They could just make out a large stupa ahead and could hear prayer flags flapping in the breeze.

"We're being followed," said Indigo.

"I know," said Ignatius. "For some time now. We can rest at the stupa and see what comes of it."

As they reached the monument, it was still brightly painted, but ill maintained. Piles of rocks purposely stacked lay around it, offerings for the deceased. A ruined temple lay further beyond, and the party decided to rest there. The land rose gently towards the temple and was softer than the track they had been following. The snow crunched under foot and as Ignatius took another step whatever was beneath the snow cover broke. A long leg bone moved upwards into view, just peeking out of the snow. As they advanced it soon became clear they were walking on a mass of bones. A femur, a humerus, a sternum all came into view and then a mandible. They were all stripped of flesh, and soon they were all ankle deep in human bones.

Sumata seemed oblivious to them. A shudder went down Indigo's spine. Quickening their pace, they all exited the boneyard and entered the temple. It had been abandoned long ago, but it offered some protection from the biting wind.

Indigo decided to look around, curious at some of the statues of idols. She had never seen them before. To some extent, they were in a typical Tibetan style, angry-looking gods in a dance pose with multiple arms and three eyes with their tongues hanging out. But instead of the traditional black or red skin, they were hairy. It looked like white hair, but it was difficult to tell, the grime of years had sullied them too much. One painting had an inscription that read *Meh-Teh*.

The storm had gathered full force, and the harsh snow blew in almost horizontally through the open window holes and broken walls. Ignatius wrapped his scarf around his face and peered through a gap in the wall.

Without warning an enormous, clawed hand reached in and grabbed him by his coat and tried to pull him through the aperture. Foul hot breath engulfed Ignatius, and he struggled to breathe as he came face to face with an angry ape-like face, and yellow, bloodshot eyes. Terrifying fangs slavered at his face. White matted fur covered a conical shaped head, and the beast let out a thunderous roar that echoed around the valley.

"Yeti!" shouted Indigo.

The beast released his grip and moved around to the front of the temple, his huge hairy body filling the doorway, curious as to how many more humans had entered his domain. Entering, he quieted down, no longer roaring with rage, and curiosity took over as he spied the unwanted visitors. As he looked around, Indigo took the opportunity to strike, lunging forward to attack with her short sword, but the beast was too fast, and his gigantic black fist struck out to hit her but missed as she reeled backwards, astonished at her own speed. But in doing so, she fell and lay on her back wheezing.

Primitive superstition filled Sumata, and he fell to his knees, prostrating himself as if in worship, his arms outstretched and his forehead touching the ground. "Meh-Teh! Meh-Teh. Do not anger him," he whispered.

The creature lowered his head and took Indigo into his gaze, moving his head through various angles to observe and study her.

"I don't think he has seen a female human before. I guess he is only used to the monks who used to frequent this temple," she whispered, trying not to make any sudden moves.

During the distraction, Ignatius had pulled out his sonic blaster and was busy adjusting the dials. As he pointed it, Indigo got to her feet and rushed into the line of fire.

"No! You cannot!"

Fortunately, Ignatius had been a little too slow or she would have been injured or probably killed. She could feel her heart pounding in her chest and hear the rush of blood in her ears. Ignatius looked at her in astonishment.

"I will not allow it! This beast, and ones just like him, have walked unhindered on this planet, in these mountains for thousands of years, unknown to science, I will not allow you to kill it."

Still on the ground, Sumata added, "Valley of the Deities. These creatures are rarely seen and must be revered."

The beast's expression changed, his eyes drooped at the sides to try and gauge what was going on.

"He communicates via telepathy. His name is Meh-Teh," explained Indigo. "He tells me he can read my aura. He is a highly intelligent creature, able to read our astral trace and most likely communicate with minor spirits. Therefore, he doesn't see us as any threat. He knows we are not his enemy."

"Can you understand him?" asked Ignatius.

"Yes, a little. He will not attack us. He is curious about us and doesn't wish us any harm. He says the bones outside are not his prey. This is the Forbidden Temple, and we are in danger here. This temple lies in a beyul which is a hidden valley. A scared place where the spiritual world and physical world overlap. It is sacred and protected by the lords of the land, elementals who are connected with the natural world around. They often appear in other forms such as sprites, nymphs or birds of prey and sometimes butterflies. But there is one, the most powerful of them all, who manifests as a snow leopard."

"Did the snow leopard create the pile of bones?"

Indigo looked at Meh-Teh with an expression that suggested a question. "He did. He also caused the monks to abandon this place a long time ago, terrified of the ghost leopard that stalked and killed most of them. The rest fled. He says we need to be on guard, leopards are masters at stealth. We are in danger if he discovers us. Although if we rest here until the storm has passed, he says he can keep watch and show us a safe passage."

They decided to make camp and as they settled in, they realised that Sumata had vanished. He had presumably run away. "Typical coward," scathed Ignatius. "I only hope we can travel alone using the map."

It soon became obvious the beast seemed to follow Indigo around or sit just staring at her.

"If we leave, is that thing going to follow us?"

Indigo looked on and laughed. "He may be of some use if we get into a fight!"

When the storm had passed, a bright yellow moon came up over the craggy grey mountain tops and illuminated the area with an eerie glow.

"I'll keep watch," said Ignatius. He walked off towards the doorway and stood looking towards the moon, his pale face clothed in his usual moody look, and it glowed unnaturally. He was motionless, lost in his own thoughts. He examined the past, his encounters with gods, and thought about his future with Indigo, his future with the Union Jacks. Is this the life he wanted? His expression didn't change, and he continued his watch.

Indigo was cold and lay in restless sleep, her eyes closed and her torso raising rhythmically as she gently breathed. Halfway between sleep and wakefulness, she could see in her mind's eye seven beings on horseback, riding through a golden field of wheat being harvested by locals. And as she continued to observe with hope in her heart, the golden wheat turned red. A fountain of blood spurted skyward in several areas of the field and seven riders were now seven reavers with hawk heads and bloodied beaks. The air swished with the sound of scythes as they curved through the crisp air and bone and entrails flew with them on the upward arc. A tear rolled down the lead reaver's cheek. She was beginning to think she would never be rid of the Charon.

For most of the night, nothing stirred. Ignatius was still motionless at his post and Indigo slept. Abruptly, she was wakened as the darkness of night was split by the shrill squawk of an eagle as it swooped in. She felt icy cold on her cheeks as the bird's wings beat the air as it came in with its flesh-tearing talons before it. It was so fast Ignatius couldn't respond quickly enough. He drew his steam cannon, but it was too late. Indigo felt the bird slice her cheek and she saw her reflection in the bird's black eyes. She felt its beak touch her nose and she knew, the bird was trying to get a long close look at her, to identify her. To peer directly into her eyes, looking for her soul.

The yeti was swifter in his movements, and a great black hand grabbed the bird of prey and flung it towards the nearest crumbling wall. As the bird hit, it squawked again and a plume of golden-brown feathers flew into the air, descending in a random fashion to the dusty floor.

After a moment or two, the bird regained its composure and flew directly upwards, turning to circle above Indigo before heading out of the temple.

"An Elemental?" asked Ignatius.

Indigo looked at the yeti for an answer. "Yes!"

"Why did an elemental attack us? And why just you? The eagle was clearly trying to get a good look at you." Indigo hesitated for a while before simply saying she didn't know. But she had her suspicions.

"What kind of sorcery was that, do you think?"

Agitated she responded, "I don't know, but it's gone now, let's just get some rest shall we?"

He lay down and made himself comfortable with Indigo next to him, there was an awkward distance between them. Although they were lovers now, sometimes the role they played as Union Jacks was an obstacle

The great bulk that was the yeti sat next to her watching her breathe rhythmically. She didn't know how in the morning she was going to lose this gentle giant.

Chapter 14: Elementals

They had been asleep for about an hour. The air was damp and chill, and the skies were clear. A myriad of stars spattered the deep blue sky. The Milky Way split the heavens in two as the line of stars arched across the velvet background and illuminated the temple through the holes in the roof.

Except for the rise and fall of his muscular chest, Ignatius didn't stir. Close by, Indigo was restless, tossing and turning, her sleep filled with the usual constant dream. She felt the burning white light hit the centre of her back, and a purple aura enveloped her. She felt the cosmos scream as she felt every atom of her body separate and become at one with the fabric of space. Energy flew from her fingertips and destroyed anything it came into contact with. A silent scream in her own voice filled her consciousness, threatening to send her mad. But she didn't wake. Instead, she experienced an out-of-body episode as she stood looking down on both herself and Ignatius. He stirred and started to panic, pushing his arms out before him as if he was fighting against some invisible force. His eyes were wide open, and terror filled them. It was like he couldn't breathe, he kept pushing as if being enveloped. All colour drained from the scene as if he was being wrapped in a thin translucent membrane. It shimmered like mother of pearl and pulsed as if it was alive. A rich spectrum of colours danced across the membrane and then burst into brilliant white light. Indigo couldn't look at it any longer, it temporarily blinded her. The intensity grew and she could feel the heat from it warming her face and as the strange skin grew even brighter it exploded and Indigo sat bolt upright in her bedding, screaming as she did so.

The yeti growled and was shifting nervously from one foot to the other, agitated, not knowing what had happened. He began pacing around, throwing his arms in the air. Indigo was sobbing as Ignatius took her in his arms and looked on her face with sympathy. "Same dream? It's alright, I'm here. It's ok."

"Yes," she lied, "same dream." She didn't know how to explain what she had witnessed. She didn't want to alarm him.

Silence filled the air once more as they lay down in each other's arms, falling back to sleep. As they slumbered, a supple beast crept along the snow-covered ground with its belly close to the floor. Not a sound was heard as the snow leopard stalked the temple ruins. Not even the carpet of bones surrounding it stirred. Its piercing green eyes reflected the moonlight and shone like emeralds in the gloom. He moved with such agility and stealth, any normal human would not hear or see anything until it was too late.

Indigo knew something was imminent, her senses were heightened and on high alert since the eagle attacked. She released herself from Ignatius and peered into the blackness of night.

"What is it?" whispered Ignatius

"I'm not sure, but it will be upon us soon."

They both sat bolt upright and were soon on their feet, as a loud growl split the icy air and the cat pounced, its front paws hitting

Ignatius in the chest. He staggered backwards but kept his balance. Indigo's blade sliced past him, and she felt the hind quarters of the cat crunch and blood erupted. The angry cat turned and she felt claws rip across her shoulder, tearing her coat and white blouse which was now stained scarlet with her own gore. Her shoulder burned.

Landing gracefully on his front paws, the leopard dragged her back legs behind her, growling and flashing his fangs in a show of aggression. This mighty creature, as white as the snow with black spots, readied for another pounce but never made it. Indigo lunged forward with her short sword and split the leopard's skull in half, its keen edge creating sparks on the old, tiled floor as she followed through. The majestic cat fell, motionless and the air was silent once more.

Behind them the yeti had sadness in his eyes as he communicated with Indigo telepathically. His head swivelled from side to side as usual, but this time he looked anxious with panic etched on his leathery face.

"What's he saying?" asked Ignatius.

"We are in danger. We shouldn't have killed the leopard. More will come, we have to move on, now."

"More leopards?"

"No! Elementals. They will combine their force and attack."

Ignatius looked at Indigo. "are elementals bad? Aren't they just air or tree spirits?"

At this point, she answered. "Oh yes. Just air, just tree spirits." She grinned sardonically, "and water nymphs, and storm giants, and lightning, and the plants and the fire sprites. Just about everything in the natural world, really. Have you seen what the elements can do to the planet?"

Ignatius looked a little sheepish, he got the message, but Indigo continued. "The spirits of the forests could be anything, leopards, bears, wild boar, but only if we are lucky, otherwise they might be a giant troll, the kind that uses oak trees for clubs."

"How do you know this?"

Indigo thought briefly, genuinely trying to figure it out, "I don't know. Somehow, I just do."

They gathered their things and made for the doorway. During this time, Indigo was still trying to understand how she seemed to have newfound knowledge of supernatural things that she had never encountered, and she had never studied. The Yeti stood before Indigo. The beast had sadness in his eyes and shook his head at her.

"He says we shouldn't go on in the direction we were going. It's too dangerous."

Indigo ignored him and continued, but the beast kept moving in front of her to block her progression.

"I must." She looked at the yeti and held his giant leathery hand, giving his finger a gentle squeeze. "I must continue. Don't worry. Perhaps we will see you again on our return."

His shoulders slumped and he turned away, shaking his head, resigning himself to the fact Indigo was not going to stop and without any more actions, he picked up his pace and left the temple. As she followed, she couldn't see the yeti anymore. He had vanished into the snowy hills like magic.

Without any more delay, they continued their journey. Every so often, Ignatius would consult his map, using just the light of the stars to see and to check they were still on course. In the darkness it was hard to tell if they were on track. As Indigo was concentrating on her foot positions on the rock edge, she felt a sudden urge to jump. She jolted and stopped, with Ignatius walking into her.

"What is it? What's wrong?"

"I don't know. I feel the need to just jump!"

Ignatius caught her arm with a firm grip. "What do you mean, jump? Are you crazy?"

"I know, it's just… it's just…."

She fell silent and her eyes rolled into her head so only the whites remained.

"Indigo, what's happening?"

She turned to him with an eerie expression. "Sylphs. It's sylphs. Air elementals. They are in my head, influencing, taking over."

The trees that carpeted the slopes either side of the valley began to rustle, but not with any wind. They appeared to be moving rhythmically and in unison, noises getting louder and louder as if something was coming through the trees towards them. Tendrils of white mist snaked through the trunks and joined forces. Some shot up into the air and others travelled like serpents towards them.

If Ignatius hated anything, it was an enemy he couldn't see, grab hold of, or one that lacked solidity. And the Elementals were just that. Ignatius felt his feet rise involuntarily, and the rock beneath him began to rumble and move like waves on the sea. He struggled to keep his balance, then out the corner of his eye he caught a glimpse of another snow leopard, its shoulders rising and falling as it approached with a hunting stance.

"The mate of the leopard we killed," said Indigo.

Ignatius made eye contact, ignoring whatever was happening beneath his feet, so he didn't have to break his gaze. The leopard bared her fangs, getting ready to pounce. Slowly, Ignatius took out his steam cannon and sonic blaster, trying to decide who would be fastest when the dual began.

Forest nymphs began to float from the trees and gather around

Indigo, their tiny delicate wings glowing silver as they fluttered in the breeze. Indigo had drawn her short sword and steam cannon and had started to move towards Ignatius so eventually they stood back-to-back.

Without warning and as quick as lightning, the leopard pushed off of its hind legs and razor-sharp claws slashed at Ignatius, just catching his cheek and tearing through his coat. Ignatius felt his cheek sting and warm blood tricked down his chin and his neck, staining his collar red. Fangs dripped saliva right next to his face as he fought desperately to hold the beast off, which was difficult whilst holding two weapons. Ignatius ducked and swung himself beneath the front paws and pushed his steam cannon into the cat's ribs, but before he had time to pull the trigger the supple leopard had turned and was clawing at him again.

Indigo's sword whistled past his head as she was now slicing at the nymphs who had changed from looking angelic to scowling faces with enormous sharp teeth. Several nymphs fell from the air, some clutching their abdomens and separated from their wings, which drifted slowly to the floor like feathers. These nymphs, though, were not dead and as they hit the ground, they were very quickly up and biting at Indigo's ankles, ripping tiny holes in the leather of her boots. Some were crawling up her legs and she had to beat them off with the flat of her sword. Blasts from her steam cannon split the air and echoed off the sides of the distant mountains and fire bolts splattered through a group of nymphs, the hiss of steam being the last thing they heard before they died. The floor was rapidly becoming littered with tiny bodies and dismembered wings.

The leopard began to get the better of Ignatius. Blood seeped through his shredded clothing in places, and he could feel the big cat overpowering him. For a time, the two rolled around, sometimes the cat was on top, other times it was Ignatius.

Out the corner of his eye, Ignatius could see there were far fewer forest nymphs trying to attack Indigo; some had met their end, whilst others retreated to the cover of the forest, nursing limbs or wings.

With some desperation, Ignatius remarked, "Indigo, I could use some help here, please."

Knowing it was too dangerous to use her steam cannon for fear of shooting Ignatius, a sword whistled past his face, striking the leopard, not enough to wound it, but enough for the cat to snarl and momentarily turn her attention elsewhere. Ignatius seized his chance and threw the cat to the side, managing to fire a shot. The cat whimpered and ran off into the forest.

Ignatius lay on his back panting for breath. "Fighting humans is one thing, even gods, but wild animals is totally different! I wonder what these Elementals wanted, or do they just attack anyone who is passing through?"

Indigo didn't reply, she thought the question was rhetorical. Holding out her hand, she offered to help Ignatius back on his feet. "Come on," she said, "we need to get out of here in case any of them return."

Chapter 15: The Crone

A little further, and Ignatius had the feeling they were being watched. Squinting, he tried to pierce the darkness amongst the trees either side of them. Concerned the leopard might have returned.

Before he could speak, Indigo was ahead of him. "I know. We are being followed. But it's not the leopard. I can sense it."

As if by magic, an old woman appeared right in front of them, too close for comfort. Startled, neither one of the Union Jacks saw her arrive. "Crone!" exclaimed Ignatius, feeling a little embarrassed, but he couldn't help himself. He had heard of local medicine women who lived in Tibet, local shamans who were not to be trusted or conferred with for any length of time, and you certainly didn't accept medicine from them unless you wanted to be incapacitated for a good length of time, paralysed from the neck down, or sent mad, screaming at the voices in your head or the illusionary shadows that attacked you whilst you slept.

The old woman looked like she was a thousand years old. She had brown leather-like skin all over her, the vertical creases in her face and the flatness of unsupple skin between gave her the appearance that she was made from an old saddle. She was wizened and stood with a stoop, perched on top of scrawny bowed legs, a slight hump on her back. Her only hair was wispy and white, matted and hardly covered any of her head. She grinned and what few teeth she had were yellow with a pipe stuck between some of them; it emitted great plumes of aromatic smoke every so often. They could hear her breathe as her ancient lungs wheezed and crackled from the years of abuse at the hands of the tobacco and herbs she smoked.

"Where goes you?" she asked in a husky low-toned voice.

It sent a shiver down Ignatius's spine. "Greetings. We did not expect to see anybody in these parts, let alone a dwelling. You live here?"

She cackled like a witch but didn't answer.

"You look injured, you are bleeding." She rummaged around in her dirty clothing and pulled out some herbs. "I can fix that for you."

Ignatius was more worried than when the leopard attacked. "No, thank you. It's very kind of you, but I shall be ok."

She didn't reply, but sneered and removing her pipe for a second, put some of the herbs in her mouth to chew, loudly and disgustingly, and stuffed the remainder back into her clothing. Then she turned to Ignatius with one eye enlarged and her eyebrow raised. "Turn back! Turn back! You may travel in number, but you have no place here. You are not worthy!"

"Worthy for what?" asked Ignatius.

Again, she cackled. A vicious laugh that was starting to irritate Ignatius.

"Worthy to be here. In the here and now. To be on your quest." Another laugh split the icy air and echoed off the valley sides. "Worthy to be in Rahasya."

She ran towards Ignatius, her ancient, bowed legs causing her to hobble from side to side, made worse by a wound on one of her legs. As she reached him, she stood on tip toe and closed one eye, spying him with her other that was wide and round and black like the burning coals of hell, her brow and one side of her face wrinkled tight. Ignatius stood back a little, she unnerved him. Smoke billowed in his face from her pipe, and he coughed.

"Worthy to be in the presence of gods and the Pearl of Life, the Pearl of all creation. It will not end well. Turn back! Turn back! Turn back, I tell thee thrice. I can see into the spaces between the worlds, and I can see that you will have the potential to destroy Rahasya, and both die. And your death shall be repeated over and over throughout all eternity."

As she became animated, it was like a mirage, she faded and changed into a leopard, then back again. It was so quick it was difficult to believe it had happened. The hairs on the back of Ignatius's neck stood on end. Indigo looked at him, she had seen it too. She placed her hand on the pommel of her short sword.

"You won't need that dear," she scowled at Indigo. "It is past the moon time," and she looked heavenward. Indigo followed her gaze just in time to see the moon disappear behind a thick blanket of cloud that extended as far as the eye could see.

"There is a reason why the Knights of Himavala exist. They kill all adventurers like you. You should be dead by now!"

Curious, Ignatius asked, "how do you know of the Knights?"

She cackled, a laugh that seemed to last forever. She coughed and wheezed, "I was the Mother Superior for a time." She waited for a reaction. Ignatius and Indigo were too stunned to speak, so she continued. "Yes, I dared to step out of line, to question the Knight's purpose and methods. As Mother Superior, I should have been leading the order, writing and demonstrating law, showing how they should live and protect. But I became curious about the Pearl. But I was exiled, my soul captured and tethered to an elemental for all eternity. An unbreakable curse placed upon me. I was once beautiful, now I have to hide in the shadows, living in a cave with the nymphs and sprites, constantly in danger as the rocks leak poisonous gas."

"So why did you attack us?" asked Indigo.

"I was trying to stop you from venturing further. But as a leopard, I have limitations and animal instinct takes over. You have injured me and killed my mate, so I no longer care, go ahead, meet your demise."

She turned and pointed, her thin outstretched arm looking like loose skin hanging from her bones with a scrawny hand and talonlike fingers. "Travel that way and it is certain death immediately. There lie the poisonous gases in the Forbidden Territory." She shifted her direction, "travel that direction you may survive… for now."

"Why should we believe you?" asked Ignatius suspiciously.

"You have no choice!" She cackled a hideous laugh that turned Ignatius cold. She hobbled away and soon vanished amongst the rocks.

Chapter 16: The Mystic

Deciding to follow the crone's directions, they continued with caution. In the dawn light they could see a dense forest made of rhododendrons.

"These are some of the most beautiful flowers I have seen," said Indigo as she buried her nose deep into one of the blooms to drink in its aroma.

Flowers of bright red, orange, pink and mauve filled the landscape, dotted around the sides of the valley, sweeping down to fill the valley floor on which they travelled. The scent brought back memories of running around in her mother's garden. Despite the cold atmosphere, internally she felt warm and happy. Pleasant memories of childhood and summer days. But the feeling didn't last long before a shadow swept through her mind and thoughts of the terrible deed that had brought about her birth from an immortal, a beast, a demon. An image of a dark figure taking her mother, the act of which turned the flowers around them brown and wilted. She had no idea how her birth came about, whether it was consensual or forced, but her childhood memories were now forever sullied.

She refocused and every time Indigo saw another colour, or a slightly different specimen, she couldn't resist stopping to admire it and take in the scent which now filled the air. Neither of the Union Jacks noticed at first, but as they continued their journey, the rhododendrons were more numerous and their leaves longer and wider. The light had dimmed and without any perception, they found themselves in a forest so thick they could hardly move and were without much light.

As they turned to retreat, it was as if the plants had converged on them. A mass of branches and blooms whipped across their faces at every turn. Ignatius noticed that pollen coated Indigo's face.

"I feel drowsy," she said, and the world began to spin. She felt her legs go heavy and she felt lightheaded. She found it difficult to stay awake. She looked over at Ignatius. His face blurred and when he did come back into focus, she noticed, "Your face. It's yellow. Pollen…"

At which point, she was overcome and fainted. Ignatius caught her although wasn't feeling too great himself. Feeling nauseated, he dragged himself and Indigo through the thick forest, trying to retrace their steps, until at last he found the rhododendrons were beginning to thin out again. He placed Indigo down on the floor and slumped against some rocks. Gasping for air, he wiped his face to remove as much pollen as he could. Then, as he wiped Indigo's she began to rouse, opening her eyes again. She sneezed, and again. She wiped her face with her sleeve and sat upright.

"Mystical pollen?"

"It would seem so. Hopefully not poisonous. Which is going to make it difficult to continue as the entire region is filled with the same plant. If we go around it, I'm not sure how far out of our way we will be going, plus it will be uphill to get away from the valley floor."

They sat and thought for a while. "I'm going to try my sonic blaster. Trouble is, I don't know how far this forest goes." He took the map out of his pocket. "There isn't even a forest shown on here. But this is the correct path, look." Pointing out other features the two of them agreed, this must be correct. "This land is so uncharted."

Ignatius got to his feet; the effects of the pollen not quite worn off yet. He took his sonic blaster from its holster and adjusted some dials. Holding his arm out in front, he took aim and pulled the trigger. The first bolt hit the nearest rhododendron, and it vibrated, letting out a high-pitched screech that nearly burst their ear drums. Part of the plant disintegrated, and the rest shook violently and retreated to clear a path. Ignatius took aim at another plant and the same scenario repeated. Then another, and another, after which the remaining rhododendrons seemed to retreat by their own choice.

He turned to Indigo. "Come on, quick, let's make a run before they change their minds."

Indigo pulled herself up and the two of them made haste. "What if they close in on us?"

"Then I'll just shoot them," grinned Ignatius.

Before long, the two Union Jacks emerged from the forest at the other side and were greeted with bright light and cool fresh air. The whole atmosphere seemed to have changed. Everything was easier, the air not quite so cold, the light brighter and the pathway now a gravel path, banked on both sides by light-grey rocks dotted with yellow lichen. Up ahead, either side of the path were two carvings of a crowned lion and a heavenly bird.

Continuing, they didn't notice a man sat on a rock nearby. He almost blended with the surroundings. He was dressed in a simple natural linen robe that reached the ground and, on his feet, he wore leather sandals. He was tall and slim with a sweet-looking face. His hair was shoulder length, and he wore a moustache and small neatly trimmed triangular beard. He had an aura about him which intensified around his head, and his face seemed to glow. He seemed to exude a calmness that Ignatius had never experienced before, and when he spoke his voice was soft like velvet and mesmerising.

As indigo addressed him, all she could think was how the man glowed. He exuded an aura of gold and his face shone like the sun. Indigo had observed auras before, but never one of gold.

"Can you see what I see?" she whispered to Ignatius.

"See what?"

"His aura?"

Ignatius looked on. He couldn't see an aura, but knew this man, this being, was special. He appeared as if in soft focus and it seemed like gentle music filled his ears. Was this what Indigo meant?

"I'm not sure. But he is spellbinding. Does he have a halo?"

"That's it. Part of his aura."

The mystic smiled gently, his eyes seemed to smile, to draw them in.

"Greetings, weary travellers. I am Issa, it is good to meet another two travelling the same path." He paused, and then in a knowing way added as if reading their minds, "I may appear strange to you, an aura, perhaps? I don't know."

"Are you one of the Descended Masters?" queried Ignatius.

"I am what am. I am not always in control of my qualities. Like you, I am a pawn, we are all pawns in the great cosmic game. I walk this land in search… I believe there have been others before me, the blue-skinned man of India, born of Queen Devaki, and the wandering ascetic born in Nepal, and many others, all of whom searched."

"In search of what?" asked Ignatius, impatiently.

"The truth. Nothing more, nothing less. Life, all life, in the entire cosmos, must search for the truth. There is nothing else. The truth is all that matters. And the truth is now. Yesterday has gone, tomorrow does not yet exist, at least on this plane. Time is complicated. Time is separate and yet flows all at once, but for this instant, here where we stand, there is only now."

"Then I think we are similar; we are seeking the truth. It concerns…" He didn't get a chance to finish.

"I know. I know what you seek, Ignatius." He sighed and smiled, causing his face to emanate even more of a glow. Ignatius didn't know how he knew his name. "I have knowledge of it. Although I do not consider it wise. You have been on a long journey, and you now have knowledge that is of enormous importance, not just to humanity, but the whole cosmos and all life within it. Some of what you know is painful. You are the offspring of a god, a demon, a terrible immortal who seeks to destroy the cosmos and all within it. You know the truth about consciousness, about how the cosmos works, and your soul has been forever changed, but it is too early to say if this is a good or a bad thing. Let's just say, it is distorted. But tell me, what good do you think will come of your search for the Pearl? The enigmatic Flaming Celestial Pearl."

Indigo looked shocked; Ignatius was speechless. How did he know his heritage, the history of their adventures and what they were seeking. Ignatius felt his head swirl, beads of sweat broke out on his forehead and the hairs stood up on the back of his neck. "How do…"

"How do I know?" the mystic smiled, that same blissful, at-ease-with-the-cosmos smile that was starting to irritate Ignatius.

"I am blessed with second sight. I am not from here or this plane. I come from the land of the Duranki, the same land Viveka the Librarian came from. The destruction you wrought on his library has had a devastating effect on the balance of the cosmos. So much knowledge has been lost to the whole of creation. Viveka has been set adrift and is set on revenge, should he ever discover your whereabouts. He knows the girl died and has found some comfort to satisfy his anger for a while. But fear not, I shall not betray you.”

That same sweet smile appeared again, his sapphire-blue eyes sparkling.

Indigo felt a little uneasy but said nothing. But felt a little reassured that even the mystic didn’t know everything, despite his second sight. He believed her to be dead, overcome by her trial in Oxford at the hands of the High Priestess of the Administorium.

“I do not believe your adventure is advised, and to bring another,” he gestured to Indigo.

“Eliza,” said Ignatius.

“To bring Eliza into this is reckless.”

“What do you mean the balance of the cosmos has been devastated?”

“The cosmos must exist in a state of neutrality. The spheres, the thirty-one planes of existence, must be in harmony. The rhythms of the cosmos must be orchestrated by the Omnisoul and vibrate at exactly the right frequency. The infinity shards created by yourself and the Charon caused disruption, but merely provided an amplification to the harmony, nothing the Omnisoul couldn’t contain. But that harmony has been disrupted by the hyperquakes that have rippled out from the opening of the Book of Shadows, and the aftermath of the battle with Calabi-Ya has permanently damaged the plane that your earth spins through. That damage has caused the music of the spheres to distort. That distortion has affected the thoughts of the Omnisoul, and… as you know… all life, the history of the cosmos, what is, what has been and what will be, is made manifest by the thoughts of the Omnisoul.

When the Omnisoul dreams, the cosmos expands. When the Omnisoul sings, when the Omnisoul plays the Cosmic Sitar, a whole new part of creation is made manifest. And when the Omnisoul screams, the cosmos shakes and the Elder God is given another chance at superiority, at control of the cosmos as his dark matter swells from the anger and dark thoughts the Omnisoul generates. The Omnisoul has grown bored and lazy. That is why some events pass by unnoticed. They are not really unregistered in the mind of the Omnisoul, but apathy has grown, and complacency.

But you know this. And regardless of what I say here and now, you shall not err from your task. I know this.”

“Then we must continue our journey, but our map has become unclear and we only have a vague notion of where to go. I was informed you would be able to help us.”

The mystic smiled again and silently turned away. “I cannot help you directly. I am but a simple mystic, a shaman, a holy man on his travels to seek further knowledge. To some, I am a redeemer, a saviour.”

“Then if you are seeking knowledge, travel with us and you can learn all there is about the cosmos.”

That same sweet smile prevailed and his eyes sparkled. “The knowledge I seek is not the same as yours. I know how the cosmos works, for I have studied at the place you seek. My journey must take me elsewhere. I am headed towards India, although my journey is within, so I seek solitude. But I can point you in the right direction. However, I shall repeat, you are best advised not to go. Do you really want to seek out the final truth? Can you live with yourselves after that?”

Ignatius and Indigo had frowns on their faces, confused by what the mystic was telling them. "What can we expect to find? Is it so terrible?"

"A sane man should never open the doors to perception. It will drive him to insanity. Your lives will not be the same, for although they have already been irreparably changed, this adventure may end with your life!"

The two Union Jacks were speechless, both contemplating their adventure.

"One of you has already travelled death's dark corridor." He looked at Indigo, "And it is with great sadness I say, your soul, Indigo, is no longer your own. It has become blackened through no fault of your own and lies prisoner somewhere I cannot see. Your only hope may lie with the demon who took your mother and whatever magic he can summon to free you."

Indigo's knees went weak, and she nearly passed out. How did the mystic know who she really was? She didn't have time to speak.

"Oh, I know what you are thinking. How do I know you are both descended of bad blood born of the most terrible and merciless demons in the cosmos. They will stop at nothing in their eternal quest to end their immortality, but eventually they will have done with you because their fate is almost fulfilled, and your death shall be imminent. Anything other than death shall be a vile abomination wrought against you and your blackened souls shall be lost forever. You shall no longer be human."

Both Union Jacks had turned pale, cold sweat trickled down their backs. Neither one could speak. Indigo's thoughts turned to the Charon and how she wished she had never met them. But she knew in her heart that regardless of what Skye's actions had been to secure the Book of Consciousness, she would have eventually met with her father, Atman. She had been bred specially for these events. Horrific images kept flashing through her mind of her poor mother being molested by the god, the hawk-headed demon, tearing at her flesh with his beak, forcing himself upon her. She had no idea if this was the truth, but it was too terrible to think her birth had been with consent. Ignatius was silent, internalising what he now knew. He wasn't quite as repulsed by the knowledge he had carried for some time now, but his birthmark gave him a sudden pain, much sharper than the burning he usually experienced on the back of his hand. Ignoring it, his thoughts went back to his heritage. He was descended from an immortal, despite the Charon's actions, their quest and fate, he knew this could be an opportunity. The Union Jacks might be able to elevate the British Empire beyond all recognition with whatever knowledge he and Indigo could take back with them. All other Empires would crumble. This was their job, to protect the Empire, and he took his responsibilities very seriously.

"So does our fate mean we are damned?" asked Indigo.

He smiled again. "That I do not know. Only the Omnisoul knows that, and the Book of Consciousness."

"And the Book of Shadows, what of that?"

He still smiled. "Again, that I do not know. But I would think not. As you know, that great tome is made from the dark thoughts of all in the cosmos, your fears and your thoughts of your conception are feeding it even now."

"So how do you know why we are travelling this path?"

The whole valley knows why you are here. It was prophesied millennia ago.

Ignatius was speechless. The mystic knew everything. "So who prophesied it?" he asked.

"Enoch Slipnot, from the Land of the Duranki."

Ignatius rummaged around in his bag and pulled out the Tamas Codex written by Enoch. "Is his prophesy in this?"

The mystic walked on. "So many questions." He smiled.

"Tell me! Is the prophesy in this book?"

"Perhaps. I don't know. I do not read; I prefer to discover life for myself. I only know what I can see, in the mind's eye and walking across the planes. I have come to earth to convey, let's say, certain knowledge. There have been a few like me."

Ignatius was obviously irritated. Indigo held his arm, for fear he would get angry, so she continued with the questions.

"Forgive us, but we are bound to have many questions. We are merely human, then one day suddenly we discover we are godlings, demigods, call us what you will. We are in possession of a rare book and are seeking an artefact used in the creation. None of this is normal. Tell us, where is this Land of the Duranki? And how would Enoch Slipnot be capable of a prophecy?"

The mystic laughed heartily, which was even more annoying than his usual smile. He placed his hand to his chin and thought for a while. "Let me think…" And they continued their journey along the path together.

At length, the mystic declared, "the land of the Duranki existed at the time of the last great cataclysm. The world undergoes changes and every so often, it shall cleanse itself of all that is and has been and begin again. In some respect, that is the quest you are on. What you seek shall be knowledge beyond all other beings at this moment in time, here on earth, at least. It is knowledge that is beyond most beings' comprehension, so you need to decide if you wish to continue. But in doing so, you may lose your lives. You may lose each other. Your love for each other may not survive."

With concern, Indigo asked, "are we on a fruitless quest? Do we even need to be here? I have got to the point where I no longer care much for cosmic quests and artefacts." She looked at Ignatius for some response, but none came forth, clearly he thought differently.

The mystic replied simply, "I cannot tell you what you should do, your choices are yours. You are lucky to have free will. However, be wary of those who claim to be wise, and those that claim to be loyal, and those you fear the most, but most of all, be wary of those whom you love, for they may betray you!"

Ignatius shifted a little from foot to foot and Indigo spied him with suspicion, becoming concerned when he didn't make eye contact.

Chapter 17: Enlightenment

As they journeyed on, the mystic enlightened them with tales of antiquity. "Before I tell you of Enoch Slipnot, you must first understand the importance of the Land of the Duranki, and Enoch's role in its history."

His aura darkened and his smile seemed to fade a little. "Millenia ago, the land of the Duranki was visited by seven cosmic beings, the Celestials. They were sorcerer lords from an advanced and extinct civilisation located in the Netherworlds. They formed a covenant with the Duranki and a bond was formed between themselves and the earth. They were worshipped as gods and after gaining entry to the cosmos from the Netherworlds, their power increased several fold. No other sorcerers were as skilled in the dark arts and alchemy. Using their sorcery and cunning, their god-like status became manifest, immortal and able to operate outside of time."

"Presumably, just like the Omnisoul had laid down in the Book of Consciousness?" enquired Ignatius.

"Quite. It soon became clear that they were to play an important role at the end of the cosmos, when the Great Cycle ends and begins again. Their role is to wait until that moment, at which point they have been tasked with bearing witness to the collapse and destruction of all things, all matter, to record the evidence for the next cycle. Their presence on earth caused great changes to the people of that land and new religions and cults grew up around the presence of these strange beings from the sky. The Celestials encouraged it, rejoicing in their newfound status. This caused the collapse of the Duranki's society, and their true heritage faded into obscurity."

"What was their heritage, who were they?"

"Originally, they were descended from the Ti-Botta. They left Rahasya in search of new lands to populate, and upon finding them, they settled them, but this all went to waste when the Celestials arrived, who demanded worship and were feared. Great monuments to their existence were built, temples and tombs all worshipping the new gods from the sky. Over time, worship of these gods caused factions amongst the people and they became competitive, making their god the only one to worship and wars broke out amongst the Duranki people. Brother fought brother and much of the architecture was destroyed in the fighting, leaving little trace of their civilisation and the Celestials.

"But why would the Omnisoul need somebody to record their histories? The great god of creation has already written it."

"That is true, but the theory has it that these histories must be recorded for future generations on earth and because the end will bring about the end of the Omnisoul, and so to start again requires a history to follow. A starting point for the new epoch. If the cosmos is the consciousness of every living being, then complete entropy of the cosmos shall bring about the demise of the Omnisoul. You can't have one without the other."

"It's the Omnisoul's insurance policy," added Indigo.

"Quite!"

Ignatius thought for a while before asking, "so, what about Enoch Slipnot? I have read in his Tamax Codex that he was the last remaining warrior-priest of the Charon. So where did he come from, to be recording events concerning the Charon?"

"It is true Enoch is the scribe for the Charon, he records for the Ti-Botta. His origins are shrouded in obscurity."

"You said is, you mean was?"

"Is, was, is yet to be. All time runs parallel and simultaneously. Yesterday, today, tomorrow all exist at the same time. All sentient beings can only live in the moment, their timeframe is just *now*. Nothing more, nothing less. Unless you are a wizard, a sorcerer, or a witch and can astral surf, move between the planes and transform yourself to higher realms, but even then, once in place, all time is just *now*! And even upon their return, they must be in the *now*. Only the Omnsisoul can occupy the cosmos in all places at all times." The mystic thought for a moment. "And the Elder God, Calabi-Ya"

"So, who is Calabi-Ya? I have heard him say he is the brother to the Omnisoul."

"Ah! Yes, it is complicated. Only the two gods themselves know the truth. But I have my own belief."

"Which is what?"

The mystic thought for a little while. "I cannot say. This quest is yours and yours alone. You and Indigo must find your own path, your own reasoning and draw your own conclusions. There are two paths, one to the Field of Truths and one to the Field of Untruths, and you must choose wisely. Whichever path you choose, my advice is to make sure you do not separate yourself from creation. Those who live a fruitless life full of regrets and hopelessness, their mind is infected by their bodies. Do not let your emotions, created by your senses, rule your consciousness. You should just *be*. Life is too enormous and intricate for you to understand, you should just live your life blissfully and value every single moment. These moments are your past, your present and your future. Earthly time is an illusion created by humans to try and make sense of their world. The truth, not the reality your mind creates for you, is that all roads lead to the individual, the self. So, my advice is you should abandon your quest and if you value your life, you should not explore the source of life. The man who forsakes all desires and abandons the self will reach the ultimate goal of eternal peace."

His smile was so annoying at that moment, his calm soft voice was about to make Ignatius erupt. None of this made sense.

"What do you mean, the source of life? We have not come here for that; we are in search of an ancient relic."

The mystic returned his usual smile. "So be it. I must leave you now, but if you continue your journey, then you must continue heading west. There you will encounter the Sea of Palms. If you can cross it, and nobody ever has, then your life will have been extended only briefly because you will encounter the Gatekeeper. He will surely kill you. Nobody enters Rahasya, the land of the Worthy Ones. It is forbidden. But remember, your gift of vision is far greater than that of action, you need not search for answers, when you can see them before you."

For the first time since meeting him, the mystic seemed not to smile. Indigo thought a darkness fell across his face, and for a brief moment his aura flickered and turned a dark green, and then was gone, his usual aura reinstated.

"Now I must leave you. May the wind be at your back and the sun upon your face. Safe journey, Ignatius". He turned to Indigo and his face appeared to be even more of a glow and, producing a large grin across his unblemished face, he took her by the hand

and spoke so softly he was hardly audible. "Safe journey, Indigo, you must take care of yourself, your troubles are not your own, and Ignatius must remove the pain and anguish you find in your soul. You have a most important part to play in this cosmic game of chess. But you shall fail unless your blackened soul is healed."

Indigo pulled her hand free in shock and had a surprised expression fixed to her face. She still didn't understand how he knew her real name.

"Farewell, Ignatius, farewell... Eliza. You have passed my tests."

"What tests?" they asked in unison.

"Never mind..." And with that, he turned and walked in the opposite direction. Ignatius was surprised, too, and in the split second it took for him to glance at Indigo to try and read her thoughts and expression, the mystic vanished, perhaps blending into the rocky surroundings once more.

Chapter 18: Trapped

They were both weary due to the thin air; it was difficult to breathe. Indigo was chilled to the core, and Ignatius could feel pains in his hands and legs. The mountain atmosphere was no place to spend long periods of time. But they were now descending again and would soon be back below the snow line. They picked up the red granite seam again and after a couple more hours were walking amongst some greenery. Mountain springs erupted occasionally from the ground and watered an abundance of exotic plant life.

"There!" said Indigo. "Look over there." Pointing she indicated to Ignatius a village.

Consulting the map, Ignatius responded, "this was the last dwelling place before the Sea of Palms and then Rahasya."

"At least we can rest and find some fresh food," replied Indigo. "We might even find some hot water to soak our limbs and regain feeling in them."

He smiled and his sun-scorched face showed more lines than Indigo had ever noticed before. She studied him, he was a good man and although she sometimes disagreed with his decisions, she respected him, loved him.

They travelled deeper into the city, a fascinating old city, ancient beyond anyone's imagination. It was a bustling labyrinth of narrow alleyways, market stalls and taverns or tea houses. It was impossible to move freely, the dense population side by side trading and praying. The whole atmosphere was charged with a mystical history and spirituality that Ignatius couldn't quite pinpoint. Above all of this, the unmistakable smell of incense filled the air, along with the pungent smell of butter tea, made from yak milk.

The buildings were whitewashed with brightly coloured woodwork and equally bright prayer flags fluttering in the crisp mountain breeze. Indigo found the whole place caused sensory overload, along with the stares she attracted and several clawing hands that had never seen such fair female skin and auburn hair before. But mainly the inhabitants were all calm and contented, their faces with fixed expressions and skin like heavily creased leather. The harsh environment looked like it had taken its toll. The twisting alleyways seemed to narrow even further, and the two Union Jacks became aware they were alone. Making their way along the high-walled corridor, slippery cobble stones under foot, the alley went on for about a quarter of a mile. After travelling about halfway along, Ignatius became aware the already murky light had dimmed behind them. He turned to see a group of people blocking the light. Three came running at them. They were all dressed like the pirates had been, black hooded cloaks, cummerbunds and leather belts at the waist and a scarf hiding their faces. Just tempestuous eyes stared out, with dilated pupils in which burned determination.

"Ignatius," said Indigo, "warrior priestesses!"

As Ignatius looked back, more were attacking from the front. There was no escape, and the alleyway offered such restrictions that fighting was going to be difficult. Indigo drew her short sword, ideal for close combat, and a steam cannon. A hiss of steam was followed by a loud crack as the first shot was fired. The leading knight fell to her knees. Those behind her leapt over the dead body and were brandishing some sort of rotating blade attached to what looked like a prayer wheel. This would make short work of slicing into flesh. The dim light was split once more as steam hissed and fire lit the area as another shot was fired. The same came from behind Indigo as Ignatius followed suit. The floor was slippery with thick blood where they fell. More assailants were gaining ground.

Too close now to shoot, Indigo pulled a dagger from her boot and began to slash and parry with both her sword and dagger. A black-hooded knight came at her with full force. Indigo jabbed and felt her dagger glance off the leather breast plate, but she quickly followed up with her sword and felt it bite into flesh and shoulder bone. Blood spurted, spraying the whitewashed walls. The knight staggered backwards and fought back with a cutlass. Indigo ducked her left shoulder, and the blade missed. Bringing her dagger upwards she pierced the assailant's throat and, wild eyed, she slumped to the floor.

But there was no time for rest, two more came at her with a quarterstaff and the point hit her breastbone, knocking her off balance. As she fell, her dagger bit into the thigh of one knight, whose legs buckled and she fell on top of Indigo, which probably saved Indigo's life as the blue crystal tip of the other's quarterstaff crackled and sparked intense azure light as it hit her partner in the back. She fell limp immediately, and Indigo had to haul her dead weight off so she could retaliate. Gaining her feet, she thrust her short sword into the gut of the second knight, finding soft belly flesh between her leather jerkin and belt. Blood gurgled from her mouth, and she fell on top of the other corpse.

A cutlass came whistling past Indigo's right ear and caught her shoulder, glancing off as she used her agility to sidestep. Using her expertise as a swordswoman, Indigo was soon standing with a firm stance, her sword, albeit a bit short, held out in front of her, demonstrating she knew how to use it. In an instant, she was thrusting, parrying the heavier cutlass, and advancing forward until her opponent had backed up against two more knights. One quick thrust and the blade sunk deep between ribs, piercing her heart. The other two didn't have time to think and soon lay in a heap on top of their comrade-in-arms.

Behind Indigo, Ignatius was fighting three more. When he pointed his steam cannon, the lead knight caught the end with the crystal on the tip of her quarterstaff. Blue fire circled the gun and danced up Ignatius's arm. With a yelp, he let the gun go as his body jolted with the shock. Stumbling backwards, he pulled two derringers from his belt and fired. He hit one knight in the forehead, killing her instantly and another in the shoulder, temporarily stopping her. The third used her quarterstaff to vault and hit Ignatius full on in the chest with her boots. As Ignatius landed on his back, Indigo filled the gap and the knight landed on the point of Indigo's dagger and sword.

It was now difficult to move for dead bodies littering the alleyway, but there seemed to be an endless stream of knights entering from both ends, dimming the only light available in the narrowness. Sunlight was replaced by the eerie blue glow of some crystal-tipped quarterstaffs.

"What are we going to do?" said Indigo in a low growl.

"I don't know. Grab a quarterstaff from one of the dead. At least they are longer, and we can use them to hold them at more of a distance."

They both picked up the weapons and Ignatius retrieved his steam cannon, but it had been put out of action until he could repair it. Meanwhile, Indigo had pulled out her steam cannon once more and was pointing the quarterstaff at the horde and firing shot after shot. But it was like the colonial wars in Africa, they just kept coming, climbing over the dead to gain some ground. She felt Ignatius push his back against hers and they waited.

"I'm still not sure what we are going to do," she said.

Then Ignatius sprang into action. "There's nothing for it!" he cried.

"What do you mean? I have no intention of dying in this filthy hell hole!"

"No, I mean, we're going to have to call for help!"

Indigo looked at him with a puzzled expression as she saw Ignatius drop to one knee. He dragged the nearest corpse to him and, opening the mouth of an already grimacing face, he placed a coin under the tongue of the knight.

"No! No, Ignatius…" Indigo grabbed him by the sleeve, her face contorted with horror. "I shall never forgive you!" She bared her teeth, and every muscle of her face convulsed to form a mask of sheer repulsion. But it was too late. Ignatius felt the weight of guilt in his heart but could see no escape. If they were to live, he believed this was the only option. Indigo grabbed him by the lapels and shook his huge frame back and forth, crying, "No! No! No! You can't! You just can't."

All Ignatius could feel was a heavy sinking feeling in the pit of his stomach. His head swirled; guilt overcame him, and he could feel a lump in his throat. He knew he shouldn't, and deep down didn't want to but he had no intention of dying this day, not here, not before he and Indigo had experienced some life together other than that of the Union. Indigo sank to her knees, her arms limp beside her, her heart broken and pounding so loud she could hear it, feel it trying to burst from her chest. It was pounding in rhythm with the footfalls as the knight ran towards her. Tears stung her face and froze in the cool mountain air. She sat back on her haunches and closed her eyes. Dropping her weapons, she removed her scarf and pulled her collar apart to show her breastbone, awaiting the sharp stabbing burning pain that would come, preferring the inevitability of her own death.

Chapter 19: Limbo

The smell of sulphur filled the Void. A permanent red mist obscured any view. Just a red mosaic of fire and brimstone continuously tumbled and writhed for all eternity. Shapes shifted, and vague outlines of bodies writhed against each other in constant search of an end to the eternal monotony that was, is and will be. Faint groans and mumblings emanated from the sea of flesh and could just be heard above the hiss of the odd vent that erupted with yet more lava and damnation. Here, all souls merged into one organic shape with shared agony and despair. The throng appeared to be nearly all body, with very few limbs. Resistance to the imprisonment was of no use. Heavy chains bound some of the inhabitants, but others were so weak-willed, restraints were not necessary. Here, constant pain was the only solace and reminder to these beings they were not dead. Occasionally, a horned beast would rise from the mound, appear to feed from the limp forms before it then sunk back down again, only to rise again, perhaps after an immense span of time, and appear to feed from the same forms again. Whatever the beings here had done in life, their punishment was the same for them all, and Limbo was their abode, with no escape. At times, it was even more unbearable, when the gnashing of teeth was so loud it became deafening. Bleeding ears and the scratching of eyes made blood flow enough to mix with the lava and feed the four rivers of the Underworld.

Amongst the mound of flesh that seemed to go on forever, far off into the hazy distance, a single eye opened. Terrified and angry in equal measure. Although this was Limbo, dreams and nightmares still occurred, giving off more vibes to help sustain the dark energy that was always trying to subsume the cosmos. Adonai's skin burned and blistered. This was the life of the Charon unless summoned to carry out the will of the Omnisoul, when the Keeper would release them from their fate. His metallic and bejewelled eyepatch singed his beautiful cheek, and his orange hair was matted with dried blood and burnt at the tips. He tensed his chest and arm muscles, becoming aware that his clothing was, as usual, torn and tattered, sinew and muscle burst from his red garments. The repeated nightmare that he had to endure for all eternity was still fresh in his mind. In his mind's eye, Adonai could see and relive that he held an enormous pearl in his hand. It throbbed and murmured and somehow caressed his skin. But all around him he could see a war raging.

He could feel Devi lying next to him and several unknown shapeless blasphemies, scarlet and black and oozing with vitriol. Beings of no consequence, thieves, vagabonds, paupers and criminals who had carried out the vilest of deeds to the innocent. If he could move, if he knew it would make a difference, he would inflict more pain and suffering on them. But what was the point, eternal damnation was their sentence. It didn't matter if you were a god or the lowest level of being in the cosmos, in Limbo you were all the same, immortal and vulnerable and punished.

Devi groaned and awakened. As she tried to move, heavy chains made from links as thick as a man's arm clanked. Adonai felt his own enchanted chains weighing him down and unable to move due to the close proximity of others, contemplated his nightmare. It was a reccurring nightmare he had experienced thousands of times before. This was part of his punishment, to relive a single battle over and over, without any change to the outcome. When the cosmos finally reached oblivion, he knew he would still be experiencing this same dream.

Adonai remembered this event well, despite his great age and how long ago this had been. Seven sages stood before him and the other Charon. This was the scene just prior to a battle that would seal the fate of the Charon and have terrible consequences for them. The seven sages, the Celestials, stood tall and proud in their brightly coloured robes that were a sign of their status and their sorcerous power. It would often appear in his nightmares, like this one today. But each time, it was fresh in his memory, the heavy feeling that somehow, all the gods had ignored the rise of these seven from the Land of the Duranki, somehow, missed all the signs until it was too late.

During the first flush of battle, Aryas used his mystical powers to contain the seven wizards by entering their minds and driving them to the point of madness. But this was not enough. Lighting fires within his great bronze prayer wheels, Paladin joined Aryas at his side and together they began to warp the fabric of space that surrounded them. Paladin began to spin his prayer wheel, smoke and flames spitting from the relic as it rotated. Aryas was chanting, a deep low mumble and without pause. It resonated with the air and his eyes had rolled back into his head. The atmosphere surrounding them was smoke-filled and electrified with magical fire that cracked and fizzed and seemed to warp everything it touched. The Celestials rearranged themselves into a triangular formation, with the Master at its helm, his arms raised and poised ready to strike. Magical runes glowed around him, forming a halo of turquoise light and circles of blue fire circled his hands with fingers held in curious positions.

Startled, Adonai felt a firm grip on his shoulder. Turning, he saw it was Devi looking concerned, a frown upon her brow. The images receded from Adonai's mind, and he was present again, in Limbo, heavy chains weighing him down, captive and waiting for instruction, which might be imminent or a thousand years from now.

Somewhere in the mound of fire and flesh lay Paladin, his bronze armour covered in detritus, his bald pate just protruding above his breast plate, his ancient face splashed with blood and the ornate carvings on his armour engrained with gore. Tara lay near him, her platinum hair stained red, her beautiful features full of woe, her mouth fixed in a grimace. The Charon detested their immortality and had long sought to end it, but always unsuccessfully. Aryas was oblivious to his surroundings, as usual. His mind and body drug-filled to forget. His eyes were closed and the gold brocade on his purple velvet suit was stained and dirty. He looked more like a vagrant than a dandy or a wizard. There was no sign of Darshan and Atman, buried somewhere by the sheer number of bodies confined to Limbo.

At some point, Adonai couldn't tell if any time had passed, boredom was worse than the fire and brimstone, but it became evident there was a stirring in the crimson void above. The mists swirled and the blood that occasionally rained upon them stopped. A huge yellow eye appeared, then two more, all with eyebrows of fire. The familiar wide-open mouth appeared and lolloping tongue.

A sinister grin split the abyss, and the Keeper obeyed the calling and set the Charon free.

Adonai chose his moment. A moment that was seldom available, but in the past had proven invaluable. He motioned to Aryas, who was in pain, his limbs too heavy to lift, the enormous chains too much of a burden to move. Aryas closed his eyes and by his mystical power of thought, released Adonai from his body, liberating his astral form so he could move through Limbo freely and search the planes for the one who could redeem them. The one who had been born of Adonai and represented the Charon's only hope.

Adonai moved through the planes, interacting with nobody and nothing. He crossed vast distances and visited several worlds, seeking clues to discover the plane on which the earth rotated. Since the fragmenting of time, and the creation of the Infinity Shards, it had become unclear on which of these copies of the cosmos the one true earth resided and the one true offspring of Adonai would be found. He learned that it was the dawning of the Great Alignment, which meant the earth would soon be in position with other significant cosmic bodies on several planes. A cyclic event divided by millennia, and he knew the time had come. Adonai had no indication of how long he had been gone from Limbo, knowing if he was absent for too long, the Keeper would sense it, so having learned what he needed he returned as the Keeper released the seven immortals.

The Charon soared across a dark blue-black sky where the air was ice cold and dry. Below were snowcapped mountains with rocky grey valleys beneath, with the occasional red granite outcrop. They passed white temples and stupas, and simple shrines erected to the spirit world, the forest nymphs and water guardians, and a host of other elementals before arriving in a nebulous black cloud.

The alleyway grew darker as a thick swirling mass of black matter filled it, swirling with sentience. A tiny red spark emanated from deep within, growing until its red light, like liquid marble, lit the faces of all around. The knights slowed their attack, wary of what was growing before them. Scarlet bodies writhed in agony and ecstasy as the scene merged into an evil stream of gore. A large, hooded head could just be seen through the black cloud, three yellow eyes blinking at the humans in the alleyway. The Keeper had set free the seven deadly damned souls whose very existence meant merciless death to most who encountered them. The red haze continued to grow, engulfing the blackness, and the Keeper faded away once more. Red rivers of blood and the smell of brimstone and pitch filled the alley, making it difficult to breathe in such an enclosed space. A dreadful weeping could be heard as bodies merged into one shapeless mass of life, an abomination to the very cosmos. Through the squirming, treacherous souls appeared the familiar hawk-headed beings of the Charon. All hell tumbled forth and the Dukes of Hell became manifest.

The hesitant knights began to back away slowly as seven terrible beings appeared before them, transforming to human shapes. The lead one was extremely beautiful, his eye-patched face pale with long flowing locks of orange, at odds with his huge muscular frame. Veins popped on his large biceps, and sinews pulled in tension as his pectoral muscles flexed as with one smooth movement a wide-bladed sword was pulled from its sheath on his back, and in one continuous arc it sliced through the knight closest to him. Bone could be heard crunching and blood splattered the walls. The knight fell to her knees and her arm fell away from her torso, a look of complete terror fixed on her dead face. Within seconds, the other Charon had made quick work of the remaining knights as broad swords and a scimitar flashed in the low light, scraping on the enclosing walls. Flesh split and limbs fell from their victims. Devi was overcome with blood lust and stood surrounded by corpses. Darshan had fallen to her knees to bury her scimitar deep into the fallen knight beneath her. Another was disembowelled, another headless, until finally all the corpses were lying in pieces leaking scarlet gore onto the cobbles. The walls of the alleyway were painted red with the carnage.

Adonai turned to the Union Jacks and gave a dark sinister grin, his jewelled eye patch glistening moist with some blood. "At your service, Ignatius."

Standing behind him was Tara in her black leather combats, her platinum blonde hair stained red at the end with blood. She gave a dark smile, the kind a psychopathic killer might give before she releases your soul from this world.

Indigo trembled in secret. She disliked these beings with all her heart, especially her father, Atman, dressed in his usual powder-blue clothing, black leather jacket and a blue satin cape. He was the most silent of the Charon, but cold-hearted and, like the others, a deadly killing machine.

"Now we have been summoned, what are we to do? We are inclined, are we not, to keep killing? Such a joyous prospect. Surely you haven't just called us to get out of a scrape?" scowled Adonai.

The dandy, Aryas, stepped forward, his purple velvet spattered with scarlet. "Greetings, daughter of Atman."

Indigo's face was flushed with anger. Bile rose in her mouth, but she said nothing. She turned and thumped Ignatius with her full might, catching him cleanly on the jaw. She pulled her hand away quickly, shaking it with the pain as it spread through her wrist and up her forearm.

"I guess I deserve that," he whispered to himself, holding his face.

Saying nothing, he turned to the Charon and addressed Adonai. He felt a little uneasy. In truth, he had indeed just summoned them to get out of a scrape. Thinking fast he said, "We are on another quest. It seems that there is another artefact that may be of interest. An artefact from the creation. In addition to the Book of Consciousness and the Book of Shadows, there is the Flaming Celestial Pearl. We are led to believe it is here on earth also. We are trying to find our way to Rahasya, to the Sacred City of Kalapa. The priestesses that attacked us are from the Knights of Himavala, the Sisterhood of the Celestial Pearl."

"Ah, yes! The four artefacts created by the Omnisoul at the dawning of time," Devi replied, vibrantly dressed in red leather combats and a red cloak. "The fourth was Keisu, the singing bowl."

"We need to get out of here," said Paladin. "Besides, with this armour, I hardly fit this alleyway." As he turned, the ancient bronze armour, glistening with blood, scraped the sides of the alleyway, flaking powdery render off the stone walls. As they emerged at the other end of the alley, frightened locals were running for safety after hearing the fighting and seeing the rivulets of blood running out into the square. An old woman who looked like a witch gave an ear-splitting and shrill cry as she gathered her skirts and ran as best she could with her ancient bent legs.

"We cannot stay here. There will be too many questions," said Ignatius. "We must journey on as quickly as we can."

Chapter 20: The Sea of Palms

Indigo had no time for the Charon and was still displeased with Ignatius. She led the way as they came out of the mountain valley and into the open, where the clouds were dark grey and deep purple, filling the moody-looking sky. The only sound was the whistle of the chill wind that scorched her cheeks. She saw the pale blue cloak of Atman, her biological father, blowing in the breeze as he walked several yards in front. The hairs on the back of her neck stood on end, and her face contorted with disgust. What kind of trickery had led to her mother coupling with an immortal, a god, a demon? Or was she forced? She couldn't get the question out of her head. Did her father, the explorer, know? She thought about what her father would think, seeing her in the snow, in the foothills of the Himalayas. She thought he would have been proud.

She was revulsed as she saw Adonai. The most merciless and mighty demon possible, who seemed to revel in death and destruction. What vile event led to the birth of Ignatius? It didn't bear thinking about. The thought of sleeping with demon spawn made her shudder. As they continued, they eventually came to flat terrain very different to anything they had encountered before.

"I think this is it," declared Ignatius, "I think this is the Sea of Palms. According to the map, we are in the correct place.

Ignatius looked out at the barren wasteland across the vastness of the desert. It was a vast area of flatness that stretched in all directions as far as the eye could see. The land looked like a polar desert and had a strange pinkish tinge to it, but otherwise looked like frozen snow.

The air was still, and only thin cloud cover afforded any protection. Ignatius looked skyward.

"As the sun gets up, this will be like crossing a real desert and if the rest of those clouds disperse, we will be affected by the heat and may have to contend with snow blindness. This surface is going to be difficult."

"Why is it called the Sea of Palms?" asked Indigo. "I don't see any trees, let alone palms. Besides, it's too cold for tropical plants. I thought, as we are probably getting close to the paradise world of Rahasya, it might be surrounded by lush vegetation, palms. A sea of palms."

Adonai suggested they skirt the edge for a while. The frozen snow had a definite edge and in places it was stained red. Ignatius bent down to examine the peculiar discolouration. He stood back upright in alarm. "I think it's blood!"

He looked at the Charon, who were all curious. Nobody set foot on the snow.

"Well, it's too big to go around, so we have no choice but to cross," said Indigo.

Adonai stepped to the edge of the sea. "I don't like the look of this," he said.

"I'm told that it's impossible to cross. Those that try never return. It is the last great test before Rahasya," replied Ignatius.

"Enough of this procrastination." Tara came forward. "We are immortal, we can't die, and nothing can be worse than eternity in Limbo. We go, and deal with the consequences."

She set foot onto the surface of the sea. Just as Ignatius was about to follow, he heard a voice shouting from behind them. "Stop right there, Ignatius. You have no right to be on this quest, it has not been sanctioned by the Administorium. Your reckless travels will not aid the Empire."

Incredibly, Aelfric had somehow escaped the airship and followed them. Ignatius was flabbergasted. "You've got to be kidding. How? Aelfric, what has become of Lambeth?"

"Oh, he is ok. I used my magic and escaped, but he is safe, trust me."

True to the ways of the Charon, Aelfric didn't get any further. His last view of the world was a red blur with long wild orange hair as Adonai showed no mercy in true Charon style. His broad blade arced through the air and Adonai felt bone crunch as he sliced easily through Aelfric's collar bone, cracking ribs and cutting his heart in two. The blood poured out and Aelfric fell to his knees, a pale version of himself, his gaunt face frozen with horror before lying face down in the dirt.

Indigo was raging inside. She didn't like the cleric either, but that was a cold death. She snarled at Adonai and then Ignatius with disdain. Ignatius felt sorrow for the cleric, who was pompous but didn't deserve to die like that. He'd had no idea what he had just walked into.

Without delay, they continued. Paladin was already ahead of them. He stepped out and didn't look back. The rest followed. As they did, Ignatius could feel the texture of the sea underfoot. It was odd. A strange surface that seemed to move under his weight, but not like sand, and it didn't crunch like snow. The texture was like small waves or ripples on the surface, perhaps formed by the wind like the ripples on sand.

As they continued, Ignatius noticed that with each step his movements were getting more difficult. It was like his boots were picking up mud and getting heavier. The ground was tugging at his feet. A little further and it felt like his calves had been gripped by someone.

Indigo was walking alongside him. "Ignatius, there is something not quite right here."

Then she saw it, several hands grew out of the ground and gripped Ignatius by the calves and ankles.

"Ignatius!" she yelled as she felt a hand grip her right calf, then several more imprisoned her left foot.

Ignatius looked down, unable to move, and saw dozens of hands reach up and start clawing at his knees, then lower thighs.

"The palms of the Sea of Palms are hands. It's a sea of upturned hands."

Looking more closely, Indigo could see the little ripples were fingers, and the creases in the palms of millions of hands. She looked around and could see the Charon were under attack, too. Reaching up and behind him, Adonai withdrew this wide-bladed sword from its sheath and began to slice through the unwanted limbs. Fingers flew in all directions and blood flowed, splattering his white-stockinged shins. Devi and Tara had both drawn their broadswords and were slashing their way through the hands, but there was no escape, the entire surface of the land was alive with disembodied hands.

Paladin decided to try and use his musical weapon. He lifted the halberd-like weapon to his lips and blew with all his might. From the trumpet-shaped end, sound emerged, blasting the surface of the Sea and dispersing it so it spread outwards away from him, but the surface flowed like water and the gap left behind was soon filled again with more hands.

Indigo looked behind her to see how far they had come and whether it was possible to make it back to the shore, but it was no use. Hands had gathered like waves behind them and a ripple was moving towards them, gathering height as it did so like a huge tidal wave of flesh. As it hit them, Indigo struggled to stay upright, knowing to fall would probably mean death. She could feel hands all over her, trying to pull her down. Ignatius was struggling with hands all over his back and could feel them pulling him trying to topple him and pull him beneath the surface to some unknown terror. Despite being overwhelmed and being waist-deep in hands, Atman stood his ground and was calmly slicing through the fleshy surface with methodical and swift movements of his sword.

Ignatius pulled out his sonic blaster and, adjusting the dials, aimed at the surface of the sea in front of him. Pulling the trigger the sonic wave hit the surface, tearing a bloody hole in the pinkish surface of the Sea, but as with Paladin, more hands flowed in to fill the void left behind. Somewhat panicked, he turned to Adonai. "Is there anything we can do? I fear that at any moment we will be overcome and be pulled under the surface to who knows what!"

Adonai didn't respond, but turned to Aryas. "Aryas, do you have anything? Any spell that can save us from this?"

Aryas was already working on it. He said nothing and cooly, from nowhere, he conjured his carpet bag, ornate luggage of brocade and gold embroidery. He dug deep, his arm pushed inside it right up to his armpit and pulled out what looked like a roll of heavy fabric. The carpet bag vanished with a small cloud of smoke and with the roll tucked under his arm, he pulled out his long glass-bowled pipe and began to smoke his usual greenish liquid. The hands were increasing, and Ignatius and Indigo could feel them pulling at waist height. Trying not to fall over, for fear of the consequences, they altered their stances against the incredible force that threatened to overwhelm them.

Aryas calmy rolled out his fabric. "A carpet?" exclaimed Indigo. "You've brought a carpet for us to walk on?"

It was a hand-woven Persian kilim rug with bright bold geometric designs in blues and purples with intricate patterns of scarlet and dark blue.

Aryas was no longer silent and had closed his eyes, muttering some incantation, hands now as high as his chest, but he seemed unmoved by the predicament. The carpet grew to three times its original size and was hovering a little above the surface of the Sea. Then opening his eyes, he shook himself free of the hands that gripped him and said, "quickly, all on the carpet." He jumped, and as he did the remaining hands fell back to the surface of the sea. Landing on the carpet, it swayed but still hovered in its position. One by one, the Charon freed themselves from the hands and made their way to the carpet. The hands were so strong, Indigo could feel herself being pulled under. She tried moving her legs but it was like trying to run in a viscous liquid. Making use of her short sword, she had to individually stab at each hand until it released her. When she'd made it to the edge of the carpet, Darshan pulled her aboard. Turning, she saw Ignatius blasting himself a path, blood spurting in all directions as he shot into the surface of the sea to open up a pathway. Reaching the edge of the carpet, he pulled himself onto it.

Without wasting any more time, Aryas, who was now sat cross-legged at the leading edge of the carpet, a cloud of greenish smoke around his head, was reciting a chant and the carpet swiftly took flight, gaining altitude and speed.

Ignatius and Indigo held on to the leading edge of the carpet for some security. As they travelled, the Sea of Palms didn't want to let them escape. Before them rose tall angry-looking waves that threatened to grab the carpet and pull them back down to the surface. Aryas caused the carpet to weave and skirt around the waves, but more developed ahead. Eventually, one of the waves was successful and Ignatius felt the carpet being tugged lower. Hands splashed out over onto the surface of the carpet and began to grab at any limbs they could find. Other hands pulled more from below to multiply the threat. Ignatius took out his steam cannon and was about to shoot at a group of hands pulling at his leg. Adonai grabbed him. "No! If you blow a hole in this carpet, we will fall into the Sea. Find other means."

Ignatius felt uncomfortable as the hands wriggled across his boots and thigh. It was an eerie feeling from a very unnatural foe. It made his skin crawl.

"What would happen if we were pulled into the Sea?" he asked.

Adonai answered. "To us, probably not much as we are immortal, but we may find ourselves in some kind of hell worse than Limbo. I don't want to take that chance. To you and Indigo, probably death. I am guessing your hands would join those that make up the Sea, and the rest of your body would be absorbed to nourish it. But I don't really know."

Ignatius felt chilled to the core, as if somebody had walked across his grave. Indigo turned to him, still annoyed. "Did you have to ask?"

They continued in silence, slapping hands away or carefully

swiping them with the flats of their sword. Aryas was still sat at the helm commanding and steering the carpet. Eventually the Sea seemed to settle and the hands gently formed waves on the surface and left them alone. It seemed like several hours passed and the carpet was still travelling above the sea.

The sun had risen at the start of their journey, had reached high noon, and was on its way down to sink below the horizon. Nobody had spoken much; all were deep in their own thoughts. The Charon still longing for the demise of their immortality, Ignatius still longing to win back the affections of Indigo, and Indigo still hating everyone else she was travelling with, but with a heavy heart where Ignatius was concerned. She loved him but couldn't find it in her to do so at that moment.

As the sun began to disappear, Ignatius could see an end to the Sea of Palms. Lush green growth could be seen ahead. An emerald valley with trees growing on its slopes and grass covering the earth. Aryas took the carpet lower until they hovered just above the grass and eventually it came to a gentle stop. Stepping off the carpet, Aryas soon had it rolled up and placed back into his carpet bag.

"I think we are here; this is where we can expect to find the Gatekeeper," said Ignatius.

Chapter 21: The Gatekeeper

After resting, they waited until dawn broke before continuing their journey. It wasn't long before they encountered a tall figure ahead. The Gatekeeper stood on high ground and was silhouetted by the rising sun. He was a giant and looked ancient, history etched on his face with every line and wrinkle. He was naked from the waist up, showing his huge muscular frame, covered only by the long grey beard that terminated halfway down his sternum. His biceps bulged, making even Adonia's look small in comparison, and in his right hand he grasped the handle of a long-handled broadsword that must have stood as tall as Paladin. In his left hand he carried an enormous war axe with a keen curved blade at one end and a hammerhead at the other. He wore furs on his lower half and had a large leather belt with chains, a row of human skulls and a prayer wheel hanging from it. Around his neck he wore a necklace of human bones. His bulk blocked out the dawn and his stature made even more intimidating by the horned helmet he wore.

Ignatus approached cautiously and as he did so it was as though the Gatekeeper grew even larger. He didn't move, he just stood staring at Ignatius with eyes that burned like embers in the remnants of a coal fire. Ignatius could hear his heavy breathing. As the sun rose higher, it produced a halo and Ignatius struggled to see the Gatekeeper's face. All he could see were those same burning eyes. Behind him, the morning mists were rolling away to show the lush green hills of this hidden valley and in the distance the lush green turning to a golden glow. Now only the Gatekeeper stood before them and the sacred land of Rahasya.

Ignatius tried the friendly approach in his typical English style, although the Gatekeeper looked anything but friendly.

"Good morning, and what a beautiful morning it is." He dipped his head slightly with a courteous bow. The Gatekeeper didn't move or speak. He was a solid roadblock, an unmovable mountain.

"My friends and I were just wondering if we may pass. We are on our way to find…" He paused momentarily, "to find a certain destination." He didn't want to be too specific.

The Gatekeeper was motionless. Adonai moved forward, impatient. "Enough of this. We go now and nothing and no one is going to stand in our way."

He brushed past Ignatius, knocking his shoulder, and was followed by Devi, Tara and Paladin. As they approached the Gatekeeper, it became even more obvious how big he really was. Adonai looked much smaller in comparison.

Without warning and with surprising speed and agility, the Gatekeeper took a fighting stance and his large broadsword sliced through the air, just missing the heads of the Charon. Ignatius felt the air whistle past his shock of blond hair. He gasped. The Gatekeeper returned to his previous stance. This was clearly a warning.

Adonai didn't wait, his two arms reached for the wide blade strapped to his back and in one smooth continuous arc he lunged at the Gatekeeper who stood his ground and with a swift parry of his broadsword swiped Adonai away. He attacked again, followed this time by Tara, and again the Gatekeeper parried with ease whilst standing his ground. Again, the two Charon attacked, followed by Paladin. This time, the Gatekeeper took a stance and brought his broad sword down to deflect Adonai and Tara's swords whilst simultaneously smashing his war axe into Paladin's chest. Paladin was thrust backwards to fall to the floor, the breastplate of his ancient bronze armour cracked down the middle. He lay there wheezing, winded by the impact. In all his immortal life, Paladin had never encountered such force, and with such little effort.

"I can see why they say nobody, unless worthy, ever gets past the Gatekeeper," said Indigo, her eyes wide in awe.

Adonai and Tara attacked again as the giant of a man came from atop his mound and, thrusting his sword into the ground, which cracked with the force, took his position, holding his war axe in two hands.

"Enough!" the air was split by the voice of a child.

A young girl with pigtails and three eyes, two in the usual position and the third in the centre of her forehead, came from behind him. She was no bigger than the height of the Gatekeeper's knees. Holding onto his lower leg like a toddler, she looked at the two Union Jacks, then the Charon in turn and spoke with a soft, infantile voice. "You must stop. My brother will not surrender his position. You shall not pass this valley. Only the worthy may pass, and even then, if you reach the land you seek, there may be no return for you. If you value your lives, you must turn back."

Adonai laughed, turning to the Charon at his side, who laughed also. The two Union Jacks looked on, puzzled.

"What do you make of this Third Eyed Girl?" declared Adonai to the Charon.

Darshan stepped forward. "My dear, we don't know who you are, but we do not value our lives. That is precisely why we are here. We are immortal. Do you know what it means to be immortal? The aeons we must suffer, the boredom, the repetitiveness, the lives we see come and go whilst we sit out our lives as prisoners? On earth, we may be gods, but we have no desire to value our status, our existence. If only a blow from your brother's hammerhead would kill me, I would lay down my head right now for him to smash."

"And you?" spoke the girl, looking at Ignatius and Indigo.

"I don't know," replied Indigo. "We value our lives, certainly, and don't wish to lose them here in the snowy mountains of this barren place. But I am unsure about being worthy. How will we know if we are worthy?"

The girl giggled, "The Gatekeeper has not yet met anyone who is worthy. I am beginning to think such a being does not exist. The rocks over there are stained red with all the blood he has spilt, and the vultures here usually find rich pickings enough to make sure that no trace is left behind and the bones are usually claimed by the Elementals who sometimes travel this far."

"Then I guess we are not worthy," replied Indigo.

"It's too late to decide. As you can see, your friends are no match for the Gatekeeper's strength, so you must play the game."

"The game? What game? What do you mean?" replied Indigo.

The girl produced some odd-shaped dice made from blue crystal. One was eight-sided, another was twelve-sided and another was ten-sided.

"You must throw the dice, your score will decide on the Gatekeeper's actions." She gave a cruel laugh. "It usually results in sudden death by a blow from his hammer."

"We're not playing that, no way. Come on, we're leaving,"

said Ignatius.

"Oh no! It's too late to leave, you're here now. The Gatekeeper shall kill you anyway if you try to leave."

Adonai was starting to grow impatient. "Quickly, throw the dice and let's get out of here!"

The Gatekeeper leaned over form the mound on which he stood, scowling at Adonai. The girl held onto his calf, half hiding. "Gods, immortals and demons cannot play. Which are you?"

Before she knew it, Adonai was face to face with her, his beautiful face now creased with rage. "I am all three, now move your beast or I will kill you and then him!"

The girl was clearly terrified. She didn't have to say anything as Adonai felt a huge blow to his skull from the Gatekeeper's hammer. He retaliated immediately and was hanging onto the giant's back pulling with all his might at the bone necklace around the Gatekeeper's neck, trying to strangle him. Every sinew and muscle bulged through Adonai's close-fitting attire. Thick veins bulged in his neck and throbbed in his temples. The Gatekeeper began to gasp and stagger a little, clawing with his gigantic hands at the necklace and Adonai's arms. He couldn't release himself, so as a desperate measure he swung his hammer behind him, trying to rain blows onto Adonai's back. His sword flailed about indiscriminately as he swiped at the other Charon. Devi retaliated and drew her broadsword. Even though he was otherwise distracted, the Gatekeeper managed to fend off her blows, and those that did get though left barely a mark on his skin.

The girl moved out of harm's way and started pulling at Indigo's clothing. "Quickly, you must throw the dice. Now, come, come!"

Aryas pulled Indigo by the shoulder, holding her back. "Leave the dice. It's a trick. I do not know the consequences, but clearly it won't be good. They were both distracted by the sound of the Gatekeeper's sword as he dropped it and the fine steel rang out against the rocks, echoing around the valley. Adonai was using all his might, his single eye almost popping from his head. His neck muscles stood out as his arms tightened their grip even more, then swiftly with his right arm he reached behind him and pulled his wide-bladed sword from its sheath and sliced across the Gatekeeper's neck. Blood spewed forth from both sides as Adonai threw himself backwards away from the Gatekeeper, still holding his head, and the great giant fell forwards heavily, landing on the girl, crushing her. Two legs could be seen twitching in their death throes as she suffocated beneath his bulk. Adonai landed on his back and quickly discarded the severed head, wiping the blood from his hands.

"Now we can pass! Now you are worthy!" he said, scowling at Indigo.

Ignatius and Indigo made their way, not wishing to look at the crushed young girl. Adonai turned around. "Save your judgement, she was a demon disguised as a girl. She would have killed you and eaten your soul. Don't waste your energies on sympathy. Demons cannot decide if you are worthy, it is all a trick."

The two Union Jacks said nothing, and as they all continued on the path. Ignatius checked his map. "Not far now. We should be entering another valley where we should find Rahasya."

Chapter 22: The Place of Silence

The valley was lush and green, juxtaposed against the snow-covered mountains and cerulean sky surrounding it. Emerald, sage and veridian growth covered the sides of the valley, every tree and plant imaginable. It became apparent that the whistle of the mountain air had ceased, and all was silent. Continuing through the valley, the two Union Jacks were amazed at the exotic plant life. Large blooms of every colour grew in abundance and their way was paved with lots of blue poppies. Plants that neither Union Jack had ever seen before, the Royal Society would be able to spend years cataloguing the plant life. Butterflies big and small flitted across the flowerheads and at times the buzz of the bees was deafening. The trees that lined the slopes of the valley were odd-looking coniferous specimens with bark of many colours, the usual browns, grey and greens, but also oranges and pinks.

"I don't think the lifeforms here grow anywhere else on earth," remarked Indigo.

Crystal-clear streams ran down the sides of the valley to form an azure river that flowed off into the distance. As Indigo peered in, she saw fish swimming and negotiating the currents. Along the embankment, voles and newts could be seen through the rushes and long grasses. The place looked idyllic. There was something about it that made even England's green and pleasant land rather on the dull side in comparison.

They followed the river for a time, not knowing if they needed to traverse it at any point. Ignatius judged that at no point was it too wide or too deep to cross. Their answer came soon enough, for in the distance they were getting closer to the source of the golden glow they had seen earlier. As they got closer, the glow intensified. The plant life had diminished except for the carpet of blue poppies. Closer still, and Ignatius eventually identified what they were looking at. "It's a city. We've found it, it's Rahasya!"

As he continued to travel closer still, the city developed more detail. It was breathtaking in its construction. Tall towers of gold with organic-looking roofs, other buildings of white marble veined with orange and golds of all shades. Some towers were capped with a mushroom-shaped roof and had irregularly shaped windows spiralling up the length of them. It was colossal. Around its tallest towers flew exotic birds with bright green or turquoise feathers. Birdsong filled the air, which also seemed to be slightly perfumed. Ignatius couldn't tell if it emanated from the city itself or the flowers around him that seemed to have bloomed bigger and better the nearer they were to the city. A winding road lined either side with pink flowers led to its double gates that looked like they were solid gold with rivets the same thickness as a man's forearm. The whole city seemed to generate and emanate its own light, and it hovered just above the surface of the earth. The city was laid out in a square and the city walls surrounding it were made from rubies. There was a gate on each of the four sides, all made from a precious metal or precious stones.

"It reminds me of Sagharta," said Indigo.

As she spoke, the city appeared to fade as if cloaked in a veil of fog. Then it returned to its original brilliance, then half of it faded again and returned once more with some of the tallest towers fading so badly they completely vanished.

"Its presence is unstable," said Adonai. "It's because it lies at the crossroads of several planes. It lies on none of them and all of them at the same time. Before we even get to the city gates, it may have vanished completely."

"And we have come so far, we need to make haste," remarked Ignatius.

As they approached the pathway to the gate, a white hart stepped out of the surrounding forest and onto the golden path. It stood staring at the Union Jacks, intelligent eyes trying to work out who the visitors were. It wasn't spooked by the visitors, instead it just stood defiantly studying them until it began to dance and prance amongst the blue poppies as if beckoning them to follow him. The hart led the way through the long grasses and wildflowers, stopping occasionally to look back and see if the visitors were following.

As they approached the city, the glow intensified. Indigo felt its warmth on her face like that of the sun. Its towers soared high above them into the blue sky. Continuing along the path, the hart disappeared into the lush greenery to the left and two riders came out of the gate to greet them. They were dressed identically, in simple white linen robes and nothing else, no adornment of any kind, no belt or weapon. They looked like simple monks. Each carried a banner blowing in the breeze, flying from a golden pole. On one of the triangular white banners was a depiction of a black eagle, on the other a silver sword. As they drew near, they pulled their horses up and with smiles stretching across their faces greeted the travellers.

"Welcome. Please, come. You must be weary. It has been a long time since we have entertained any visitors," said the man with the eagle banner. "I am Vraja and this is my brother Vamza." The other spied Adonai suspiciously but remained silent.

They led the visitors to what looked like a grand palace nine stories high built on a platform of mother of pearl. The roof was constructed of plants carved from crystal through which the sun shone, causing a spectrum of colours to dance and shift across their surface. Either side of the palace was a crescent-moon-shaped lake with clear turquoise water.

Once through the golden gates to the palace, they found themselves in a great hall. "Welcome to the Palace of Kalapa. I must say, it's probably been about one hundred years since we received a visitor. Most simply perish before they find us," said Vraja. "I should warn you, of course, if the city leaves this plane, which it tends to do, then you will have no way back, unless of course you can traverse the planes and with pinpoint accuracy." He chuckled, making Ignatius and Indigo feel uneasy.

"Oh! And of course you must leave your weapons at the gatehouse. There are no weapons in Rahasya. This is a place of peace, harmony and, for the most part, silence."

Nobody protested, not even the Charon. Indigo handed over her short sword, dagger and steam cannon. But as she turned to walk away, Vamza cleared his throat. "And the pistols, please, miss." Indigo looked embarrassed and removed the two derringers she had hidden in her clothing.

"You haven't yet introduced yourselves," said Vraja, his eyebrows raised in expectation.

"Ah, forgive me, I am Ignatius, this is Elza and…"

He didn't get a chance to finish before Vraja spoke for him.

"These are the Charon. Yes! We know, although I am not sure what would bring the merciless Charon to our peace-loving abode!"

The Charon said nothing. They were used to contempt. They would expect nothing less. They thrived on it along with the bloodshed and death,. In fact, Adonai secretly thrilled in it, thinking that as soon as was appropriate he would kill all the inhabitants of the city.

Vraja turned to some other city dwellers who were all dressed similarly. "Please. Some refreshments for our guests."

They were taken to a smaller room richly decorated with silks and brocade of many colours where a feast had been prepared. As they sat down to eat, Ignatius started up a conversation about the city.

"Tell me, what is the purpose of this great city?"

Vraja smiled. "It is a place of peace where humanity is preserved from self-destruction. We live in peace and harmony. I suppose you could call this place heaven on earth. It is said that the palace of Kalapa was built by the gods, and it lies at the heart of our paradise that is Rahasya. Here, mortals, immortals and deities can all inhabit a happy place, free from the shackles of the mind and daily life.

But enough talk, this is a place of silence. Now, I must take my leave, we await the arrival of the King."

Then Vraja left the travellers to eat and drink and relax, perhaps for the first time in a long time.

Chapter 23: The King of Kalapa

As the party continued their refreshments and relaxation, the inhabitants of Rahasya came to visit one by one. Most looked at them with distrust and seemed amazed they had survived and successfully completed the journey.

More and more folk came to look and eventually their frowns and mistrust turned to warm smiles. A young boy approached, saying, "We don't get many strangers here. Where have you come from?" But before Indigo could answer, the boy was quickly whisked away.

Eventually an old man, presumably the wise elder of the region, greeted them all with a grin from ear to ear and by repeatedly bowing his head. "Greetings, travellers, you must have come a long way."

By now, it looked like the entire population had come to look at the spectacle of the strangers.

Ignatius, Indigo and the Charon were all guided to sit on chairs that looked like they were thrones with ornate arms with golden carvings with deep silk and linen upholstery. They sat there for a while, unsure of what they were waiting for. Ignatius began to grow suspicious and wanted to move on, to look for the Flaming

Celestial Pearl.

"What are we waiting for?" he asked.

Vraja came scurrying over. "For the King, of course. He will soon be here. But we must wait for his presence. There will be no proceedings without him."

"Proceedings?" Ignatius didn't get any answer.

He was beginning to grow impatient and worried that the Charon were even more so. Then, without any warning, those from the city all looked skyward and gasped before throwing themselves onto the floor in exaltation of their King.

Ignatius looked around and couldn't understand what was happening. Where was the King? He looked at Adonai, who by now was sitting there with white knuckles, longing to stand and smash everything in sight and then kill every city dweller around him. But he sat motionless and just shrugged his shoulders at Ignatius.

Ignatius sensed a dark shadow move across his face. Then again. So did Indigo. "What's that?" she asked, fearing that some Shadow Demon had escaped the Book of Shadows and followed them here. Beads of sweat broke out on her forehead. She didn't want to fight them again, she wasn't sure she had the determination any longer, she wanted to go home and be rid of all demons, including the Charon, forever, if indeed that was possible.

Ignatius looked up, and then he saw it. The large black silhouette of an eagle soared above him in the vaulted ceiling of the chamber, circling as if looking for prey. Vraja and his brother were both looking up and holding their hands as if in prayer. After chanting in unison in some unknown tongue, they lay on the ground with outstretched arms and raised buttocks.

As the bird of prey circled, it got lower and lower until Ignatius could feel the breeze of its wings on his hair. The bird came around one more time as if heading straight for Ignatius, at which point Ignatius thought he knew who the bird was. At the last moment, the bird flew higher then came around again and circled to take a look at Indigo. He did this repeatedly, still trying to work out who she was, why there was a familiarity. Then, without warning, the great bird aimed for the throne with outstretched talons. As the eagle was just about to collide with the throne, he pulled up and magically the bird morphed into the shape of a lean muscular man dressed in fine silk of royal purple with gold thread and a golden jewel-encrusted crown on his head. Gracefully, his flight ended, and he glided into position to sit on the throne facing the two Union Jacks. He had large black wings and four arms and in one of his right hands he grasped a long, ornate silver sword. He placed the sword into two ornate golden clasps at the head of the throne. The acolytes around all remained with their foreheads touching the ground in humble obedience to their king.

Three steps led up to the throne, which looked like an enormous ice sculpture but was carved from rock crystal. The whole structure sparkled and reflected the light, so it looked like it was its own light source. Shadows of pale blue and turquoise, aqua and silver brought forth the exquisite detailing. The back had two great wings carved in fine detail to represent two folded wings that were designed to almost engulf the king.

"It's ok, Vraja, Vamza, you may rise!" said Manjushri, after which a sharp prod in the back brought Ignatius and Indigo to their knees and a hand roughly pushed their heads to the cold marble floor. "Kneel before Manjushri, the King! First of the Kalki Kings who shall bring about the Golden Age."

With their heads lowered, their foreheads growing cold, Ignatius gave Indigo a sideways glance. "The Librarian's bird is the king of Rahasya!"

A soft voice spoke that almost had a dream-like quality to it. "You may rise. The curse placed on me by the Celestials is lifted in my own kingdom."

Two acolytes grabbed the two Union Jacks abruptly by the hair and pulled them back up and on their feet.

"My dear Ignatius, we meet again. And in my home, too."

"What happened to peaceful?" Ignatius bawled.

Manjushri ignored him. "Not many people make it this far."

It was difficult to tell, but Ignatius thought he could see a sly smile spread across Manjushri's face.

"I thought it a great pity that your partner, Indigo, perished at the hands of the High Priestess. Although it was necessary. The library wasn't complete until the Book of Shadows had been curated and catalogued, the wisdom of the cosmos contained within would then have triumphed all other libraries in the whole of creation. Even with its contents spilling out! So I guess her death had cause. But you humans are too small, too tiny-minded to grasp the importance of such works, to understand true sacrifice to further the great wheel of time and perpetuate existence as the Omnisoul and Calabi-Ya intended. To bring about that balance between light and dark, that contrast in the energies of the cosmos so it may continue in harmony once more."

Ignatius realised that he was clenching his fists. His knuckles were white, and he raged inside.

"So tell me, who is your new sidekick? A dainty morsel, but I'm guessing with a wild streak."

Manjushri flapped his wings in a demonstration of their size and strength. Now Indigo was raging internally and as her fists clenched, she moved as if to strike, then remembered herself and remained still.

"This is Eliza."

Indigo gave Manjushri a scowl. He looked at her quizzically, "welcome to Rahasya, Eliza. Your friend here owes me much. I was left alone when the Librarian retreated to the stars, which left me without a purpose. My keenness of eye and the wisdom I enclose within my wings meant I was his seeker, to find new manuscripts, new tomes, ancient tablets to be discovered and catalogued. It meant that I knew more than the Librarian. More than anybody else around me. Now I am left with nothing. Still, it will make it easier to exact my revenge should I wish to do so, for Ignatius is to blame for leaving me abandoned. However, I can also thank him, for Ignatius is responsible for me returning home at last, after all these millennia. Although I am still cursed to remain as an eagle should I leave Rahasya, at least for now, until I can break the spell placed on me by the Celestials.

I shall further my own library, methinks. But first I must grieve, for the loss of my brother, Jeeva. He sacrificed himself to create the runesword, his life force contained therein, which the Charon used to try and destroy the Well at the Centre of Time. Do you know what became of him?"

Indigo shook her head.

"When the Cosmic Sitar was taken back by the Omnisoul, he was sent to the Ghost Worlds, each and every piece of him to a separate part of the Void, which is so vast his parts can never be reassembled, never be found to create him whole again."

Ignatius was feeling uncomfortable. He was preparing to move quickly, every sinew tensed in his body. Manjushri was likely to strike, to exact his revenge.

"So, tell me, what brings you here? You didn't know this was my abode, so you didn't come for me. So, what purpose?"

Ignatius thought for a while, unsure whether he should be truthful or not, until eventually he decided. "We seek the Flaming Celestial Pearl and believe it is here in your kingdom."

Indigo glanced with a frown, not sure if the truth was necessary.

Manjushri laughed, a very heartfelt belly laugh, eventually composing himself, folding his wings neatly and replied, "You are either brave or stupid, I am not sure which, but you have no means of obtaining the Pearl. Yes, it is here in my Kingdom, but I am not sure you have the means of obtaining it. If, indeed, I was to tell you where it is. But nobody can obtain the Pearl. They usually don't make it this far."

He looked at the Charon, "and I should warn you, my dear immortals, in this Kingdom, your powers are diminished. One of the limitations placed on you by the Omnisoul should you ever come here. But then, the Omnisoul already knows the outcome. It is written in the Book of Consciousness. That must make life very dull for the Omnisoul if everything is already ordained and you know what is to come." He laughed again.

Ignatius was not pleased. "You have said it yourself, not many make it this far. So, we have more than a chance to obtain the Pearl, surely?"

Without thinking, Manushri blurted out, "Only if you can survive the Void. And nobody survives that. And what's more, you are just human, not even a god, and believe me, gods cannot survive the Void."

"What is the Void?"

"Just that! There is nothing there, a complete abyss, devoid of anything. Just the infinite blackness that will swallow you and from which there is no escape."

Adonai looked at Aryas and Atman. Both gave a knowing look.

Manjushri was shrewd and spotted their glances, "You may think you have created for yourselves some kind of salvation. I repeat, the humans are just that, human! Not even you, Adonai, could survive. It would be a worse eternal damnation than that of Limbo."

Adonai responded in an elaborate and ostentatious way fitting for one in the court of a king. "And have you ever visited the Void?"

"I have not, but there is no need, it's a void. There is no call for anyone to enter it. The Pearl is merely a tool used at the creation, like the two books and the singing bowl."

"So you don't actually know what is in the Void, or the purpose of the Pearl."

"I guess not, but then nobody does, only the Omnisoul knows that."

"So why do you think the Pearl has been placed in a void?"

Manjushri was started to grow agitated. "I know not, nor care to know. I am not prepared to waste any more time on this subject. I have returned to my Kingdom and need to take stock after aeons away serving the Librarian. Now, if I was you, I would be more concerned about the Stalker, who is likely to arrive at any moment to find you and take you back to the Keeper in Limbo!"

"You take care of your own affairs, Manjushri. And we will take care of ours. As you say, let's not waste any more time," responded Adonai.

Ignatius intervened. "King Manjushri, we have travelled far and have successfully negotiated many perils to get here. May we ask for some refreshment and rest, if it pleases you?"

"Very well, very well. Vraja, take them to some lodgings and give them refreshment as they require. It grows late and we can discuss this matter further tomorrow."

Vraja beckoned them to follow, and they were shown to some beds for the night. "Food will arrive shortly. Get some rest." Vraja scurried out, leaving them for the night.

Chapter 24: The Sword of Wisdom

Once they had been left alone, Ignatius was the first to speak. "Well, he doesn't seem to recognise you, Indigo."

"Are you sure or is he bluffing? I am not so sure," she replied.

The Charon were huddled together, with Adonai, Atman and Aryas in quiet discussion. Darshan was the first to break away. "The secret to you entering the Void safely and obtaining the Pearl lies in Manjushri's sword. He knows that but will not say. You will have to steal it if you are to be successful."

Ignatius felt his nerve tested. "And how do we do that? Can you not steal it, the mighty merciless Charon?"

Adonai came over and towered above Ignatius, angry but mainly frustrated. "As Manjushri says, our powers here are limited. We are not sure how exactly, but we knew this when we entered the realm. The only person who may be powerful enough to help is Aryas. As the city is constantly drifting in and out of different planes, he can walk across them and between them if necessary to try and remain on the plane that the city lies on the most. That way he may still be able to use some magic to assist."

Indigo resigned herself to the fact that this was now their quest, to steal a sword, but wanted to know why, what use was it?

"So, if we steal this sword, what use is it? What will we do with it?"

Adonai turned to Aryas. "Aryas, please explain!"

As nimble and aristocratic as usual, Aryas responded, "the sword is known as Khadga, the Sword of Wisdom." He moved dramatically playing to an unseen audience, and for once was not smoking his pipe. "I cannot tell for sure, the Omnisoul has blocked my astral sight a little, but it is my belief the sword is what will gain you access to the Pearl."

Indigo was growing impatient due to all the theatrics "But how…" She didn't get to finish before Adonai cut her off.

"As you know, our plight is to end the futile lives we have. We knew the Book of Consciousness held the story of our fate and believed that if we could destroy time, we could end of lives. We didn't know about the Book of Shadows, but when the spawning of all the hell-stuff occurred, again we believed the End Times had arrived and we joined in to start the Apocalypse. But that was just opportune. The long game has been this, to obtain the Flaming Celestial Pearl and to find its secret. That secret lies at its very heart, within the Pearl itself. We have created you two with enormous powers, powers that can be used for this one last try to discover our fate. Powers that did not come into full effect until you entered this plane, this realm. Here, you are strongest. Aryas has worked his magic over aeons for this very moment, for you. You know you have powers, but they are a fraction of what you have become simply by entering this realm."

Aryas took his hat off and made an ostentatious bow. "At your service!"

"What do you mean?" enquired Indigo.

"Exactly as I said. Here, you are probably more powerful than any of us."

Ignatius had grown worried. Indigo already hated him for summoning the Charon. Now this, he wasn't sure if she would ever forgive him. He hesitated, but eventually asked, "What are these powers?"

Adonai slowly shook his head. "That's the problem, we don't exactly know. But Aryas has assured me your powers will come into play when required. With the Sword of Wisdom and the Eye of Adonai, you should be able to penetrate the Pearl and find our destiny."

Indigo was scowling, her face distorted with crease lines and anger. "Ignatius, we have been played. Just pawns to get these, these vile demons what they want. This has nothing to do with us, the Union Jacks or the Empire. We should have stopped after the Book of Shadows!"

Ignatius tried to put his arm around her, but she shrugged him off. "I don't know what to say, Indigo. I'm sorry. But we had intelligence about these artefacts and Lawrence sent us on the mission. We have our orders."

"Orders! Orders! You can stick your or—" Indigo had started to glow; her aura was visible. Purple light bathed the wall of the chamber. She looked down at her hands and violet sparks flew from her fingertips. She had a pain in her chest. It burned. She opened her blouse and the gem-shaped burn mark left behind permanently from her previous ordeal was glowing like fire.

Ignatius wasn't sure what was going to happen. "Indigo, you need to calm down. You don't know what will happen. You have powers you may not be able to control. Calm is called for."

She made a shrieking noise in annoyance, then started to take deep breaths and calm her inner self. The aura began to recede and the pain in her chest diminished. She looked at Atman, her father. "You did this to me, You! I'm some sort of freak! I hope you return to Limbo and are never let back out. You disgust me, my poor mother, who knows what hellish ordeal you put her through!"

Atman remained silent.

"So, what now?" asked Ignatius.

Adonai replied, unmoved by what he had witnessed and as cold as ever. "We steal the Sword of Wisdom. But we must wait for nightfall."

Hours went by, Ignatius tried to work out a plan, his mind working overtime. He avoided Indigo, who avoided everyone else.

Eventually, Adonai gathered Aryas, Tara and Ignatius with him. "It's time. You will need to grab the sword on my command."

Keeping to the shadows, they headed back to the gatehouse. Left unguarded, as this was a place of peace, the weapons could easily be retrieved. There wasn't any guard. Society in Rahasya was based around love and trust. The inhabitants had clearly never encountered immortal demons before. Armed, they returned stealthily, working their way down the corridor, trying not to make any sound. They made their way back to the throne room, where Manjushri was still sat on his throne, asleep. Ignatius wasn't sure how this would work out.

Looking to Aryas, Adonai asked, "well, what magic can you perform here to obtain the sword?"

Aryas said nothing, instead he opened his coat and pulled out some herbs and an ornate ivory pipe. Stuffing the herbs into the bowl, he lit them and began to smoke.

Ignatius was growing impatient. "How is this going to help?" he whispered.

Aryas the dandy looked at him with disdain. He sat himself down cross-legged and began searching his mind for an incantation. Tara was keeping watch in all directions. Eventually, Aryas began to mutter some alien syllables, but nothing happened. He shifted his position and began again with some frustration. Nothing. He began to recite a different chant, and the sword, still held in its brackets, began to vibrate a little. This continued for some time but resulted in nothing.

Aryas looked up at Adonai and declared, "That's it. My powers here are truly diminished. You are going to have to obtain the sword by traditional means."

Tara began to approach the throne, knowing full well that if Manjushri woke up there would be a full-scale fight and she wasn't sure of her strength against the Sword of Wisdom and a king with four arms in his own realm. As she got nearer, the Sword of Wisdom began to glow with intense silver light. It began to vibrate, then it moved away from Manjushri and hovered in the air. It began to glide through the air slowly, until it reached Ignatius, who took the Sword and held it in his arms.

"You're welcome!" came a voice from behind them. The purple burn mark on Indigo's chest was aglow but diminishing as she finished her magic. Her chest looked like hot coals at the end of the night, as they are cooling but still burn with some heat.

Indigo scowled at them all, then turned and walked away, adding, "although I am not sure what you are going to do when he wakes up!"

That was true. Backing away, they made to head back to their quarters. Without warning, a large angry face came nose to nose with Indigo. Four arms grabbed her, and fierce teeth growled as Manjushri vented his displeasure.

"How dare you? How have you…?" He then paused, studying Indigo's face at close quarters.

"It's you! You! Indigo! You almost fooled me. Your soul is so black, no wonder I didn't recognise you. You were dead! And you soon will be again!"

He grabbed her two arms and threw her backwards with such force she landed on the cold tiled floor with a thud. He turned to Ignatius to grab the Sword of Wisdom whilst two of his arms had conjured up scimitars. The blades sliced dangerously close to Ignatius's shoulder and face. Adonai swung his wide-bladed sword, but Manjushri was too fast, one of his swords ringing as steel on steel clashed as he defended himself. His other sword caught Adonai across the thighs, and Adonai fell. Tara's broadsword struck Manjushri on the shoulder and he turned to duel with her for a moment. Devi caught him off guard, but again Manjushri was showing what the Charon had already guessed, their powers in this realm were much diminished.

Paladin joined the fray, and his halberd swung high, aiming for Manjushri's head. But Indigo wasn't prepared to let this continue. She wanted to go home, to figure out if her soul could be healed. She just wanted to be Indigo again. She took the sword from Ignatius and silver fire began to emanate from the blade, travelling up her arms and terminating at the point of her burn mark. She felt like she had the strength of a thousand warriors.

Shouting out some uncomprehensible battle cry, she lunged forward, bringing the blade down to crash through Devi and Tara's blades, breaking the two scimitars Manjushri was fighting with. She lifted the blade again and swung it over the top of her head and brought the blade down on Manjushri's head, stopping dead just a hair's breadth away.

"Stop! Stop! All of this. Manjushri, I don't want to kill you, but I will if I must. You have just returned to your own realm, and I can respect that, and wish you well, to prosper again, but I want to end this quest and that can either be peacefully or with violence.

Which is it to be?"

Manjushri bowed. "I have been beaten and I thank you for your mercy. I value my life which I now have back. I wish to live so I can take revenge upon the Celestials. They betrayed me and imprisoned me in the form of an eagle, and I have not been my true form for so long."

Indigo's face lit up. "Then let me take the sword, for I believe I can capture the Celestials and avenge you."

"Then take it, return it to me if you can, but go. If I can assist any further, I shall. Go and do what you must. At this moment, you are clearly the most powerful being in this realm."

He bowed again with his eyes half shut and his hands joined as if in prayer. The Charon were astonished and parted to make way for Indigo to walk through. Addressing Ignatius, Adonai spoke. "She will need the sword when the time comes, don't let her be parted from it."

"Time? What time? What do you mean?" answered Ignatius.

"I don't have time to explain, just do it. We need to get out of here."

Indigo tried to hand the sword to Ignatius. "Here take it. I don't want it. What am I going to do with it?"

Nobody answered. Instead, Atman grabbed her. "Take it, my daughter, you will know what to do with it when the time is right. All events so far have led us to this. Somehow, you were born for this moment. Regardless of what you think of me or the Charon, your life now depends on this, and your moment of greatness is upon you. The sword will allow you to cut through ignorance and delusion. You can either oblige or die here, never to return home. Your corpse will perish here."

An icy chill ran down her spine. She took hold of the sword

and her whole being was filled with a warmth like she had never felt before. Her arms tingled and she grew lightheaded as a myriad of stories and knowledge began to run through her mind. She thought her head would explode; she couldn't keep up. The Sword of Wisdom had chosen to divulge the knowledge it had absorbed from Manjushri, knowledge that originated from the Librarian's bookcases beneath the Administorium in Oxford. Ignatius stood by, not knowing what was happening. Indigo began to glow with an aura that constantly changed colour at lightning speed. Indigo began to cry, then laugh, then sob again, then horror showed on her face, then she laughed again. She could feel her heart racing, pounding in her chest and she thought it would give way. Tears continued to flow and eventually she fell to the floor, exhausted but strangely invigorated. Composing herself, she looked at Atman then Adonai with contempt.

"I hate you both! You need to see to it that I don't send you back to Limbo permanently, given my powers here seem to outweigh yours."

Darshan, who was always the gentlest towards Ignatius and Indigo, placed a hand on her shoulder to comfort her. Indigo grabbed it and threw her aside with remarkable strength.

"Leave me be, you demon whore! After this, whatever this quest is all about, I want nothing to do with any of you, even if that means through my own demise."

She looked around, finding Ignatius to see if he took that to mean him also, although even she wasn't sure if it did.

Adonai was indifferent to any of these actions or words. After this, he decided, he might just kill her anyway if she had no further use. In fact, he was finding the idea quite satisfying. Indigo was staring at him with the usual distaste, and he wasn't sure if she knew what he was thinking.

Chapter 25: Agartha

After receiving knowledge from the sword, and without a moment's hesitation, Indigo declared she knew where to go and locate the Pearl.

"It's beneath the palace, in a place called Agartha. Come on, we need to find the entrance."

They began searching for a hidden doorway, an easy task as there were no guards, there was never any need for guards in Rahasya. Looking behind silk curtains, behind ornate pillars and even the richly decorated floor, they didn't find anything. Persevering, Indigo sensed strongly it was somewhere in the throne room.

"I think it's behind or beneath the throne," she exclaimed.

"How are we going to move that enormous throne?" asked Ignatius.

Manjushri was busy moving out of the way, a smile on his face, wondering how this would be achieved.

"With my transformation at the hands of the Queen of Shadows and the knowledge gained from the sword, I can manipulate matter and interdimensional cosmic energy."

"What does that mean?"

Ignatius didn't get any further asking when Indigo held her hands out in front of her. She closed her eyes and spoke an incantation that was as new to her as it was to Ignatius hearing it. After some repetition, the crystal throne began to fade as if it didn't exist. She had moved matter to another plane without any disturbance. Beneath the throne, it was clear there were steps leading down into the bowels of the earth.

"The path to Agartha!" she declared. She took a few steps with Ignatius close behind. But no one else followed. Looking back quizzically, Ignatius questioned the Charon with just a look, not even saying anything.

"This is where you leave us," said Adonai. "Our work here is done. We are not permitted to enter Agartha; you are the only hope now. We will wait. We may see you again, we may be retrieved by the Stalker and taken back to Limbo. Who knows?"

Without any word, Indigo and Ignatius descended the steps. It was pitch black and they had to feel their way down using their feet. Each moved in silence, not sure how to start a conversation with the other. Part way down, Indigo wondered if she had the power to light the way. Holding her left hand out, the Sword of Wisdom in her right, she willed a purple flame at her fingertips, dispelling the gloom.

"I can see light in the distance," declared Ignatius.

"Indigo said nothing but turned around and kissed him full on the lips. Warmth and love ran through Ignatius's body and without uttering a single word she continued, leading the way.

As they approached the light source, it was purplish in colour just like the light Indigo generated. A minute or two passed and the light grew until eventually Indigo came crashing into a reflection of herself.

"A black mirror," she declared. She pushed her hand against it, feeling for an opening or a handle. Using her flame-generating fingertips, she tried again, and her hand pushed through the obsidian surface, then her arm. Holding open some invisible doorway, she let out a large involuntary sigh and her eyes rolled back into her head, condensation like that caused by a cold room left her mouth as she spoke. "Quickly, Ignatius, go and I will follow. Keep your guard up."

Unsettled, Ignatius did as he was told. Entering the blackness, they emerged into a place that glowed golden again, just like the city. As if leaving a tunnel, they were suddenly standing in a great hall. The ceiling was so high it was almost impossible to see. The walls were ornate with side chapels set into them occasionally. The walls of these chapels were painted with images of King Manjushri achieving wonderful feats and providing the people of Rahasya with exotic gifts in abundance. Other scenes showed the Palace of Kalapa and the surrounding lush vegetation. Quartz, ruby and emeralds embellished these scenes and gold, more gold than either Union Jack had ever seen in one place.

"What are we looking for?" asked Ignatius.

"I'm not sure. The Truth, I suppose. The Sword of Wisdom will be our key to finding the Pearl. It only ever serves up the truth, never delusion."

"But there's nobody here. So how do we proceed?"

"I'm not sure. But does this place remind you of anywhere?"

At that moment, the hall shifted and began to fade from view. Parts of it returned, other parts didn't.

"We must be crossing planes," said Ignatius. "But you are right, it does remind of somewhere."

The whole hall turned crimson and then vanished, returning to its original form and glory.

"Or there's been a Timequake," added Ignatius.

A faint moaning sound could be heard in the distance. A harmonic moan that changed pitch now and again, and possibly the sound of prayer flags fluttering in the breeze.

"Wind harps," said Indigo.

An old, wizened man with a long white beard appeared from the shadows, dressed in maroon and gold. The Union Jacks recognised him immediately. He was the High Priest of the Ti-Botta.

"Greetings, greetings. It is good to see you again." He didn't wait for any reply but turned to lead them elsewhere. Following, they walked into an adjoining hall.

"Sagharta, we are in Sagharta!" said the Union Jacks in unison.

The old man turned around. "Yes, quite. Sagharta. Where did you think you were?"

"Agartha," said Indigo.

"Ah! Yes Sagartha and Agartha are forever linked, intertwined across the planes. For an eternity now, we have shared the same space, the same timeframes, the same fragment of the cosmos. For the most part, we are totally separate, we live our life, the King of Kalapa lives his, but he has been absent for aeons. We know of his return. We also know of your reason for coming. The heavens have aligned only once every few thousand years. We know you are now aware of your purpose, and we are here to help you fulfil your destiny. Adonai has been very cunning in his plan. Oh, yes for the most part he did not know how this would play out, and at times he knew nothing of the relics you have sought out. But he has been wily in his attempts until the time came when he could see your true potential your true fate."

Ignatius wasn't sure he understood what the High Priest meant by their fate. "What does he mean, Indigo, our fate? You seem to understand more of this than I."

The old man looked on, intrigued, awaiting Indigo's answer.

"Our fate, Ignatius, is to find the Pearl but there is more. There is something extremely significant about the Pearl. But I am not sure what, yet. My mind is searching for answers amongst the knowledge given to me by the Sword. But it is going to take us both to fulfil this quest."

The old man just smiled, his wrinkled face looking like an old paper bag. "No time to waste. You will find the Pearl in the Void. Once in the Void you are on your own. If you die, you die!"

"Are we likely to encounter the Knights of Himavala? Do you know of them? Will we have to fight them?"

The old man raised his hand and frowned a little, although it was difficult to tell given his wrinkled face. "I have heard of them and know a little. But I don't think they will be able to attack you as you continue on your journey. Where you must go is a very special place few have ever visited."

"What can you tell me about the knights? I would like to know in case they are a threat to the Empire."

"They will not be interested by your Empire," he laughed. "They are from an obscure religious sect hidden deep in the Himalayan mountains, the Order are fanatical warrior nuns who have sworn an oath to protect, to the death if needed, the Flaming Celestial Pearl. They dwell in the Kingdom of Trigarta and in prehistory, they openly walked the earth, but now live their lives in hiding, partly because their raison d'etre has almost been wiped out as very few humans have any memory of the Pearl. From time to time, they resurface under the guise of other names and work towards influencing other organisations.

Trigarta lies in a hidden valley away from the outside world.

Anyone who accidentally stumbles upon its existence, and there have been a few, are never allowed to leave. Many explorers have entered the realm and were never heard from again.

All female, these fierce Knights are divided into two classes, military and sacerdotal. The cleric branch possesses the inner knowledge of the order regarding the secrets of the Pearl and only their Mother Superior knows all the secrets, which are passed down master to master. The military branch protects the clerics and therefore the knowledge they possess.

Working in secrecy, the Knights await the time of the Great Alignment when the Great Cataclysm will occur again, and the Pearl will be brought forth to restore balance to the cosmos.

The last Great Cataclysm was caused by dark magic and a meteorite striking the earth, forming the crater that now holds the city of Sagharta."

"Sounds familiar," said Ignatius, thinking of events that had taken place in Oxford recently. "And this Great Alignment, do we know when the next is due?"

The High Priests expression changed. "It may have already begun! But events can take millennia to complete the cycle."

Chapter 26: The Seven Sages

Intrigued, and concerned that another cataclysm was about to occur or that their actions might cause a cataclysm, Ignatius started to analyse their position. They still had to complete their quest, but not knowing if the Celestial Pearl had the power to cause damage, he needed to know more. After some quiet dialogue with Indigo, he asked "Are we about to enter another destructive phase and destroy all life on earth?"

The old man made a face somewhere between a grimace and his usual smile. "I do not think so. But you may be the spark that ignites these events. We should not be due another cataclysm for millennia. But one will come for sure. Although I fear you will encounter those who travelled on that meteor."

"Travelled on it? Who were they?" said Ignatius.

"Travelling on that interstellar rock were the seven beings who founded the city and then went on to conquer and take control of the Duranki. The incident caused a weak point in the fabric of space, which is why the city drifts in and out of the thirty-one planes."

Ignatius was growing impatient. "So, who were the seven beings?"

"You know them as the Celestials."

"So, who are the Celestials, exactly, and why did they come to earth?"

"They had travelled to earth from space. For what purpose, no one knows. From where, no one knows, probably the Netherworlds. Some say it was to seed the planet with their own genetic experiments. They were seven sages of great learning and magic gained by innumerable hours of study, the most powerful wizards amongst their people, and had risen to become the elders of their community. Their leader was Nipuna, or as you know him, the Master. However, they didn't cause the cataclysm but were definitely the final blow.

The Great Cataclysm occurs every few aeons or so. This is when the earth renews itself and all trace of humanity is wiped from its face, as if they had never been. This may be due to natural disasters, the movement of the tectonic plates, or the poles or even a great flood. Or it may be due to conflict. War so terrible it destroys everything in its wake. Such is man's fate. The fragility of life is constantly under threat. In this case, there had been a devastating war, brought about by sorcerers trained but unskilled in the art of Al Kimiya.

The last Great Cataclysm was initiated when an unknown and powerful sorcerer, a natural spell caster able to draw power from the elements around him, conjured up a gateway, blackened by the unholy spawn that came pouring through the portal. The great dragon, the Unholy One, Calabi-Ya poured his venom across civilisation, causing a great war, burning everything in his path, turning fertile lands to ash.

To escape, the entire population of the Duranki travelled East in a great exodus. They spotted a bright light in the heavens, like a star, but more brilliant in its luminosity. They decided to follow it, using it to navigate by, without really knowing where they were going, the journey made increasingly more difficult by the blanket of ash that had engulfed the globe, reducing the light. But the star was so brilliant, it was plainly visible.

The star grew bigger and bigger and more brilliant, until the elders could feel its warmth on their faces, until it became apparent that this was a meteor about to impact the earth. Whether this was a coincidence, that it arrived just after the war, or whether it came through the same portal as the dragon or whether it was his final blow, directing a huge piece of space debris towards the earth, no one knew, but it caused such a fracture in the earth's crust when it hit that whatever life remained was wiped out by fire and brimstone.

The elders found themselves riding a shockwave that took them through a fracture in space-time, and they escaped annihilation. It soon became apparent that whatever plane they were now on was unstable, and they were able to drift across the thirty-one planes. It's not known how they survived and how long passed, but eventually the crater caused by the meteor cooled. After the impact, the temperature plummeted due to the debris thrown into the air, which blocked out the sun completely, and the land became a barren ice land with rivers of lava running through it where the earth had split due to the impact. The elders were now in a land of fire and ice, surrounded completely by huge mountain peaks that formed the edge of the crater with a central peak where the land had rebounded. The Celestials then took control of the Duranki using their magic and impressing the Duranki with their knowledge and wisdom.

Knowing the land the Celestials left had been destroyed and they could never return, the Duranki allowed the Celestials to use their magic and build a city of unrivalled splendour on the central peak. That city was Sagharta, surrounded by the lava lake of the Celestial Lotus. Because the city sits directly on the cosmic fracture, it can easily drift in and out of planes, never being in the same place for very long, making the city impossible to find.

There the Celestials lived in peace and became known by the gods as the Faithful. But they became restless and their thirst for more knowledge led them to become reckless with their magic. Eventually, boredom set in, and they began to grow resentful of the gods with whom they sometimes interacted when using their sorcery. They became conceited and would do anything to increase their power and further their influence on the thirty-one planes, until eventually they deemed themselves as powerful as any god.

Their conjuring had brought the attention of both Calabi-Ya and the Omnisoul, who thought the seven sages an amusement to be toyed with. Eventually, they made a bargain with Calabi-Ya to steal the Flaming Celestial Pearl to weaken the Omnisoul's power over the cosmos; in return he would make them immortal. A terrible war raged, sometimes referred to by mere mortals as the War in Heaven.

Using their sorcery, they were able to cloak themselves in secrecy across many planes until they came upon the Omnisoul, who was making music and dancing. After some merriment and entertainment with Svara and Dravaka, they were able to distract the god while Zayika administered a powerful potion to put the god to sleep just long enough for Palaka and Antapala to steal the Pearl.

When they presented their treasure to Calabi-Ya, he double-crossed them and, taking the Pearl, began to build his army of dark forces using its magic. He refused any discourse with the sages and began to weaken their powers by depleting their magical life force. Raksa never let Calabi-Ya leave his sight, vowing revenge when the time was right.

When the Omnisoul discovered what they had done, he decreed they owed a debt and would therefore be the guiding force for the Charon, the seven terrible beings that carry out the will of the Omnisoul, enslaved and held in Limbo for the most part. The Omnisoul brought forth his wrath and disfigured them all except Nipuna the Master, who would serve as a lasting reminder of their treachery. Dravaka was transformed into the Stalker, blind with hideous tree-like growths emerging from his head and abdomen. Zayika was transformed into the Sleeper, faceless and with black wings. Antapala had her beauty taken away from her and she was transformed into the Guardian, grotesque and covered in sores, then posted to the remotest part of the cosmos to protect the Well at the Centre of Time, and over the aeons she became obese out of boredom and lack of any interaction with any lifeforms save for the creatures and insects that fed off her sores. Svara was made bodiless and exists as only a mouth with foul black and yellow teeth, used to simply convey messages. Palaka was sent to Limbo to the eternal fires to keep guard over the Charon, and Raksa was transfigured into the Watcher with a blank face and head shaped like a fan that contains many eyes to watch the cosmos.

But this didn't stop them, and those who could retreated to Sagharta, where they developed dark rituals and could conjure the darkest magic without the aid of any gods. They discovered the secret to immortality. Apart from the gods, they became the most powerful beings in the cosmos. No other entity could rival their power, and when they worked together their combined power could match that of Calabi-Ya. Only then did they become known as the Celestials.

When the land split, four rivers of lava were created and flowed from the lake that surrounded the central peak. One of the rivers became known as the River of Woes that linked the crater with the Underworld, giving the Celestials access to the Charon. Jealous of the Charon, the Celestials decided they would try and destroy them.

During their war with the Charon, Adonai lost his eye. It was removed as a trophy by the Watcher, who now wears it on a harness about his body and uses it to see infinite distances across the planes."

"That's a lot to take in. I still cannot understand how the Celestials have become more powerful than the Charon," said Ignatius. "I mean, the Charon are gods, immortals, demons, call them what you will."

The old man intervened. "Who said they are more powerful? It is complicated, but you will see. You will see and understand."

And the old man continued to lead them past more side chapels and into another chamber.

Chapter 27: The Celestials

Indigo was growing a little impatient waiting. She cared little for tales of the Celestials or who was the greater. "Then I guess we should continue. This Void, where will we find it?"

The old man's voice dropped to barely a whisper. "Of course, I will show you. If you can find the Pearl and discover its secret, you can free the Charon and fulfil their only desire. If you can make it out of the Void, we can help you get home." He took a long pause. "And the Charon will be gone, forever. What will happen to the people of Sagharta, I'm not sure, we live to serve the Charon."

Indigo turned to Ignatius. "There would be no greater pleasure. Give the Charon what they want, and I will not have to deal with those demons again."

Ignatius had mixed feelings. He did want to be free of the burden given to them by the Charon, and to return to some sort of normal life again. But he wasn't sure he knew what normal was anymore, or if normal would be too boring. However, he wasn't sure whether the Charon would just kill them both once they had fulfilled their quest, and apparently their destiny. In fact, he wasn't sure if their own death might just be easier. He was so confused right now he didn't know what to think. Confused was an emotion new to him, he was always sure of himself, sure of the decisions he made on missions, sure of his purpose within the Empire. But now, their lives had been turned upside down.

The High Priest led them to a side chapel. Scenes on the wall were of the Charon fighting monsters, a gory scene with more scarlet paint than Indigo thought was necessary. It was a stomach-churning scene created with fine detail. Looking down to avert her eyes, she realised they had walked across a complex mandala created on the floor in coloured sands and were now standing at its centre. The old man opened his robes and pulled out an orb that looked suspiciously like a steam grenade. He hurled in at the altar and a portal opened. A velvet black portal that grew continuously.

"Nobody has seen the Celestial Pearl since it was stolen by Calabi-Ya. He took the Pearl trying to steal its wisdom, but it became lost in the Void after the long Battle of the Dawn, when Calabi-Ya tried to seize control of the cosmos. Step into the Void and your destiny, your search for the Pearl, if it is there, will begin. The choice is yours."

Before Ignatius and Indigo could make any decision or even have time to think, the whole citadel began to quake. The skies outside turned dark grey, and moody clouds began to swirl. The tiled flooring inside cracked and the High Priest looked shaken. A deep blue mist began to gather before them and a seated figure gradually appeared, cross-legged with turquoise clothing, his hair, midnight black, swept back and with a tiny triangular beard and waxed moustache.

"The Master," said the High Priest.

Immediately, the nebulous cloud swirled and sparked and fragmented into six other clouds and the remaining Celestials appeared.

"This is not usual. I have never been in the presence of all the Celestials at once. They must be concerned about your presence or the quest you are on. You are in danger."

The High Priest took Ignatius by the arm. "I have to get you out of here, quickly." But before they could flee, the seven Celestials had emerged from the ether and had gathered in a semi-circle about them. The Master was tapping his fingertips together.

The Master spoke. "Greetings, Vidus. I see you have met our meddling Asura. Humans are getting too troublesome recently. I am here to relieve you of them. I am sure the Keeper has a place for them to be kept safe."

The three-eyed Keeper pushed his head out from under his hooded cloak and gave a sinister grin. The giant disembodied mouth known as the Voice gave an eerie laugh, long yellow fangs and teeth dripping vile saliva to the floor.

Ignatius snatched his hand away from Vidus. "I am not prepared to run, High Priest. Master, you have no jurisdiction over humans, you cannot hide us away. Tell me, for what reason do you need to imprison us? What have we done?"

The Master twitched his moustache, and the Stalker reached out his long, thin, taloned fingers to grope at Ignatius, his cold deathly touch sending chills down Ignatius's spine. Ignatius pulled away from his touch.

"It's quite simple," replied the Master. "You meddle in the affairs of the Charon, for what purpose I do not know. But you are an irritation, a thorn in our side and today, it shall end. Sleeper, work your magic so the Keeper can take them away!"

Indigo was tired and frustrated at anyone or anything that would slow her journey to get home. "What makes you think we are just going to capitulate?"

The Master laughed, a wholehearted cruel laugh. "After the Omnisoul and Calabi-Ya, we are the most powerful beings in the cosmos. Even the mighty Charon must kneel before us and do our bidding, so two puny humans are nothing more than an insect to us."

That was what Indigo was hoping for, complete underestimation. The perfect element for surprise of the highest order. Ignatius was growing nervous at this point; he didn't know what Indigo had planned. He knew he could fight, he was a Union Jack, fearless in the line of duty, but these were powerful beings.

"We defeated Calabi-Ya…" She didn't finish.

"Only with the help of the Charon, you fool."

'No. No, you obviously don't know. I took his soul."

Fear flickered across the Master's face, but just momentarily. most people would not have seen it. Now, Indigo knew she had the upper hand.

"Impossible!"

"No, quite possible! He is probably still searching the Ghost Worlds for it. You see, if there is anything I have learned it is that all beings, even gods, have their limitations or their restrictions."

The Watcher took his telescope and placed it to his eye and began moving as if scanning some invisible horizon. After some time, he confirmed what Indigo was telling him.

"I also know that through the manipulation and transformations of matter and time I am capable of achieving, I am capable of destroying you all, regardless of your god-like status, because I am a godling, a demigod."

"You do not have the courage to face me. I am the Master, the leader of the most powerful beings in the cosmos, besides the gods. How dare you face us? You shall fear my wrath."

"You think you frighten me, sorcerer? For you are nought but that, a thaumaturge working with wonders and illusions."

"Brave words!" came the reply in his usual pompous manner.

Indigo said no more, instead chose to demonstrate her powers. Holding her arms out in front of her, she began rotating her hands as if moving some invisible ball. Amethyst flames began to form like a fireball and her aura glowed intensely with her power. Ignatius wasn't sure what she was doing but thought he saw her vanish just briefly, at which point all the Celestials jumped a little as if jolted by some electrical charge. Indigo was completely immersed in the aura surrounding her. Nobody else could see this, but her aura began to swirl and eddy and mix with what looked like star stuff, cosmic material from the death of stars and formation of heavy metals. She was engulfed by the light of a thousand newborn stars, causing pleasure and pain and a primeval memory of something before the creation of the earth. All she could hear was the thundering rush of her own blood and it all felt like a dream. Then she was static again and smiling, a big self-satisfied smile from ear to ear, looking extremely pleased with herself, standing with her arms behind her back. Even she was surprised at how much her powers had grown.

"That was too easy. I guess it always is against those who don't suspect and dismiss immediately, such is your arrogance and your aeons of dealing with the lame Charon and any other underling you deem weak and feeble."

The Master pulled out a singing bowl from his robes and began to peer inside. Looking alarmed, he began searching inside the bowl, looking for something precious.

"Looking for this?" Indigo brought her right hand from behind her back, holding a vermilion mass, pulsing and irregular in her palm. It writhed and changed shape, it fizzed and gave the odd spark and deep within a fire burned, illuminating the whole mass.

"Your soul, I believe? That's the beauty of time, it all runs alongside each other, and I can cross time, borders and planes in an instant. Like I said, you may be god-like, but I am a godling!"

She was finding her newfound magical strength was vast but not necessarily infinite, so she brazened it out. At that moment in time, she was feeling invincible.

Ignatius had pulled his sonic blaster out, ready should he need it. Feeling extremely inadequate at that moment, knowing that somewhere deep within he had powers, too, though maybe not as strong as Indigo's. He didn't know how to access them, and he wasn't sure of Indigo's plan or of the strength of her powers. He wasn't comfortable antagonising the beings that held the Charon captive. If they were no match for the Celestials, what chance did he and Indigo have?

The Master was stunned at how events were starting to develop. But Indigo continued. The Stalker was next. Indigo didn't appear to move anywhere, but somewhere on another pane, Indigo's astral self crept up on the Stalker and, reaching into his torso, which was cold like ice and sinuous like tree roots, she took hold of his soul. It was red and pulsing but cold to touch. Removing it, she returned to the present plane with Ignatius, holding the soul for all to see. Two souls were now in her possession.

Next was the Keeper. Her astral form slid into his hooded cloak and, despite his three eyes, she remained unseen. Clawing her way through his ribs and sinuous flesh, she removed his soul. It was hot and pulsing like the fires of Limbo where he resided. The Sleeper was next. She appeared right up close to his faceless face and could see her own reflection in his silver mask-like visage. He had no eyes, just four holes in his pearlescent face. Indigo could see her own reflection, not really liking what she saw, her face, although it was only her astral form, seemed haggard, stressed, older than she cared to think she looked in reality. These cosmic adventures and the magic she was using were taking its toll on her flesh. Despite her love for Ignatius, yet again she felt resentful because of the situation she now found herself in because he had called the Charon once more. The Sleeper's soul was warm to touch but seemed to snake its way around her arm, sending tremors down her spine.

The Voice was going to be trickier. Just a bodiless mouth with foul breath, and yellowed teeth, and blue lips. As she stood before him, Indigo pushed her head inside the mouth, between the foul fangs and nearly vomited. Groping about, she finally found his soul, black to the core and covered in nodules like it was diseased or had some king of fungus growing on its surface.

Indigo knew the Guardian had been killed, but as time runs parallel, here she was, her midnight skin still crawling with parasites and pus-oozing sores. She knew she was going to need a strong stomach to search for her soul. Even her astral form needed some persuading for this. Initially, she closed her eyes and went for it. Her hand could feel the sticky foul-smelling ooze, but she persevered, until eventually she found the slimy remnants of her soul, green and filthy. As she removed it, tendrils of liquid came with it. It was the grossest thing Indigo had ever experienced.

That just left the Watcher remaining. For him, she needed more time. Her astral form began to glow and grow in stature. She began drawing more energy from the aether, from the cosmos, drawing in star stuff and the organic material that swirled in space to eventually form life. She knew the Watcher could see her; he was the only one who could see her astral form. He lurched forward to try and intimidate her, his many eyes blinking. But Indigo didn't flinch. As fast as her astral form could, she circled him over and over, looking for a way in to seek his soul. She hovered near an eye, then pushed her fingers right in, searching. He was helpless, and eventually she found it, a hard pulsing red soul. It burned as she grasped it and she let go. It moved, and she wasn't sure where it had gone, but she found it and, gripping it tightly, she removed it despite the pain it caused her. But she wasn't finished, she wanted something else. Attacking from behind, she reached around his torso and grabbed the large eye that was attached to the leather harness he wore on his chest. He screamed and tried to fight her off, but she now had both hands on the eye, her fingertips digging in either side of the orb until it popped off and she held it aloft, the original Eye of Adonai.

Making a hasty retreat, Indigo resurfaced on the plane whence she'd originally started an instant later than when she'd left, displaying before her all the souls she had stolen. They hovered, a multi-coloured array of ethereal cores that no being should ever see, and certainly should not have removed. The Celestials all looked horror-stricken, and the Watcher was searching around, looking for his eye. Indigo was desperate to return it to Adonai and return the Charon to Limbo or anywhere else they wanted to go, just so she didn't have to see them again. This desperation is what had given her the strength to do this. She might not love Ignatius right now, but she wanted to love him again.

"Here," she said as she casually tossed the Eye of Adonai to Ignatius. "I feel you may have to use this before we give it back to Adonai." She wanted to say, your father, but thought that was too cruel. Ignatius took out his goggles and, with some small tools from his engineer's waistcoat, he removed the right lens and replaced it with the eye.

"And what do you intend to do with the souls you have in your possession?" inquired the Master through gritted teeth.

Indigo gave the most sinister grin she could muster; it was unbecoming of her, and a darkness spread across her face. Her eyes watered and she meant every word she spoke. "I am going to destroy them. I have experienced my entire body being dismantled atom by atom and then reassembled. It isn't pleasant. My whole being is now something else, my soul, apparently, is blackened I'm not sure what that means to a human, or if such a result will blight me for eternity, so yours, yours, I'm going to completely squash them and tear them apart until only individual atoms remain. Then I am going to burn them and fling them to every corner of the cosmos so they shall be irretrievable. I am going to DESTROY YOU! I am the Soulslayer!"

A shiver ran down Ignatius's spine. He had never seen Indigo like this before. He was beginning to think her newfound powers were taking over and maybe destroying the woman he longed to be with forever. Looking at the Celestials, he had never seen such fear in the eyes of enemies, even on the battlefield for the Empire, the atrocities of war paled into insignificance compared to this. These were super beings, god-like, and their spirits had been torn apart, their souls removed, and they were now staring their fate in the face.

"Oh, what to do? Shall I destroy them, or show mercy? I could send them all to the Ghost worlds, and you can spend an eternity looking for them. But no, no, I think I was correct the first time. Tear them apart burn them and fling them across the planes."

Looking haughty, the Master reached out to grab his soul, but as his hand came within grabbing distance, it burned and he pulled back in pain, smoke rising from his fingertips. The rest of the Celestials appeared to be frozen, unable to move, maybe due to the lack of a soul or due to some force Indigo had inflicted upon them.

Alarmed, the High Priest gestured to Indigo. "My dear, do you know what you are doing? With the exception of the Charon, the Celestials are the most revered beings in the cosmos. I fear your fate hangs in the balance. If you are fortunate, they will kill you. If you are not, then expect to be sent to Limbo, to be tortured and burned alongside the Charon, or to be turned into fuel to power the Charon's great ship Taraka."

Ignatius intervened. "High Priest, do you know of our fate? Have you any kind of clue what we must do?"

"Only the Book of Consciousness can tell you that, and you no longer have possession of it. All other answers will come from the Pearl, but you must enter the Void first."

Indigo was growing impatient, but in truth didn't want to be too hasty, not knowing the outcome for her actions. She wanted to know the secret of the Pearl first. She paced for a little while, all eyes of the Celestials were upon her, but rendered helpless. Surprising Ignatius, she sat on the floor, cross-legged as if in meditation, her hands resting on her knees and her eyes shut. She began a low mumble, easily mistaken for deep breathing.

Ignatius had a sense of foreboding and a heavy feeling in the pit of his stomach. He was worried that he was going to lose her, either killed by the Celestials or to some illness of the mind brought on by the extreme power she now seemed to wield. He feared he would be attending her funeral for real.

As Indigo continued, a membrane grew around the Celestials, a force field to prevent them from leaving the spot where they stood, should any of them be able to use magic in their paralysed state. She then turned her mind to the souls that hovered above her head, quivering and pulsating with sentience, multiple colours flashing across their surface. Holding her arms up to the sky, she cried out and one by one the souls rushed at her and were absorbed into her chest. She felt pain rip through her body and was thrown violently backwards, cracking her head on the tiled floor. Ignatius thought for a brief moment he saw a demon, a woman possessed, her arms and legs grotesquely twisted, green blood running from her mouth, shadows slithered across her flesh, and then she screamed out and was then silent and unmoving, not a soul in sight, her body was whole once more.

Rushing over, Ignatius held her and checked she was still breathing. Opening her eyes, she smiled, "I'm ok, I'm ok. Give me a moment, then we must make our way to the Void. The Celestials won't give us any more trouble for the time being."

Helping her to her feet, Indigo felt like she had taken some kind of energy-enhancing drug. Her whole body tingled, her head was light, and she felt invincible, but secretly knew this power was affecting her own soul and wellbeing, possibly shortening her life. She had to act fast, find the Pearl then rid herself of the Celestials' souls before they caused long-lasting damage.

Without any more delay, she asked, "High Priest, where is the Void?"

The High Priest was not the fastest-moving person, but hastily took them through the portal he had opened and to a small hexagonal building standing alone on the very centre of the central peak of the crater in which Sagharta stood. A small, simple, unobtrusive doorway was the only opening. Unlike the rest of the city, it had no decoration, and looked out of place.

"Nobody has entered in thousands of years. The Void is inside. Once through the door, you will be on your own, lost amongst the thirty-one planes with no guarantee of a return. If you do not return, what must we do with the Celestials?"

Indigo shrugged her shoulders nonchalantly. "Terminate them, I suppose! I care not." Then, turning, she pushed the door open, and the two Union Jacks entered the building.

Chapter 28: The Great Void

Saying nothing more, Ignatius and Indigo stepped into the Void. Blackness filled the space all around. Nothing could be seen, and the silence was deafening. Indigo reached out and took Ignatius by the hand. He turned to look at her, and she gave a faint smile. "We don't want to lose each other. Where do you think we are?"

"I don't know, but I think we may be outside of time and space. The Great Void may be just that. Do you think it exists within or alongside the Ghost Worlds?"

Indigo Shrugged her shoulders. "If this is the Ghost Worlds, then are we expecting to meet Calabi-Ya?"

"I hope not. Without the power of the Charon with us, I don't think we would stand any chance of survival."

"Well, do we walk on? Or just stand here?" She gave the slightest of smiles.

It was all a bit too disconcerting, the empty blackness continued beneath their feet. They were standing on nothing.

"Let's try."

The two Union Jacks walked on, but the uncertainty of every footstep made them feel dizzy. It was like motion sickness. Indigo started to panic, she could feel her heart racing and hear it pumping blood rapidly through her body. She tentatively pushed her right foot forward, as if feeling for a step in the dark. Ignatius did the same. Unconsciously, she gripped his hand tighter. He looked at her, his eyes struggling to see her face in the darkness.

"Do you think the Sword is of any use?" he whispered, not sure if there were other beings in the Void with them. Was this their test, to fend off demons?

"I'm not sure how the Sword of Wisdom can help, but I can try it."

Unsheathing the great silver blade, the rasping sound it made split the silence, and its glow illuminated Indigo's face. She pushed it forward in front of them as if she was trying to pierce some invisible wall. Nothing, no resistance, just the great yawning blackness.

"Do you think we are going to be stuck here for all eternity?" asked Indigo. "Is this our Limbo, our final fate?"

Ignatius didn't answer. He couldn't, he didn't have any answers. She re-sheathed the sword. Just then something brushed his shoulder, and it wasn't Indigo. He jumped and spun around. In the gloom, he could just make out the figure of a man. He pushed his face forward and opened his eyes wide. He jumped backwards with a yell and his heart skipped a beat.

"What is it?" screamed Indigo.

"It's… it's… m… me!"

"What? A mirror, it must be your reflection."

"No, it's me! Another me."

Indigo peered as hard as she could and, sure enough, there stood Ignatius, although he vanished momentarily as the silhouette of a woman crossed in front of him.

"Aah!" she screamed, "It's me!"

Figures came and went. They both disappeared occasionally but reappeared moments later.

Ignatius appeared next to her. "Come on, we need to complete this mission and get out of here, or I feel this place will drive us both insane."

"But where are we going? We have no idea which direction, there is no direction, just a void, and we have no idea on which plane to look for the Pearl. And at this rate we are likely to lose each other if we keep disappearing and reappearing!"

Ignatius took her hand. "Let's stick together and hopefully we won't lose each other."

He felt the warmth of her hand, comforting to him, knowing she still harboured some dislike of his actions during this mission. Indigo felt warmth, too, but feared it was the burning energy of the souls she had absorbed and wondered what damage their power was doing.

As they held each other's hand, they merged and become one. Ignatius looked down and could see Indigo's clothing, feel her legs and not his own. His hair was no longer a shock of blond, but long and auburn with curls upon his shoulders. As he continued to gaze, he saw his own boots and trousers once more, he had breasts, no, now he could see his waistcoat. Indigo did the same, her feminine figure was now more muscular, bulky, she had the biceps and pectoral muscles of a man, this was all very alarming.

"I don't believe humans were meant to cross the planes like this, our bodies can't cope with the disturbance," she said.

They continued moving, although they had no idea where they were going in the darkness, becoming very disoriented.

"Is that a figure?" said Ignatius, pointing to another being. "They are dressed in blue. Can you see?"

"I can, but I have a bad feeling over this. I think it could be…" She didn't finish before the figure was upon them.

"The Omnisoul!" they both shouted. A multi-faced head leered at them in fury, clearly irritated by the presence of Asura. Flaming hair roared, and the Omnisoul's head turned so all four faces took turns to see. Two male, two female each baring teeth, with flaming hair snaking around sensuous female features and furrowed male brows with flaming eyebrows and beards. Fiery eyebrows were raised in surprise and arms waved about and the Void shook with the Omnisoul's wrath.

"Did you not see this moment, all-present one? Or can you not see into the Void? Is that why you are here, to look?" mocked Indigo.

"I see everything," came the reply. "I see it all, I created it all, you are here because I orchestrated it, my thoughts created it, and it is recorded in the Book of Consciousness."

"So, tell me, how does this end? Certain death?"

The Omnisoul didn't answer for a few moments, as if searching for the answer. Ignatius didn't wait. "I don't believe you know!"

The Void became an echo chamber as the Omnisoul gave a loud roar and anger spread across four faces, each turning to look as the Omnisoul grew in stature, towering over them, with many arms thrashing around spinning prayer wheels and slashing with curved swords. Ignatius had to duck and weave between the weapons to avoid losing his head. But he was determined to keep provoking the great creator, to see how far he could go, to see how much information he could obtain. At this moment in time, he believed he had nothing to lose, they had come this far and this time there was no way of knowing if they could ever return, they might be trapped in this Void for eternity so death might be the easy option, he had no intention of living an eternity like the Charon, trapped and bored with no free will.

A giant scimitar came crashing down beside him, just missing his left leg. The whole Void momentarily sparked, and became fiery orange for a moment. "In fact, I believe that you may not be the First Cause, I believe that may be Calabi-Ya, who says he is your brother, who carries the title Elder God! The histories record that the first seven breaths of the fiery whirlwind brought forth the Charon. I think that fiery whirlwind is Calabi-Ya, the dragon, who also owned the Flaming Celestial Pearl, the Pearl of Wisdom. This all makes sense now."

"INSOLENCE!" screamed the almighty god, "you are nothing more than a midge on the backside of a dung beetle." The whole Void quaked.

"The only reason you are here is because I have allowed it, for my own amusement. It is written in the Book of Consciousness. But I can see this may have been an error. Make no mistake about it, you are my creation, my toy, my pawn. Oh, Adonai believes you to be his, and he is your father, but only because I allowed it. Adonai is a fool! He believes he can manipulate his fate, to use you as his salvation. The hilarity of the situation is beyond belief. I can squash you at any time, erase you from the cosmos as if you had never been. You are the biggest failure in my design of pawns to play the celestial game. Do you think you could ever really look upon one such as me? To commune with a god such as me?"

Ignatius retaliated. "Then why do you allow it? Why am I here? I didn't ask for any of this. I don't wish to be a part of the Charon's miserable existence."

"It is too entertaining. To watch a puny Asura such as yourself believe you have the power, the courage, the intelligence to battle gods. Besides, I am curious, I want to see where this game ends.

Oh, it's true I create the cosmos, all that was, is and will be, but sometimes that is in my dream state, even a god needs rest. If I really wanted to, I could see what the ultimate truth is, but this is my entertainment, my reward for creating it all."

Ignatius began to understand the Omnisoul's laziness and how the Charon created one such as himself. Perhaps it was because of the Omnisoul's complacency. Perhaps this creation was not all it was meant to be. It was now obvious how the Omnisoul's dark thoughts manifested into their own, dark insidious matter, Calabi-Ya.

"I am going to remove Indigo's powers, she will be a helpless human, lowest of the lifeforms in my creation. You will be stranded here for eternity, in the empty black Void. Your fate will be worse than that of the Charon." The Omnisoul laughed a hideous, torturous mocking laugh that echoed around Ignatius's ears and reverberated through his entire body, chilling him to the core.

As if on cue, Indigo appeared next to Ignatius. "Ah!" The Omnisoul said, "The woman who believes she is capable of more than other mundane Asura. Greetings, how appropriate you should make an appearance, how easy it will be now for me to remove your powers, destroy you entirely, to smash you to your simplest constituent parts and it shall be as if you never existed, never to have interacted with the cosmos, never to have been, to be now, or to be in future. You are a disgrace to the cosmic dust that makes your puny body, the simplest of vehicles for your soul to inhabit. You will cease to be and never will be."

Beads of sweat appeared on Indigo's brow and stung her eyes. Fear filled her whole body, but she stood fast. They had come this far, and she wasn't going to die now. She thought she might never see Oxford again, she had no idea of their fate, but she held firm with the true determination of a special human, a Union Jack. She pulled at her clothing and exposed just enough of her breasts to reveal the gem-shaped burn mark on her chest, obtained at the hands of the High Priestess and her infernal machine, and began to recite an incantation that she didn't even know she knew. Where it came from was a mystery, but she suspected it was thanks to her celestial father, Atman, or perhaps Aryas the mystic. Her speech was a low mumble of incomprehensible words and syllables in a language she had never heard before, perhaps it was the high speech of the gods. The incantation grew in intensity and bass tones and the purple burn mark began to glow and appeared to dance across her chest. Her hair now formed an auburn-tinged halo around her head and her eyes rolled back into her head like a shark about to attack. Purple fire grew around her whole body until it was strong enough, before rushing forth into the Void, its velvet blackness now illuminated a violet colour, a colour showing that Indigo Gemstone now controlled this space. The Void was now hers, regardless of who or what was within. At that moment in time, Indigo was the strongest godling in the cosmos, perhaps the strongest goddess.

The blue-skinned Omnisoul now faded into the violet light and was just discernible by the fiery hair and eyebrows. Indigo's incantation could no longer be heard as the Omnisoul let out a scream of such intensity and primeval origin, it was a sound like no other. The cosmos quaked and it could be heard in nearby star systems knocking planets from their orbit and rending a tear in the fabric of the cosmos itself. Other beings appeared in the Void, drawn in through some portal created by the hyperquake. A green creature with tentacles where its nose and mouth should be, a humanoid with four arms, an amorphous blob, a priest, a man with a crocheted waistcoat, a bandana around his head of unruly black hair and the name Jimi painted on his guitar. He disappeared as quickly as he appeared and was replaced by a creature, half fish and half woman. The planes proceeded getting entangled and slid across each other interfering on occasion. A man appeared with long tight curly hair and a silver star stuck on one cheek then another with a red lightning bolt painted across his face, then they were all gone and the Void continued in its possession by Indigo. The Omnisoul had become bored and swiped a large hand across ways to try and eliminate Indigo from the Void, but she was too quick and leapt to safety. As she landed, she raised her hands out in front of her and closed her eyes. The violet light intensified and swirls of purple flame travelled around her arms, snaking around her entire body until suddenly an explosion occurred so bright even the Omnisoul was taken by surprise. Then across her hands lay the silver Sword of Wisdom. It glowed and seemed to absorb the light given off by Indigo as she took the stance of the expert swordswoman she was and, holding the sword, she was ready to fight.

The Omnisoul stopped mocking, and his eyes widened on each face. His hair and eyebrows fizzed and sparked and swirled in anger. The Void seemed to tremble and the form of the Omnisoul grew in stature and loomed bigger than ever, his yellowed teeth grinding as a gigantic face hovered directly in front of Indigo.

"What trickery is this, girl? What do you bring before me? I ordain everything!"

Indigo stood her ground, her stomach trembled, her legs were weak, but she locked her knees and stood fast. "I don't think you ordained this," she said defiantly.

"What is this? How do you possess the sword of Manjushri?"

"The Void which we now inhabit is outside of your control. It is a bubble that exists at the intersection of planes, at the heart of

Sagharta, and was created by the Pearl itself. So, great omniscient one, your powers here are diminished. How this is so I cannot tell you, but the Pearl is guiding me, the Pearl is tasking me. I am her servant!"

The Omnisoul was a whirl of arms, each brandishing a scimitar. The great blades came crashing down around Indigo, one after another. Indigo thrust and parried, matching the Omnisoul's attack. With one arm raised and the other brandishing the magical blade, she expertly drove closer and closer to the Omnisoul. When within striking distance, she held the handle with two hands and sliced horizontally, causing the Omnisoul to roar and jump backwards. She wasted no time and moved the blade with such ease it was like an extension of her own arms. She thrust and parried, sliced and stabbed and matched the Omnisoul's many blades at every turn. The fencing classes her mother had paid for in France when she was a very young girl had paid off. She was perhaps the best swordswoman in the whole of the Empire.

Whilst she kept the Omnisoul busy, Ignatius placed his goggles on and, using the Eye of Adonai, could see the Omnisoul, a rainbow of colours crashing through realms and crossing planes as he fought Indigo. Behind him in the distance was a pinpoint of light.

"I think I see it. We need to get past the Omnisoul."

Breathless with her efforts, Indigo said, "I don't think I can make it. I don't know how long I can keep this up."

"No! We go together. We are stronger as a team. And we still need to discover the secret of the Pearl. What's its purpose? We can only do that together."

He reached into his coat and pulled out his sonic blaster. Turning the dials he took aim at the Omnisoul. The familiar pressure under his finger felt greater than usual this time, probably as he was about to attack the creator god. Sound waves rang out a menacing melody of destructive notes that hit the Omnisoul in the chest. There was a large roar of anger, and a scimitar crashed where Ignatius had been standing. Fortunately, he was nimble on his feet. The two of them advanced and as they got closer to the Omnisoul, the god got bigger and bigger. Flaming hair sparked and a gigantic female face came down right in front of Ignatius.

"You dare? You dare to think you can beat me? I created you; you are mine, I know your every move, your every thought. The great Book of Consciousness is open on your page, and here you DIE!"

Indigo felt peculiar, a great warmth travelled up her arms. The gem-shaped burn on her chest throbbed. It hurt, she thought she was suffering heart failure, and it felt like she was no longer in control of her own body. Wild terror was painted on her face, her world seemed to go into slow motion. The pain. The pain was so much. She turned to Ignatius and, with tears in her wide eyes, she spoke, a slow, dull, voice that trembled with alarm at her situation and although she didn't hear her own words, she was sure she said, "you go. If I do not follow, Ignatius, I love you!"

Ignatius's heart felt heavy. "I know. I love you, too, but we have made it this far together, we are going to end it together!"

A blast hit Ignatius full on, so powerfully that he was thrown onto his back as Indigo crashed the magical sword onto the ground by the Omnisoul's feet. The blackness of the Void was now the brightness of a newborn supernova, with nothing visible, not even the Omnisoul, just pure white blinding light and the whole cosmos seemed to scream. As the light faded, so too had the Omnisoul. The Void was black once more, and only Ignatius and Indigo were present.

Chapter 29: The Pearl

With the Omnisoul gone, the two Union Jacks turned their attention to the pinpoint of light that Ignatius discovered earlier. They ran towards it, but despite their speed they didn't seem to be getting any closer. The pinpoint of light was still the same size.

Ignatius put on his googles with the Eye of Adonai over his own right eye and could see the Pearl as if it was just in front of him, but when he removed the goggles, the Pearl was still in the distance.

Vertical slits of turquoise light began to appear in the black fabric of the Void. They were lenticular in shape and roughly the same height as an average human. Then, more and more appeared, like the black fabric of the Void had been sliced repeatedly with a knife.

From one of the slits came a leg, followed by a hooded body. One by one, the same scene evolved from each slit. They were gateways created by the Knights of Himavala to access the Void and protect the Pearl.

The lead knight had a scowl upon her rune-tattooed face. Her face was mostly in shadow cast from the hooded cloak she wore, but it was still possible to see the whites of her eyes and sapphire-blue irises that burned with determination and ambition. Her dark curly locks protruded from her hood and fell about her shoulders. Dressed all in black, she almost blended with the inky atmosphere of the Void. Other knights followed, dressed similarly, their cloaks tied in at the waist with a cummerbund armed with an array of silver and obsidian knives. Some had a scimitar in each hand, and together they all advanced on Ignatius and Indigo whilst the pinpoint of light still glowed in the distance behind them.

Indigo didn't waste any time, she held the Sword of Wisdom in her right hand and a steam cannon in her left. She led with the sword, not waiting for the knights to come to her. She pounced, as graceful as any feline, and her sword was a blur of silver in the darkness and she slashed and thrust at several knights who had charged her. Blood spurted from the neck of one as Indigo felt the slight resistance of taut muscular flesh against her blade. The knight fell clutching her neck, her fingers of no use to her wound. Indigo didn't slow, she jumped through the air and both feet connected with the chest of another, sending her backwards until Indigo was standing on her chest. She felt a burning pain in her thigh as the knight thrust an obsidian blade into it. The knight was about to stab Indigo with another when Indigo slashed her several times, until her corpse was nothing more than the slight advantage of higher ground. Two more blades came whistling past her face, and as she turned to see who threw them, she saw a knight was about to thrust her blade into Indigo's ribs. But Indigo managed to connect her sword with the scimitar and parry the blow. Then, bringing her left arm up, she fired her steam cannon. With a hiss of steam and a loud bang, the shot hit the knight in her right shoulder, and she fell, her lifeless body perfectly still.

Ignatius held his ground and fired shot after shot from his steam cannon, some of which found their targets. A knight came sliding in underneath his firepower and took his legs from under him. As he fell, he took aim and watched his shot hit a knight in her chest, and she fell, twitching in her death throes. The knight who had felled him was now standing above him and slashed at his face, cutting his cheekbone. Then her blade connected with his right wrist, which held the steam cannon. Ignatius felt the blade cut deep and he dropped his weapon, but as the knight momentarily took stock, believing she had the advantage, Ignatius took a dagger from his boot and stabbed her in the thigh several times. He felt the warm blood pour over his hand, but he didn't stop. He turned his attention to the throat of his attacker and finished her.

As the two Union Jacks fought side by side, they were unaware of a new lineup of knights behind those they were fighting. They each carried a double-edged crescent blade, one in each hand, shaped like boomerangs. One came spinning through the darkness, and Ignatius had to push Indigo aside to save her from being sliced. As Indigo tried to focus her vision on what had just happened, the curved blade was already returning to its owner. Two more blades came her way and two were heading for Ignatius. One was low and Indigo jumped over it. The other was chest height, and she had to move fast to knock it aside with her sword.

Ignatius received a deep wound to his arm as a blade hit him, losing its spin and its ability to return to his assailant. The other just missed the side of his face. He picked the blade up and threw it, watching it arc through the knights until eventually it found a mark. She clutched at her arm, badly injured but still alive. Ignatius sustained a blow from a quarterstaff, knocking him off balance. As he fell, a knight leapt upon him, pinning him down. She held a silver knife between her teeth and another in her right hand. Swiftly, she plunged the blade into his side, and he groaned in pain.

Removing the other blade from her teeth, she grinned and as she went to plunge it into his other side, there was a flash of steel as the Sword of Wisdom sliced through her neck and she fell on top of Ignatius. Pushing her aside, he saw Indigo with a liberated quarterstaff knocking heads and slashing them with her blade.

The knights had diminished in number considerably. Piles of corpse lay around, with their black cloaks stained crimson. Against his better judgement, Ignatius removed the blade from his side, and blood ran down his leg. In sheer frustration and anger, he picked up his steam cannon and let loose volley after volley of shot until visibility in the Void was almost nil, steam clouds rising to obscure the view, as he killed one knight after another.

Eventually, one knight remained. She looked different to the others. She was still dressed the same, but her black cloak and hood were lined with red satin, her handleless knives were made from red obsidian and her scimitar was more ornate with a large ruby for the pommel. Standing before the two Union Jacks, she introduced herself.

"I am Rak-Saka, the Marshall of the Knights of Himavala. We have sworn an oath to protect the Pearl, fighting to the death if necessary. You fight well and have been more than a match for my knights. But I do not wish to lose any more, so let's talk."

Ignatius lowered his weapon cautiously. Indigo remained ready to strike. "What is there to talk about?" he asked.

"Firstly, why have you come? What do you want with the Pearl?"

There was a long pause before Ignatius answered, even he didn't really know. "In truth, we are not sure. We seek the Flaming Celestial Pearl because it is one of the artefacts from the creation. What power it yields, or its purpose, we do not know, but we have recently been in possession of other such artefacts, the Book of

Consciousness and the Book of Shadows, and simply want to know more about the Pearl."

Rak-Saka half closed her eyes squinting at him suspiciously. "You have no understanding of the Pearl?"

"None whatever, it's the truth."

"I think I believe you, although I don't know why. The Knights of Himavala have been sworn to protect the Pearl for all eternity. It is the most precious artefact in the cosmos. It is fragile and must not be damaged in any way."

Indigo was growing impatient. "Why?"

Rak-Saka smiled. "When you enter the Pearl, you will know why. It is something I cannot put into words. But be warned. I shall be here waiting. If you harm the Pearl in any way, I will kill you!"

"How do we enter it?" she asked.

"Ah! That is for you to work out. I am not permitted to say, it is against my sworn allegiance to protect it. You must also work out how to get to it." Turning, she gestured with her hand at the white pinpoint of light in the distance still. She then turned and stepped into a thin turquoise slit in the fabric of the Void that opened up in front of her. She stepped inside and was gone, but the slit remained shimmering and warping slightly from side to side, wavering so the knight could return at any moment.

Ignatius placed the Eye of Adonai over his right eye, and he could see the Pearl up close, close enough to touch it. But as he reached out, it wasn't there. As he tried again, he heard a voice, just a faint murmur, somewhere outside of the Void. He then realised it was the voice of Aryas.

"Do you hear that, Indigo?"

"Hear what?"

"I can hear Aryas. Can't you?"

"No, just the overwhelming silence of the Void."

He listened intently. Aryas was a mere whisper, a slightly hoarse incantation in some unknown long-forgotten high-born language. It was almost melodic as the mystic repeated it over and over. Ignatius closed his eyes and could see Aryas sat cross-legged, smoking his usual green liquid in his long-curved glass pipe hanging from the corner of his mouth. Ignatius could now smell the herbs as if Aryas was sat next to him smoking them. The invocation continued, a low mumble with the odd higher-pitched syllable. Aryas was completely still, except for his lips, chanting and letting out the odd puff of pipe smoke.

Eventually, Aryas stopped and removed his pipe before instructing Ignatius to place the Eye of Adonai to his own eye once more. As he did so, the Void was a rush of rainbow colours, and the pinpoint of light came accelerating towards Ignatius. He jumped with surprise as the great gleaming white Pearl was suddenly in front of him, bluish white flames all around it, giving the artefact its name. He removed the Eye, at which point he realised the Pearl was still there, it wasn't some kind of trickery of the Eye of Adonai. He could feel the heat from the flames, and the pair of Union Jacks had to back away slightly.

The Pearl was enormous. Ignatius and Indigo were dwarfed by its presence. The flames reduced, and it became clear the Pearl was sentient, and its surface didn't just glow with the pearlescence of other similar precious pearls. Its surface was a myriad of subtle colours, subtle energies that radiated their own light. The colours moved across its surface, pastel pink, palest blue, pastel purple and golden shimmers. Indigo felt compelled to touch it. Reaching out her hand, she leaned in, but Ignatius grabbed her arm. "We don't know if it's safe!"

"Well, there's only one way to find out, isn't there?" She snatched her arm away; she couldn't help it. There was a compulsion, a drive, a decision had been made that wasn't hers. As her long pale fingers moved through the flames unharmed and met the surface of the Pearl, an energy thrilled through her body. The surface was soft, and it murmured. The colours shot around its surface and began to congregate around the point her fingers touched. Indigo felt her legs grow weak; her head was dizzy. It was like she had lost all control of her body. Her legs trembled and her stomach fluttered, then there was a blinding flash of palest blue light. Indigo regained her composure and Ignatius thought he heard the Pearl whimper and moan in ecstasy.

Frowning, deep in thought, Ignatius spoke. "We don't even know the purpose of the Pearl. How was it used at the creation? We know nothing about it. Is it going to suddenly burst into flames? Is it dangerous? We need to analyse this, gather some intelligence."

Indigo shook her head, part in answer, yes, they didn't know what its purpose was, part in anger, for not wanting to merely find out. The Pearl was here, so too were they. They might not get another chance, where did Ignatius think they were going to get any intelligence? They were standing in a black Void with no way of knowing where they were or how to return either to Sagharta or to Oxford!

"I don't think we have any choice, Ignatius. We are alone, no Charon to assist, no other life forms, just the Void. The deep black bottomless Void. We need to just act. Trust me on this, the Sword has guidance for me, I'm sure of it. It communicates to me. The Sword is the only way in."

"And out? How do we get out?"

"We'll cross that bridge when it comes to it." She held the Sword before her and as she did so, she could feel it sharing its knowledge, divulging masses of information from the Library again. She sighed a little and closed her eyes, it was too much. She felt like her head would explode as her mind, her consciousness was crammed with data. She had knowledge of other civilisations, most of which she had never heard of, and knowledge of great monuments built to honour unknown gods or kings. New languages and writings flashed through her mind. She wanted to scream, but her voice was silent. The Sword murmured and silver light swam around her whole body, it swam about her mind and filled her vision even though her eyes were closed. Ignatius looked on, not sure what was happening, concerned for her safety.

Eventually the silver light display began to diminish and settle back to just surrounding the enchanted blade.

Indigo opened her eyes. A tear rolled down her right cheek. "Oh, Ignatius, the knowledge, the knowledge this Sword contains is immense. I don't think I should use it again; I don't think I'll be able to contain the information it is giving me. It's almost like a punishment. It is not a sustainable practice. However, I do know how we can explore the Pearl.

She touched its blade to the surface of the Pearl. It murmured again and groaned in ecstasy, and as the blade slid through its outer shell like a knife through butter, colours flashed and swirled all over the surface and travelled up along the sword and around Indigo's arms. A slit opened on its surface, widening to an elongated oval, ripples of the Pearl's surface radiating outward from the opening. Indigo felt as if the Sword was drawing energy from her and she felt faint. There was a blinding flash of brilliant white light and what sounded like a chorus of angels singing, heralding the start of something special. Then, Indigo and Ignatius were inside the

Pearl and the singing was a distant faint song somewhere in the distance, or perhaps outside the Pearl. The blackness of the Void had been replaced by the brilliant white of its interior. It was like snow blindness, neither Union Jack could see. Their eyes hurt and a pain throbbed at the backs of their eyeballs.

"Goggles, put your goggles on," cried Ignatius in desperation. Both pulled on their brass-rimmed protective goggles. They helped to dull the light, but it was still too bright. They closed their eyes, but it didn't help, the light penetrated their eyelids.

Ignatius noticed what could only be described as a warm, moist feeling. Except for the light, he felt comfortable, cosy as if he sat in a soft armchair, by a dying but warm fire. He opened his right eye and, using the Eye of Adonai once more, peered into the light. He gasped and held Indigo by the hand.

Chapter 30: The Eversoul

The two Union Jacks were overwhelmed by the warmth and softness of the Pearl's interior. It was a strange feeling, but they both had the impression of being loved. All the anxieties and mental struggles they had accumulated over the past missions seemed to have dissolved away. Indigo no longer felt ill at ease with the fact she had encountered gods, immortals and demons of the worst kind. Within her heart, she felt regret at letting the absinthe and drugs take over and change her. Her internal warmth continued to grow, and her breathing slowed until she was taking big deep breaths. She no longer cared if her soul was indeed black, whatever she was experiencing meant she didn't care because she had found peace.

Ignatius felt similar. He was uncomfortable at his recent actions, he knew drugs were not the answer, and definitely not the ladies who frequent the night to earn their living. Indigo deserved better than that. He knew he loved her, that was all that mattered. He also regretted his reliance upon using the Charon to aid them, knowing this made Indigo uneasy. He needed to apologise when the time was right. Without realising it, he had a big smile on his face, a smile of contentment.

Without any more distractions, they both knew they had to focus on the interior of the Pearl, but the intensity of its light was too severe, too much. They were both shielding their eyes, despite their goggles. Eventually, Ignatius revealed what he could see with the Eye of Adonai.

"I see, I can see."

"See what? What's causing this feeling? I'm comfortable, kind of floating on a warm sofa like those of the Bedouin caravans we've experienced before, all fur and rugs or floating in a warm bath."

Ignatius didn't know how to reply. Silence remained for a while. He was totally absorbed.

"She's beautiful, the most beautiful creature I have ever seen." His voice trailed off in a soft sigh. "It's like a womb, we are in a womb!"

Not able to see, Indigo wasn't sure what to make of Ignatius's comments so remained silent. The warmth intensified; Ignatius's body felt like it was bathing in warm but viscous water. It penetrated his whole being.

"It's a goddess, lying. She's, she's naked, birthing. It's like the cosmos is being given life, flowing from her loins."

She was lying back on what looked like a mix of clouds and velvet and brocade cushions. Barely visible, transparent, she looked like an ethereal outline of a goddess, an outline that glowed. Her limbs were faintly alight with a myriad of stars and her entire abdomen glowed with the light that was so intense and blinding. The goddess smiled the sweetest smile Ignatius had ever seen. Even more so than that of the Mystic. Her face was golden, like that of an angel, but she was no angel, it was a goddess. She had a beautiful oval face, perfectly symmetrical, her eyes were golden and sparkled, a long straight nose ended at her perfect heart-shaped lips, upturned at the end in a smile. Her hair was silver and flowed down across her shoulders and mingled with her surroundings. Her whole being glowed, she exuded warmth and love, and life. An aura surrounded her, pure light, the brightest, whitest untainted light ever seen.

Lying with her knees slightly raised and her feet flat on the unseen floor, her swollen stomach pulsed with the rhythm of the cosmos and from between her legs poured cosmic energy, aether and the very stuff of life. Celestial matter flowed from her like colourful nebulae. It never stopped, it was just one continuous stream of life-giving matter, fed occasionally from what looked like milk that dripped from her breasts. As each drop fell and met the flow of matter, it exploded into a little shower of sparkling light, giving birth to stardust that could be used to create celestial bodies. In an instant, the stardust and colourful gases had multiplied and travelled past Ignatius to somewhere behind him, somewhere in the cosmos, to find their nucleus and neighbours to form galaxies, stars and planets and travel on their orbit throughout space and time, settling on one of the thirty-one planes of existence, there to nourish new life, new civilisations, to seed the cosmos. The birthing continued; it was eternal.

Ignatius was mesmerised and confused. This looked like it was the place where all life began, all life was created. He removed his goggles, letting go of Indigo's hand in his panic to shield his eyes again, and when he replaced the Eye of Adonai once more to look again, he could see the same goddess, the same life-creating process. He looked to his side, unsure of where Indigo had gone. She was lying on her back, smiling her, legs apart, looking peaceful, contented. He had only ever seen her like this after their intimate moments, after they shared their hopes and dreams, their ambitions in life and shared their hearts' desire and love for each other.

She whispered in her softest, most sensuous voice, "let me see. I want to see. I want to see what has possessed my body, what has given me life."

Ignatius wasn't sure what she meant by this and was too perturbed to ask, thinking this wasn't the time or the place, they had work to do. Leaning down, he raised Indigo's upper body and placed his birthmarked hand over Indigo's right eye. She gasped. "Oh, she's beautiful, this whole vision is beautiful beyond all imagining. Is this truly the stuff of life? Is this where we all began our existence, from the loins of the goddess?"

Ignatius was trying to be a gentleman and couldn't find the right words., he stumbled over some and eventually could only say, "Yes, I guess this is it. It's amazing. But what about the Omnisoul? The creation is the Omnisoul's."

He stood, once more removing his hand from Indigo's face, and she protested as the light blinded her again.

"This doesn't make sense, Indigo. Is this just a vision? Is it trickery? Or is this really the beginnings of creation?" He turned and saw that Indigo had vanished. He looked around, but she had gone. He started to panic a little. To his surprise, Indigo had climbed up onto the goddess and was currently nestling up against her like a small child, and a wide smile stretched across her face.

"Indigo! Indigo, what are you doing? It's not safe!"

In her contentment, Indigo was slow to respond. Still smiling she looked at Ignatius, somehow seeing through the light. "It's ok, Ignatius, it's ok, she's our mother and wishes us no harm. Why would she? She is the Mother Goddess of all the cosmos, the true creator. She is soft and gentle and shares her love for all beings in the cosmos."

"How do you know this? I still don't understand."

"She told me!"

Before he saw it coming, a gigantic soft warm hand scooped him up. The goddess moved him towards her. Smiling, she spoke to him in the softest, warmest, most love-exuding tone he had ever heard, merely a whisper. He felt his whole body thrill and be nourished at the same time.

"Greetings, little one. I see you have made it past the Void of Truth and entered Prajnana, the Flaming Celestial Pearl. You can open your eyes now; it is safe momentarily. I am the Goddess Supreme, the Eversoul. Forgive me for not stopping my birthing whilst I speak with you. I cannot, I am here just to birth, to spawn the stuff that makes the cosmos, to keep it eternal, to sustain it, give it energy. My body is made to just keep delivering eternally. This is my role, and I am happy with that. I am surprised to see you. I cannot remember when I last had a visitor, it has been aeons. But I do not get lonely, I have the produce of my loins to keep me company.

The last visitor was a god, an immortal. One of my earliest creations. A dashing handsome god with a beautiful face and lovely flowing hair, built with a magnificent muscular frame, I recall. Adonai was his name, yes that's it, Adonai."

Ignatius and Indigo were astounded. They looked at each other. "Is this part of the plan, do you think?" asked Ignatius. "Adonai has played us all along, like cosmic pawns?"

The Goddess laughed lightly. "He was always mischievous and cunning. I am sure if Adonai is involved, you are part of a greater plan."

She was so matter-of-fact. Ignatius and Indigo were reverential in their approach. They had encountered gods, goddesses and demons, but never a goddess that seemed so significant, so important and so powerful, she was creating cosmic matter, the very aether.

The goddess smiled sweetly again; her gaze was almost hypnotic. Sweet music filled their ears. It was soft and haunting and reverberated off their chests. This was powerful music despite the lack of volume. It pounded their chests and interfered with the rhythm of their hearts. Both Union Jacks felt invigorated.

"Humans are a certain level of life, intellectual and exemplary in their search for the truth. However, they live their life as a dream. The energy of those thoughts grows and becomes entwined with the nature of the cosmos, gathering strength until those thoughts become dreams and those dreams you mistake for your reality."

Ignatius and Indigo were speechless, not sure how to respond.

"Your spiritual development has lost its way. The Asura, humans, are perhaps our greatest failure. Save for a few special swamis, mystics, gurus, call them what you will, who have attained enlightenment, humans have never grasped their true nature, and the nature of the cosmos."

Ignatius responded, bowing his head slightly in respect, "We have many questions, but knowing where to begin is difficult, and I fear our time here may be limited."

The goddess smiled and almost laughed. "No, you have time, it does not exist here, time is a human construct anyway. Here…" She paused, "here you have an eternity."

Indigo's heart sank, fearing they were doomed to be in the Void forever.

The goddess could read her mind. "Fear not, child, you are not prisoners here. Only I am a prisoner, cursed to remain entangled with the Pearl for all eternity. I also know your questions; you do not need to ask them."

At last, Ignatius managed to blurt out the obvious question, regardless. "Who are you? And why are you a prisoner?"

This time the goddess really did laugh and as she did the silver light grew in intensity again and it looked like more celestial matter poured forth in a gush greater than they had seen before.

"I have been confined by Calabi-Ya, who sought the Pearl aeons ago, chasing its wisdom. Upon gaining it, any wisdom he acquired was overshadowed by his greed and darkness, and when he realised he could not gain overall dominion over the whole cosmos, he captured me and I was cursed to spend the rest of eternity in the Pearl like some kind of genie in a lamp.

I am, as I said, the Goddess Supreme, Queen of the Cosmos, the Eversoul. My name is Maha-Devi, and I hold dominion over all creation. I am the First, initially the Unmanifest Absolute, from when time slept during the eternal embrace of darkness, the original Void, the great abyss. And at the time of bright space and reawakened energies, I became manifest and from me all the cosmos is born. You would probably call me God. There is nothing else but me, just my consciousness and my soul. All the spiritual worlds that exist are my soul, we are all *One,* connected in this cosmos of bliss. Each thought you have is *my* thought. These thoughts manifest the physical world around you. I am your inner voice and there is a plan for your life, nothing is random."

Ignatius was confused. He tried to interject but didn't get a chance to.

"I know what you are thinking. I told you, I know your questions already. It is believed that another is the creator. Oh, it's true, the Omnisoul fashions and guides the cosmos to create the cosmos you know, taking charge of it, organising and developing the primordial energies I birth. That is why the fate of every lifeform in the cosmos is recorded in the Book of Consciousness. That book does belong to the Omnisoul. But like I said, time does not exist here. The Omnisoul became bored all too soon and, as you already know, those idle thoughts produced the Elder God, Calabi-Ya, but that creation was almost instantaneous with the birth of the Omnisoul, such is the length of eternity. The two split in just the blinking of an eye. The Omnisoul and Calabi-Ya are simply knowledge and ignorance, dual aspects of the one, which is why there are two books stemming back to the creation, the Book of Consciousness, knowledge, and the Book of Shadows, ignorance. Light and dark, good and evil, merely different vibrations of the fabric of the cosmos.

They are just two different manifestations of the same god, as day is to night, as lightness is to darkness. They inhabit the same consciousness. This would make sense as the Book of Shadows is the accumulation of the Omnisoul's dark thoughts and every deed, nightmare and ill thought from every being in the cosmos. It is all linked. We are all one entity. All souls across the cosmos and time and myself, the Cosmic Soul, share true Oneness. The oneness of existence and the divinity of the soul comprise the Eversoul, the Omnisoul, Calabi-Ya and you. We are all ONE. The cosmos is worked and shaped from within. You are a part of that cosmos. You are the cosmos. Every motion, gesture and thought has an effect on the cosmos. It is a living entity. For as long as there is life within the spheres, there will be a cosmos, with no beginning or end.

The only thing that saddens me is why the Charon have let the Omnisoul make them prisoners. Together they are far more powerful but seem to have forgotten. Adonai has been very cunning in his creation of you two, believing you to be their salvation.

The Omnisoul was an inevitability, a god to create using the matter I provide, but the Charon are my first seven breaths, the seven Sublime Lords, my favourite offspring. They were hope eternal and were to rule the cosmos as my heralds but fell victim to the Omnisoul. Or more accurately, victims to the Celestials who the Omnisoul allowed to become too powerful."

Still struggling with his vision, Ignatius spoke without looking at the Goddess any longer. "But why? How have the Celestials become so powerful?"

"Idleness! It's as simple as that. The Omnisoul has become Idle. I have accepted my fate. I have no free will; however, I am now in a state of bliss. My whole body thrills at the creation of something new at every moment. Time does not exist, for I am outside of the Megasphere, Although I am forever trapped inside this Pearl, I know and feel what takes place within the cosmos, on the thirty-one planes and I know your partner, she has the power to destroy the Celestials. She has already captured their souls, rendering them impotent. You must leave here and finish what Indigo has started."

She placed Ignatius down again, and Indigo climbed down from her resting place, standing beside him. She tentatively reached out without lifting her arm and her hand found his. She held it tightly, feeling his warmth. Closing the gap between them, she hugged him, forgetting all anger for summoning the Charon.

"And what will become of us?" asked Ignatius.

"You have nothing to fear, for you are me. Since the dawn of existence, the human race has only ever experienced one reality. You believe your mind and your thoughts are who you are. Any being learns through its senses which then causes their mind to create reality, to embellish it and present them with the world they see, hear and can touch or interact with. This is really an illusion, an unreal transformation of the cosmos to suit each individual.

Ultimate reality is all-pervading, self-luminous, eternal and the power behind all tangible forces. The only way to know the true cosmos, and therefore the true self, is to know the unknowable. The unknowable is to know me; to become me, I am within you all so we are forever connected. If you act as an observer of your mind, you will find the door to your true self, your true nature.

It is the same for the Charon. All the Charon have to do is step out of their minds and see they are not prisoners; they can stop this imprisonment any time they want. For aeons, they have suffered needlessly. They have led a life that is not their own, but it is of their own making. Time is an illusion, and they have interpreted it incorrectly. They created you as a means to find their own freedom, to find their door to exit their bubble within the cosmos. There is no need. In a mind with ego, there are few possibilities. Over the aeons, the Charon have grown their ego, their status amongst the gods, and have found fewer possibilities. When, in reality, their escape is simple."

Indigo was impatient to return. "Come on. I think we have learned all we need here. We have some souls to deal with and need to decide what we do with the Charon. They need to accept their free will. It is theirs for the taking. They have not yet realised that. As soon as they do, they will be free from the shackles of Limbo, although I haven't decided yet if they should be!"

She bowed at the Goddess and, turning, she raised the Sword of Wisdom once more and pierced the side of the Pearl. The same long oval slit appeared and she pulled Ignatius through the opening. He took one last look at the Goddess Supreme and the gap closed tightly behind them, sealing her in.

They stood in the Void once more, their eyes hurting, eyeballs aching, trying to get used to the dark.

"I think we have some unfinished business with the Celestials," she said in a determined voice, pulling Ignatius after her. "Come on, I'm done with this. I want to go home."

Chapter 31: Soulslayers

It was difficult to know which direction would take them back to the portal through which they had entered the Void. Using the Eye of Adonai, Ignatius scanned around, pinpointing the correct direction. The walk was long.

As they exited the building, they were greeted by the High Priest. Bowing and smiling, he said, "Did you not get any further? You have been gone only moments."

Ignatius looked puzzled, for him and Indigo, time had been much longer. "We located the Pearl and learned its secret."

The High Priest stopped him immediately. "Do not share this information. I do not wish to know. The secret is yours, and yours alone."

"Very well, but we now have the Celestials to take care of. What have you done with their souls, Indigo?"

"They're safe." She patted the gem-shaped burn mark on her chest.

Without wasting any more time, she led the way back to where the Celestials were still held captive in the bubble she had created. The Master was scowling at her, with menacing revenge etched on his face.

He spoke. "Are you done playing games?"

Indigo let out a hearty laugh. "Oh, this isn't a game. I want my life back, so I am here to end you right now. In fact, I am here to end it all." She looked around at the Charon.

"I have reached the pinnacle of the cosmos and know all there is to know. I have been enlightened and know that you have usurped your power. Taken advantage of your positions to fool the Omnisoul and the Charon and imprison Manjushri after double-crossing him. But it doesn't end there."

She looked around and noticed Manjushri had crept into the chamber and was hiding behind the Charon. "Oh no, it doesn't end there, the Omnisoul, the great Omnisoul, is a usurper, as is Calabi-Ya. None of you should hold the position you have in the cosmos."

They were all looking uneasy. The Charon looked on, confused. Ignatius was concerned for her and felt completely useless, surplus to requirements in the event taking place.

"What do you mean?" asked Adonai. "How can the Omnisoul usurp the position of creator?"

"The Eversoul herself told me. The great Goddess Supreme, Maha-Devi who births the stuff the cosmos is made from. She is the true creator, the rest of you are all imposters. Imprisoned in the Pearl by Calabi-Ya, she is the creator of the primordial matter that the rest of you fashion and pervert for your own needs."

Adonai suddenly looked enlivened and for the first time looked buoyant. Indigo and Ignatius had never seen him like this. "I remember. It was such a long time ago. I visited the Eversoul, she wanted the Charon to be at her side." A tear rolled down his cheek, and Ignatius wasn't sure if it was a tear for joy or sadness.

The Master had remained motionless all this time. "So what do you intend to do, girl?"

She thought for a while. "I intend to get my life back on track. The Charon shall be free, so I never have to see them again, and you are all nothing but conjurers. You are not gods, in fact, on the scale of things, you are less than me and Ignatius, at least we are born of gods. True godlings."

At that moment, Manjushri made his presence known. Sneering, he said, "I am going to enjoy this. I have been an eagle for far too long. It is about time the Celestials paid for all their meddling."

Indigo held her right hand to her chest and closed her eyes. One by one, she brought forth seven souls that hovered in front of her. Multiple colours flickered across their surfaces, and the heart-shaped souls moved and twisted, throbbed and distorted as if in pain.

A tremendous heat seared her skin as fire raged through the chamber and the ground shook as Calabi-Ya landed next to them all, his great clawed feet crashing down and splitting the tiled floor beneath them.

The Master grinned. "Did you really think it would be that easy, you foolish girl? Whilst you have been gone, discovering what you believe to be true, I have summoned the mighty Elder God and now this place shall burn. I will oversee the destruction of Sagharta and send you and your sidekick to the foulest part of Limbo along with the Charon. Myself and Calabi-Ya shall hold dominion over the whole cosmos."

Calabi-Ya had transformed himself into his form of the harlequin, the fine dandy with his fine features and haughty attitude. He looked at the Master and Indigo read into his expression: he didn't share the Master's plan. Calabi-Ya had no intention of sharing power, but with a wave of his hand the spell that held the Celestials vanished and they were no longer paralysed or captive.

The Master looked menacingly at Indigo and Ignatius. Ignatius readied his sonic blaster for a fight. Somewhere behind the Master, the Watcher raised his telescope to one of his eyes. Without the Eye of Adonai, he could not see as far or across as many planes, but the fear that was etched across his face gave Indigo a signal that something far bigger was about to occur.

Within seconds, the ground shook once more and the Omnisoul appeared, blue skin and flaming hair, multiple faces and four arms swinging weapons and musical instruments wildly. Upon viewing Calabi-Ya, rage took over and a battle broke out immediately. Ignatius grabbed Indigo, pulling her to safety. "This is not our fight, keep out of it, Indigo!"

The two Union Jacks crashed to the floor, away from danger, Manjushri helping them to get clear and back to their feet. "Ignatius is right. This is a battle of the gods; you need to stay clear."

The air burned as the Omnisoul clashed with Calabi-Ya, who had regained his draconic form. Leathery wings beat the air and poisonous venom dripped and burned all around. The Charon were rendered helpless, they had no intention of assisting the Omnisoul and didn't want to attack the Celestials who could send them back to Limbo in an instant. The Celestials, however, were intent on revenge against Indigo.

"I told you if I can assist you more, I shall," said Manjushri. "The time has come for you to yield the Sword of Wisdom. It is powerful beyond your imagining. It will drain your strength and the life force from your soul, but is the only weapon that will truly stop the Celestials."

Indigo felt the weight of the weapon in her hand. Manjushri put his hand on hers. "But I must warn you, if it takes too much of your life force, you will not survive. Whilst the sword gives wisdom, it requires your life force to assist."

Adonai looked on with a certain amount of glee. "Devi, this could be our end. Without the Celestials, there is no one to do the Omnisoul's bidding, and the Omnisoul won't do it, it's too lowly." Devi moved closer to Adonai and held him. Tara held on to Atman, waiting with anticipation. Aryas was in his usual state, smoking green liquid in his glass pipe. Darshan held him by the arm and Paladin was sat resting, due to his heavy armour.

Indigo looked at Ignatius. "I'm sorry, but I have to do this. For us both. If I die, then know this, I love you, Ignatius, with all my heart and soul, blackened or otherwise. But I cannot go on with the thought of the Charon forever being in our life."

Ignatius had a heavy heart and knots in his stomach. His eyes filled with tears, and he just gave a silent and gentle nod, unable to speak.

Indigo zoned out and the battle between the Omnisoul and Calabi-Ya became just background noise. As the Master lunged forwards, she swung the Sword of Wisdom on a horizontal arc, narrowly missing his soul, which still hung in the air. "Ah, ha, ha! I will destroy you!" she cried out loud.

The Master hesitated. She decided the Guardian was too fat and sluggish to worry about, she wasn't sure about the Voice, she didn't want to get too close to those teeth. She thought the Sleeper and the Stalker were the biggest threats.

"I've got you covered," said Ignatius, pointing his sonic blaster at any of the Celestials that moved.

At that moment, Indigo felt her whole body flood with an extraordinary heat and power, which felt like it was gnawing at her own soul and heart. Inside, she trembled but couldn't show any fear before the Celestials. Then the Sword took control of her limbs, and she raised the weapon high, ready to strike. Silver light danced along the blade's edge and white fire swirled about her hands, then her arms. Her own aura became visible, and it too was a dazzling field of brilliant silver and white light that sparked and twinkled like stardust. Her hair flowed in an invisible breeze and her eyes rolled back into her head, leaving just the whites exposed, leaving her looking like some kind of ghostly apparition.

The leading edge of the blade swept through the air and music filled the air, sounding like a choir of angels singing some distance away. As the keen edge touched the first soul, it erupted like a mini stellar nova, showering Indigo with sparks and lightning. The blade continued on until it reached the second soul, and again it exploded in a similar manner, then the third and fourth as Indigo became aware that behind the souls the Celestials had started to fall, with horror-stricken faces. She saw the Keeper fall first, then the Watcher and Guardian. The blade continued on its arc as Indigo felt root-like tentacles encircle her throat as the Stalker tried to retaliate. But it was a hopeless attack, as his soul burst, the root-like growths shrivelled and fell to the floor. On it continued, until all the Celestials had fallen, their souls destroyed by the Sword of Wisdom, their bodies a crumpled heap on the floor.

As Ignatius looked on, the seven bodies transformed into ancient looking necromancers. The Charon were thrilled. It was the first time Ignatius had ever seen them all smiling, shedding their dour personalities. They weren't sure if this was it, if they might finally be free of their lives being dictated to them by the Celestials. Was this an end to their immortality?

Indigo collapsed, exhausted, and Ignatius had to support her for fear she would fall. Meanwhile, the Omnisoul and Calabi-Ya battled on, blades and fire crashing all around. Unexpectedly, the whole chamber lit up with the most intense white light which interrupted the raging battle. All of them had to shield their eyes as the Eversoul appeared, a beautiful ghostly outline of motherhood, stardust and nebulous gases filling her body to give the appearance of solidity.

There was a collective gasp, and everyone feared being blinded. The Goddess smiled sweetly at Ignatius and Indigo. The Omnisoul and Calabi-Ya were still battling on, neither one stronger than the other, neither one able to get the upper hand and tip the balance in their favour.

"ENOUGH!" screamed the Eversoul. It was like thousands of choirs all singing together. Ignatius had to cover his ears as the single word seemed to last forever and was echoed by invisible angels amplifying the word.

The Omnisoul and Calabi-Ya seemed to start moving in slow motion. Indigo jolted upright from her weakened state, gasping for air as if she had momentarily died once more.

"My children, do you not see, your fighting is futile. You are but two sides of the same coin, two aspects of this great creation."

The two gods stopped their aggression and looked as if they had been scolded by their mother, which was true.

"You were born together, such is the paradox of time in this vast eternity, all things happen at once, past, present and future. Born of my loins, Omnisoul you were born genderless so there would be no rivalry, all beings would be equal in your creation using the primordial birth matter from your mother. You were to fashion creation on your anvil, building worlds and producing souls to make the cosmos magnificent. Yet you became bored so quickly, creating Calabi-Ya. He is you and you are him. Whilst you both exist, the cosmos remains in balance, light and dark, chaos and order. This is how it should be. Creation is light and shadow, and it must alternate in supremacy or life in the cosmos would never be fulfilled."

She paused and her voice softened. "Children, what am I to do with you? You are a disappointment, to me and the creation. It troubles me that you have forgotten that you are both as one. You shall set aside your differences and return the balance to the creation. Now begone!"

There was a flash of turquoise light and the two mighty gods disappeared.

Chapter 32: New Gods

Finding it difficult to see, and confused, Ignatius was the first to speak. "How did you escape?"

The Eversoul smiled with such joy as she spoke softly and sweetly. "The Sword Indigo wields left a permanent rip in the Pearl, meaning I can now escape my imprisonment. Just before I was imprisoned, I created the Sword of Wisdom. It is linked with the Pearl of Wisdom, so the cut you created will not heal, so I made my escape. That does not mean I can escape my purpose. I still must birth the primordial matter that fills the cosmos, but I can now escape the Pearl should I wish to. But I shall return. It is my abode and I am comfortable there."

"Then what will that mean for the Omnisoul now?" asked Ignatius.

"The Omnisoul can continue shaping the creation, but I must first reconcile the Omnisoul with Calabi-Ya."

Throughout the conversation, the primordial cosmic material continued to flow. It was unstoppable.

Shielding her eyes, Indigo asked, "And what of the Charon? What will happen to them?"

The Eversoul turned towards them with sadness in her eyes.

"Adonai, the Charon are free." She hesitated. "You have always been free! Know thyself and take control."

Adonai felt a crushing weight on his heart and soul. The other Charon looked on in disbelief.

"For an eternity, we have been captive in Limbo, and through the Celestials used at will by the Omnisoul. How have we been free?" Anger began to etch itself across his beautiful pale face. Devi moved forward as if she was about to strike but was restrained by Tara.

"The only eternal thing in the cosmos is one's soul, your bodies are transitory. You could have taken control of your fate aeons ago. Instead, you concocted elaborate plans that have taken millennia to fall into alignment. Ignatius and Indigo are the Great Alignment, the fate of the Charon. That Great Alignment has been fulfilled, it is here now, they are both present, as are the Charon.

The Eversoul appeared to grow in size a little as she addressed the Charon. "You allowed your free will to be taken from you, but it was all a misconception, you have always been free, you have been oppressed for so long, you believed your own illusion. Darkness and ignorance can be illuminated by three flames. Firstly, truth, you forgot what the truth is, then, nature, you chose to believe what the Celestials told you about your nature, and the third is knowledge, in which you were sadly lacking as your self-belief grew hazier in a darkness of your own making. You had no knowledge of the web of deceit you were entangled in. However, you have no one to blame but yourselves. Escape is always through wisdom. After the Omnisoul, you were the first seven breaths of the fiery whirlwind at the beginning of time. You were the chosen ones. Instead, you demonised yourselves, for which you have been punished enough. Otherwise, I would despatch you the same way as the Celestials."

Indigo gave a sigh of relief. "At last," she whispered under her breath, repeating it, "At last!"

"And what shall become of us?" asked Ignatius.

The Eversoul's sweet smile returned, although it was difficult for Ignatius to see it through the bright aura of silver light.

"You are not descended from Adonai, not really. Oh, he thinks you are, and he did have a hand in your birth, but you are mine. You are all mine. Adonai the Lord is your inner strength, your cosmic strength with the ability to conquer all obstacles in life. The same is true of Indigo, you are not born of Atman. The meaning of Atman is soul or spirit, call it what you will. Atman is the innermost *you*. This is normally so deeply hidden; most humans never discover it. He is your cosmic consciousness. Your own consciousness, the vehicle of your soul, has manipulated you.

All the Charon are aspects of you two. They are real, they are eternal, but so are you. The soul that is in all beings is immortal, and even through death, cannot die. You are the creators, the consciousness, the true essence of the cosmos. One cannot exist without the other. The Charon represent your suffering and lack of free will. You, as with all humans are not free because your mind is cluttered with all that is not important or worthy of time and attention. Free yourselves and free the Charon.

You are the New Gods, you are divine. You are the only triumph that has come from all this. The cosmos has culminated in you both. You are both special beings, special humans, our greatest achievement.

When you leave here, you must continue to view the world as entirely abstract, consciousness is the real essence of life, the consciousness that lives on in your soul when it is ready to depart your physical being. Then, you shall return to me, as will all beings, and be at one again with the cosmos."

Ignatius and Indigo were speechless. The Charon were feeling confounded, for all of this could have been avoided. The complications of the cosmos were too much to comprehend in worldly terms.

"So where does that leave Indigo and I?"

"You shall return home. Your cosmic adventures are over. And the Charon are free to roam the cosmos at will, until we all meet again someday. For now, I shall return to the Pearl. I have made it my home, but now I can exit as I wish, no longer captive."

Ignatius and Indigo didn't remember anything more after that. Instead, they became aware they were back in Lhasa with Lambeth scurrying around gathering belongings ready for the journey home aboard the *Spirit of the Empire*.

"I have your rooms ready and your clothing suitably cleaned and pressed. The captain seems to think the return home may be a little quicker due to a tailwind." The old man stood smiling, his hair still waving in the slight breeze that entered the cabin.

As the great airship took to the skies, Ignatius held Indigo tight. "I think we should take a break for a while, to rest and recuperate," he said.

She leaned into him. "I think that would be a good idea. I have had enough of gods and demons, we need to get back to what we do best, sleuthing and gathering intelligence. It should be easier now the Administorium have been disbanded. Just one thing, though. What do you think will become of our powers?"

"Well, I'm not sure I have any anymore, although I do still have this." He took a piece of linen from his pocket and, unwrapping it, showed her the Eye of Adonai.

She gasped. "I'm not sure that's such a good idea!"

"But your powers, they are strong, I guess only time will tell."

"Hmm. I'm not sure I want to know. I just want to get back to being Indigo again. I don't want to be a godling."

The journey home was uneventful. Ignatius and Indigo made the most of their time together, peaceful, no adventure, just the love and affection for each other. Lambeth was given some free time and Indigo remained in Ignatius's room for three days, neither one of them leaving.

After a few more days, Indigo was in Ignatius's study. They had agreed to spend more time together, and Indigo was toying with the idea that they should cohabitate. Ignatius was thrilled by the idea and the two of them were making plans. They hadn't reported back to Lawrence yet. They were taking a break to devote all their time to each other.

Unexpectedly, Lambeth appeared at the study door.

"You have a visitor, sir. Were you expecting anyone?"

"No. Who is it?"

"She says her name is Eliza Patience..."

Epilogue

Report Number: 01/1858

Type: Classified

Agent: Isambard Ignatius

Chapter: House of Albion

After a long and arduous journey to Tibet to look for the Flaming Celestial Pearl, I can report back that we made the rendezvous with Helena and Nicholas from the House of Esoterica and gathered intelligence for an expedition into the mountains looking for the fabled land of Rahasya, where it was believed the pearl could be found. The journey was difficult, taking us through mountain passes and abandoned temples, through uncharted lands following a granite path along which we encountered unfriendly locals. After risking our lives with the wildlife in the region and the inhospitable conditions, I can report that nothing came of our endeavour.

I regret to inform you that the expedition was of no value, and I have nothing more to report.

I. Ignatius

Oxford

Glossary

Agartha

A legendary kingdom said to be located within the earth on its inner surface, leading to the hollow earth theory. It is sometimes confused with Shambhala.

Asura

In Buddhism Asura is the lowest rank of deity or demigod.

Beyul

In Tibetan Buddhism, Beyul are hidden valleys.

Knights of Himavala

Himavala is Sanskrit for Pearl, so the Knights of Himavala are the Knights of the Pearl.

Issa

In Tibetan Buddhism, Issa is the name of Jesus.

Kalapa

Buddhist legends state Kalapa is the capital city of Shambhala. This is the name given to both the palace of Rahasya.

Maha-Devi

From Mahadevi, the name of the Supreme Goddess in Hinduism.

Manjushri

The name of the Librarians eagle in Shadowslayers. It is a Buddhist word for knowledge. It is also the name of the first king of Shambhala, a mythical Buddhist kingdom that lies somewhere between the Himalayan Mountains and the Gobi Desert.

Meh-Teh

The Tibetan name for the Yeti. It translates as 'man-bear'.

Prajnana

The name of the Flaming Celestial Pearl. Prajna in Hindu is the highest and purest form of wisdom, intelligence and understanding. Jnana is Sanskrit for the wisdom of the reality or Brahman. The Prajnana is a jewel equivalent to the philosopher's stone

Rahasya

Sanskrit for 'secret' or 'place of silence'. The name of the scared city in Tibet, home to the Kalki kings. Kalki is the Lord of the Universe born in Shambhala

Rak-Saka

The Marshall of the Knights of Himavala. The name comes from raksaka, Sanskrit for Protector.

Sumata

The name of the guide given to Ignatius and Indigo to lead them to Rahasya. An Indian name meaning gentle or kind, a friendly person.

Tashi

The name of the tavern where Ignatius and Indigo meet their contacts. It is a Tibetan word meaning good fortune or auspiciousness.

Tulpamancer

A tulpa is a conjured up imaginary friend. A tulpamancer is someone who can summon up such a being. It is believed this being then shares the mind and body of the person who created them.

Vraja & Vamza

Arriving in Rahasya Ignatius and Indigo are met by the brothers Vraja and Vamza. Both names are Sanskrit for host.